Praise fo

C000181654

'The final twists of t   tay
not reveal the outcor.   ,   _____ _.i...
A compelling and thoroughly enjoyable read' Cathy Gunn,
author and former financial journalist

'*Countdown to a Killing* takes the epistolary form into
the 21st century. MacAulay's first outing in print was the
thoroughly readable *Being Simon Haines*. Here, among
various curious and flawed characters, he gives us Lomax
Clipper. You might not want to be Lomax Clipper – but you
won't forget him' Alex Wade, writer and lawyer

'A WhatsApp whodunnit... innovative and contemporary...
A truly millennial murder mystery' Ben Wilson, author of
One Year Without Social Media and *Guardian* journalist

'A unique storytelling style... its introspective nature of
characterisation is enthralling' Hazel Butterfield, Presenter
at Riverside Radio (Get Booked), Women's Radio Station &
regular guest on BBC London

'Taking a peek into people's lives through one side of their
email and WhatsApp conversations, this amazing concept
lets us explore so many important issues like mental health,
interpersonal relationships, work ethic, and love... This was
so addictive I read it in one day!' Dean Presho, Books Boys
Podcast

Praise for *Being Simon Haines*

'Compelling' Justin Warshaw, *The Times Literary Supplement*

'Will *Being Simon Haines* by Tom Vaughan MacAulay become the defining novel for his generation about what it means to be a driven corporate lawyer?' Edward Fennell, *The Times*, *The Brief Premium*

'Beautiful, intelligent and thoroughly readable' Ian Sansom

'Pretty unputdownable' Tony Roe, *The Law Society Gazette*

'Intelligently probes the key issues preoccupying millennials in any profession, not just the law' Alex Wade, *The Times, Law*

Countdown
to a
Killing

The Selected Correspondence
of
Several Key Characters

Tom Vaughan MacAulay

Red Door

Published by RedDoor
www.reddoorpress.co.uk

ISBN 978-1-915194-08-4

A CIP catalogue record for this book is available from the British
Library

Cover design by Rawshock Design

Typesetting: Jen Parker, Fuzzy Flamingo
www.fuzzyflamingo.co.uk

Printed in the UK by CPI Group (UK), Croydon

The correspondence begins in August 2016
and ends on the night of the murder.

1

New Beginnings

London and Sicily (specifically, a damp ground-floor flat on Ambler Road, Finsbury Park; a charming, airy flat on Upper Street, Islington; and Palermo's Falcone Borsellino airport), August 2016.

————

From: Wen Li
Sent: Sunday, 14 August 2016 09:22
To: Dominic Corcoran
Subject: So sorry

Hi Dominic,

I wanted to apologise again for not being able to attend Friday's session. As I said in my WhatsApp message, please do make sure you invoice me for it. It's horrible to think that I wasted your time. Especially when you'll have countless other patients equally in need!

It's just that, despite the medication, there are still days when I simply can't take the Tube. I do understand my OCD now, and what's going on in my mind when I stand behind passengers on the platform. But, while it's a relief to understand that these are just wild fears, and that I'm not actually going to do it, this doesn't stop the feelings of despair at the thoughts I have. Asking myself if I want to push. Worrying that deep down I might.

On Friday, I just had to leave the platform in the end. It's so frustrating because my flat is super near to Finsbury Park Station and it should be such an easy journey down on the Victoria Line to Oxford Circus. It's particularly gutting because it's not just the session with you but also walking through central London that does me good. When I'm strong enough, and manage to get to Oxford Circus and come out and mingle with the crowds of shoppers under all the bright lights and then arrive at your clinic, it always feels like a dream. Cavendish Square is so grand and makes me think of Sherlock Holmes. It's like the fantasy London that I imagined as a little girl in Suzhou, after my mum first told me we were leaving for England.

Anyway, on Friday I fought my way back up the stairs of less glamorous Finsbury Park Station and, when I got outside, one of the drunk guys who always hang out there pointed at me and said he'd never seen such a sad face. I rushed back to my flat and cried myself into a state of exhaustion. I couldn't even face my mum's homemade Chinese dumplings, which is always the ultimate sign that I'm down! :)

As discussed, I start my new job tomorrow, which I agree is a positive step for me. Especially as it's a manageable bus ride to the office! (Sorry, but you're the one who told me that humour is the best medicine at times! :))

Very sorry again.

Wen

From: Lomax Clipper
Sent: Sunday, 14 August 2016 11:48
To: Katie Wetherden
Subject: A farewell to Italy

Buongiorno, Mrs Wetherden.

I'm waiting to board for London Stansted. The plane is delayed and the air conditioning has transmogrified into a gigantic hairdryer. An ancient Sicilian man is glaring at me, a look of abject fury on his face. Today is my 33rd birthday and all I really know is that the secondment is done and my six months in Italy are over.

I woke this morning to the sound of seagulls, Aurora asleep beside me. Arriving at the airport a few hours later, with my mood much changed, I joined the queue for security behind a flustered English couple. Impatient, entitled, London professional types. The man was hatefully tall and had a hatefully thick head of dark hair. The woman was blonde and sunburnt.

I couldn't help but overhear them. He declared from on high that Sicily was a bit of a shithole. She agreed and added that the natives were, like, sooo third world? As I felt the stirrings of a cold white rage, she nudged him, raising her eyebrows at the elderly Sicilian couple who were queuing side by side with us, trying to push in.

He began to complain about the heat. He said that he could use an Aperol Spritz despite it still being morning. She laughed, and said, 'Like, I TOTALLY need one?' She mused that there had better be a bar after security. Then she turned to me, and asked whether I knew if there would be.

'*Che cosa*?' I said.

She said that she was terribly sorry. That for some reason she had assumed I was English.

'*Eh*?' I insisted. I felt suddenly euphoric. But it was a short-sighted move.

'A BAR,' the man said earnestly. 'Is there a BAR after security?'

Further questions followed. My Italo-English became weird. My chest became tighter and tighter. When she asked whether there would be air conditioning once we got through, I did not reply. It was one question too many.

Instead, as if in a half-sleeping dream, I took my mobile phone from my pocket and answered a timely call from my Palermitan mamma. I carried on speaking to her until the couple had stepped forward to go through security. Only when I ended the call did I notice the glare of the old Sicilian man.

————

WhatsApp messages from Wen to Mum
Sunday, 14 August 2016

Translation from the original Chinese

Wen

Of course I ate the dumplings. Delicious

11:50

Please don't bring up too much food from the shop today

11:50

Oh, OK. Hadn't realised Dad was coming too. You two never listen to me! He should be resting

11:55

Also, he shouldn't be exaggerating to all the customers about my new job!

11:55

It's a good firm but am not going to make a fortune!

11:56

OK, see you later. Love you

11:58

———————

From: Lomax Clipper
Sent: Sunday, 14 August 2016 12:51
To: Katie Wetherden
Subject: A farewell to Italy – continued

It is increasingly hot here at the gate. A teenage girl has just pretended to faint, attracting much attention and sympathy. She too is now glaring at me. She knows that I alone saw through it.

Where is the plane, they keep asking.

The prospect of London – specifically, the leaky roof of the flat on Romilly Road; Finsbury Park Station at rush hour; and the firm of Curtain & Curtain – fills me with nausea. I've had an idyllic long weekend with Aurora, the odd moment of tricky behaviour aside. It's strange to think that I was nervous about coming down here from Milan to see her on her home turf. I suppose I'd feared that, by leaving Milan, she might have broken the spell cast over our dreamy fortnight together. To think that we met at a communist protest that I'd thought was a street party!

Anyway, it was lovely to know that the magic had held. She seemed pleased when she saw her aspiring writer here in Sicily, although I was mildly put out that she continued to chat on her phone for a good ten minutes while I stood before her, expectantly, in a dreamy sunlit *piazza*. (Incidentally, we do not talk about my job. In Italy the notarial profession is prestigious and Aurora does not approve.) She is so startlingly beautiful, her communist dress code so extreme and Palermo so exotic that, standing there, I had to blink. The Huddersfield boy had come a long way!

We took the ferry on Friday afternoon to the island of Ustica. It's about forty miles out from Palermo, and exquisite. On Saturday evening, after a fine dinner that left Aurora conflicted and a little angry, we went to sit on a low sea wall before the waves rolling back towards Palermo. Many of the men streaming past on scooters stuck out their chins at the olive-skinned, slender-waisted, voluptuous young woman in rags beside me, while she texted away. After a while she stopped, lit a roll-up and then whispered, in lyrical Italian, that the Sicilian soil was soaked with tears.

As I nodded, understanding from this that I had been forgiven for dinner, I thought how she didn't look thirty. And how her face really was so beautiful that none of this felt quite possible or true. Indeed for a moment I reflected on that unreality, noting too that it was strange, disturbing even, that her mood swings had become hardwired into my own emotional make-up; that she was able to conjure up happiness, erase the past, make me rationalise irrational behaviour, on a whim. I concluded that it was no more complicated than that I was out of my depth – which reminded me how disappointing it was that my hair had begun to recede the day before my 33rd birthday. I thought too how my life, absent this young woman who had fallen into it, was rather pathetic: how I only really had you and your husband back in London.

I told Aurora about that, and how things up in Huddersfield were equally depressing. How, since his breakdown, my dad had developed a hauntingly vacant stare. How my mother was beginning to say she missed Lille. I said that if I made it as a writer, I'd come back to live in Italy. Aurora replied that I was already a writer. Beginning to choke up, I told her that she was the first person to believe in me, leaving aside the woman to whom I'd emailed my novel. She nodded, before letting out a sweet yawn (it was late).

Aargh, got to stop. We're boarding!

———————

From: Julian Pickering
Sent: Sunday, 14 August 2016 12:56
To: Charles Curtain
Subject: Associates' arrival tomorrow

Dear Charles,

I wanted to thank you again for your generosity in allocating budget towards securing a new team member for me. As you may know, young Wen Li begins tomorrow. In addition, tomorrow marks the day of Lomax Clipper's return from secondment. He and I have had several lengthy email exchanges during his secondment in Milan. I have reiterated that I expect him to display a more positive attitude upon his return. He is perfectly competent, of course, but as our most senior associate he must cut out the constant cynicism and the rather nihilistic 'jokes' that wear me down. I will keep you updated on his performance.

In any case, I'm very glad that this period of having to fend for myself without associate support is finally over. You are aware, I know, of the toll it has taken on me. I look forward to a new beginning – hopefully with a revitalised Lomax playing a key part, and setting the right example for Wen.

Best,

Julian

―――――――

From: Lomax Clipper
Sent: Sunday, 14 August 2016 13:57
To: Katie Wetherden
Subject: Re: A farewell to Italy – continued

Hi Katie.

This plane has been stuck on the tarmac for over half an hour. Everyone is wild with anger. I will finish what I began.

It was sad, if a little melodramatic, saying goodbye to Aurora before the waves, Mount Pellegrino in the distance. She didn't accompany me to the airport because she had a march in central Palermo, but our journey back on the ferry from Ustica was the stuff of high romance. Seagulls flying alongside us. Aurora spellbindingly beautiful in the blue light. Me towering over the weather-beaten fishermen at five foot nine. A timeless city becoming big before our eyes.

A fortnight in Milan and long weekend in Sicily have provided more colour and intensity than three years with Lisa. Except perhaps for the end last year, when Lisa said that she was leaving because I was a loser. That was fairly intense.

(Incidentally, do you know Lisa is completely off the grid? One of her friends contacted me recently, asking whether I'd heard from her. Pretty weird. I told the friend to let me know when the selfish git turns up!)

The woman to whom I sent my novel – in truth, the opening chapters of a novel – was my old English lecturer at Huddersfield uni, Professor Melanie Nithercott. She wrote back just when I was setting off from Milan to Sicily, and told me that, in its current form, this particular effort was a 'no go'. She said that she had become lost by chapter two, and that the very idea of a whodunnit with time going backwards was too weird. But she added that there were several good descriptive passages, and that, as she has said before, I should certainly keep writing – indeed, she noted that my enthusiasm and perseverance were half the battle. She suggested starting afresh.

I had a very temporary, minor crisis when I re-read the feedback on the flight down here. I've always believed I can write, and last year I realised this belief, and Melanie's encouragement, were all I had going. It's my only chance to save myself from a mediocrity that I don't think is me. Call it narcissism, but I think that Lisa was wrong, I'm not a loser. I think I NEED to be a successful writer.

And I think that I just might become one. Because, when I was on Ustica, I had a sudden idea.

It goes without saying that I hope you, Ross and David are

well. I would love to pop down to Pimlico next week. Always nice to remember how you Zone One types live; always good for the self-confidence to see those gleaming stucco palaces, the private garden squares. Seriously though, it's crazy to think that David is over three months old and yet to meet Uncle Lomax.

Finally, I forgot to say congratulations. Last year it was partnership, and now you're shortlisted for the City's young business lawyer of the year! You were already a star back in Huddersfield. My dad says your story goes to show that you don't need a private education to make it in this world.

Last week when we spoke on the phone he asked me to 'just think' that he was once your headmaster. And to 'just think' that you and I were in the same class. I didn't have time to query the implication of that second comment because we were immediately back to my grandfather, the final Klopfer, Huddersfield's most reformed prisoner of war. Apparently Klopfer singled you out as ambitious and driven during one of our first sports days, you know. Anyway, after my dad's voice had undergone that subtle change that it always undergoes when he talks about Klopfer – that thing where his strong Huddersfield accent suddenly has a faint hint of a German accent – and after repeating twice that Klopfer came to love this country, he added that it was time for him to take to his bed. In the background, I heard my mother cry: '*Mon Dieu*, Norman'.

'My nerves are SHOT, Fabienne,' he said.

PS any secret to Ross retaining his brown curls? Greyish-brown hairs are suddenly jumping ship by the second here.

WhatsApp messages from Wen to Hannah
Sunday, 14 August 2016

Wen

Hey! Pete sounds lovely! So sorry about Friday, had really nasty migraine so no way I was heading into town

19:34

Yeah, am way better now. Parents have just arrived with a load of fresh vegetables from their shop!

19:39

I know, right? And they came via Chinatown so also got me some delicious steam buns!

19:41

I know, SOOO nice. They even brought me stuff for Hot Pot next Friday

19:44

No more space for food in this flat! Bit nervous about first day tomorrow btw. They all sound a bit formal and edgy!

19:44

2

Travails

England (specifically, London, Brighton and Huddersfield), August 2016 – March 2017.

———

From: Lomax Clipper
Sent: Friday, 19 August 2016 11:16
To: Katie Wetherden
Subject: Re: Apologies

Good morning from these rather comically austere offices on Gresham Street. I'd managed to forget how poky they are! Funny to think that we are now working physically close to each other again; if I shouted out of the window, could you hear me over there on Leadenhall Street? It's so thrilling to be back in the City of London. I joke, of course; horrific journey into Moorgate this morning, crammed into the carriage with all the other stressballs, all coughing and sneezing on each other with malice. It's so odd that all City workers are still forced to do this every day.

No worries about the delay in replying, by the way. I'm aware that you lawyers tend to be busier than us Scrivener Notaries. Re Pimlico tomorrow – what time works best?

Very happy to resume the Friday updates now that I'm back. I had forgotten that, now you're a partner, email is your principal form of communication with the outside world. It's amusing, but also a little melancholy, to imagine you gazing at your phone, absorbed in my little anecdotes, during your big closing meetings.

This first week back at Curtain & Curtain has been grim. Having to deal with the rodent again has been particularly soul-destroying. Disorientating too. Julian's hair was grey when I left for Milan and now it's jet-black. He's fifty-five! As a fellow bachelor (I cannot consider myself in a relationship with Aurora, given her complete lack of correspondence since I've been back), I do think I need to somehow convey my views. Women are not going to go for the look.

My social activity this week has been limited to staring at my phone, wondering why Aurora can't be bothered to reply to my messages, and getting to know Wen, my friendly (and extremely pretty – actually, beautiful) new colleague. She and I now share an office with Julian. Wen is originally from the city of Suzhou, which is apparently China's Venice. Her parents moved here when she was eleven. I found out today that she's twenty-nine, and happens to live about two minutes' walk from me, on Ambler Road – yet another colleague or uni friend who has ended up in my lovely refuge from the stress of Finsbury Park Station. It really is a wonderfully quaint maze of terraced houses in various states of modernisation or disrepair. Amazing, and mildly triggering, that you've still not visited. Anyway, Wen's keen and diligent, and the rodent has already warned me not to corrupt her with my 'silly wind-ups' and my 'nihilistic' sense of humour.

Updates on my new idea for the novel will have to wait, I'm afraid.

I want to test it first this weekend. But I think I am on to something EXTRAORDINARY – an idea that will be a game-changer for me, and possibly also for high-brow, comic fiction in this country.

You sought more information about my old English lecturer, Professor Melanie Nithercott. She's a lovely lady. Retired now and lives back in her hometown of Southampton, alone and immersed in literature. If it helps to paint a picture, she is frail-looking and has a huge halo of white hair. I know this remains true because I am one of her four Facebook friends.

Julian made a cutting remark yesterday about Huddersfield uni. So much for his new role as Chairman of the firm's Inclusion Committee. Nothing gets me more fired up – the snobbishness makes me want to kill him. It's a real university, with real people as students. I'm not saying that I would have got into Oxbridge or the other big names, but I'm glad that I didn't try. Except for you, every Cambridge graduate I've met has had a personality disorder. And every Oxford graduate has been terribly arrogant but not terribly bright!

I would go on to describe my colleague Tiggy, from Durham, and my landlord Barnaby, from Bristol, but I need to stop for a moment because I've worked myself up into a fit of rage.

––––––––

WhatsApp messages from Wen to Hannah
Friday, 19 August 2016

Wen

Hope your Friday is going well! Don't be late for Hot Pot tonight!

13:38

Cool, you're OK with spicy, right? No probs to meet Pete and his friend for drinks after but hope you've made clear I'm not necessarily on the lookout…

13:39

Perfect! Fuck, what a first week here. My boss is sooo edgy, and this colleague I sit opposite is a seriously weird guy!

13:40

————

From: Lomax Clipper
Sent: Friday, 19 August 2016 14:05
To: Katie Wetherden
Subject: Re: Apologies

Here I am with Part 2. The rodent is up in the Partners' Room at the moment, having 'luncheon'. Our very short and podgy Chairman, Mr Charles Curtain, still insists on the use of that term. The little man celebrated his 60th birthday while I was away. I bumped into him this morning in the corridor. He was wearing his trademark braces and the bald pate was shining bright. Maybe I'm paranoid, but he seems averse to all contact with such lowly beings as yours truly. His handshake came across as a tremendous testament to courage. It was as if he were afraid of catching something from me.

I sometimes fantasise about what I would say to him if I won the Booker Prize, and made millions of pounds through royalties, film rights etc. And what I would say to the rodent too. I confess I sometimes lie awake thinking about it…

Wen and I, as non-partners, have just had luncheon at our desks. Wen and her parents have never embraced British cuisine, but she is otherwise very much the foodie, with a particular penchant for the cuisine of the city of Suzhou. She does much of her food shopping in Chinatown. She brings in the most remarkable dishes. She has a hell of an appetite too – I have no idea how she remains so slim.

I'm still smarting from being humiliated earlier, on a call with a law firm. A cocky and stupid trainee lawyer said: 'I didn't know we needed notaries in England.' I said: 'SCRIVENER notaries, Henry. And my understanding is that you want the document recognised abroad.'

Lawyers should understand that the affixing of a notarial seal is a serious matter. Our seal on a document is THE LAW; it is GOD. I won't go on again about how the Scrivener Notary is more qualified than the solicitor. How we have to pass exams on foreign legal systems. But the lack of recognition of our role, and the poor pay for non-partners, at least at this firm, do strike me as bizarre. How different life is for Italian notaries!

Of course, PARTNERS of Curtain & Curtain do earn quite a bit. Some of them, like the rodent, earn a lot – maybe even over £200k. But those of us who get passed over for partnership each year earn a relative pittance. It is haunting to think that a newly qualified lawyer probably earns more.

I now have the distinction of being the oldest non-partner in the firm, by the way. Derek, who, at fifty-nine, had held that distinction for some time, was fired while I was on secondment. He had certified that a power of attorney that happened to have nothing to do with the original was a true and faithful copy; Christmas came early for a most unsavoury Belgian businessman. I had told Derek that his approach of mass certifications at 4 p.m. on a Friday would catch up with him one day.

I've just realised that you might infer from the above that I'm also now Curtain & Curtain's least effective Scrivener, but that would be to discount the Chairman himself. Mr Curtain continues to limit himself to what I believe has always been the sole task of his decades-long career, which is to ring the bell for luncheon. At the sound of the bell, the other partners stop what they're doing, pop out to Pret and then take their sandwiches up to the cramped Partners' Room.

It would be quaint if they weren't all such terrible people.

———

WhatsApp messages from Wen to Mum
Friday, 19 August 2016

Translation from the original Chinese

Wen

Yep, I know how to make the broth

14:06

Has gone OK. They're all a bit strange though

14:06

Think I'm only non-white person in the office except for two Indian guys. Boss isn't so nice. Very cold

14:06

And this colleague of mine, Lomax, is strangest of all

14:07

Nice person but a dreamer, the type Dad always warns about

14:07

Yeah. No concrete plans for life

14:10

Told me he wants to become a writer, but that I can't tell our boss

14:10

No, don't think he's ever written a book! :)

14:12

And you should see what he eats!

14:12

So, bacon sandwich at desk every morning, with coffee and expensive orange juice

14:31

Bacon sandwich is always on bad white bread with gross amounts of tomato ketchup

14:31

For lunch, another meat sandwich full of sauce, crisps, bottle of coke

14:32

I know! I asked him what he eats in evening. He said he enjoys his lunch so much that he usually repeats it for dinner

14:37

Zero vegetables every day!

14:37

Ha! Anyway, how's dad? Has he been resting, as the doctor said?

14:42

I do insist on giving you some money to help with the shop

14:42

You'll need to tell dad there was a mistake with the accounts, or you got a tax refund, something like that

14:43

Love you too

14:46

From: Julian Pickering
Sent: Friday, 19 August 2016 21:32
To: Martin Pickering
Subject: Test

Hello Dad,

Has this come through on the iPad? Call me if you're struggling with it. I do hope you come to enjoy the iPad because I much prefer sending emails than text messages etc… emails allow you to write a proper message, and they're just as fast!

Happy birthday again. Was a great evening! I've just got back to Upper Street – the worst time of the week here, with people spilling out of all the bars! We must have your plumbing seen to. I'll find a proper outfit to do it next week. You know that Mum would have never let you get away with penny-pinching like this. You have plenty of money to keep the flat well maintained. And even if you didn't, I'd pay for it myself.

A further reminder that it's a midday kick-off tomorrow, so I'll be picking you up at eleven. Will be wearing my new Charlton shirt!

Love you,

Julian

———

From: Julian Pickering
Sent: Saturday, 20 August 2016 11:07
To: Martin Pickering
Subject: RE: You're late for Charlton

Well, I see that you can certainly use an iPad…! Impatient as always! Have just parked, so will be with you in five minutes. We still have ample time to get to the stadium. I found your old scarf, by the way!

———

WhatsApp messages from Wen to Hannah
Saturday, 20 August 2016

Wen

I appreciate you were all drunk, but I could have done without the banter about me and boys, or rather my lack of boy

17:10

And if you didn't like the Hot Pot you could have just told me before we went out to meet them, instead of having a private joke later!

17:12

20

> Hey. No worries. Forgiven and forgotten. Sorry I can't join in with drinking games but I never grew up with alcohol and I go bright red!
>
> 23:07

> Cool. Yeah, onwards and upwards. Back with the 'writer' tomorrow. Maybe he's the one… at this point perhaps I should take what I can get!
>
> 23:10

From: Lomax Clipper
Sent: Friday, 26 August 2016 12:23
To: Katie Wetherden
Subject: Aurora and the novel

Another week passes, another sixty notarial seals affixed. Yesterday afternoon, while in a sort of trance, I ended up affixing seals to a number of documents I had been supposed to photocopy.

'Jesus Christ, you've invalidated my passport!' Julian shouted. 'You're going the way of Derek!'

Wen did an urgent piece of legal research for the rodent, and quite awfully it turned out that he was right: passport completely invalidated! Luckily he's already had his summer holiday!

I can't imagine how gruesome it must be to be stuck in a Goldman Sachs meeting room. It's sad if your job is preventing you from seeing David (who is GORGEOUS!) as much as you'd like. I know how much you secretly loathe the City, and that Ross is getting fed up of London – he told me so last weekend when I came over. Your less ambitious husband misses Huddersfield, and why shouldn't he?

Aurora has finally replied. Her English is sub-optimal, but she managed: 'Stop stress me, freak!' However, I was soon lifted from my depression by a follow-up message in Italian that said it was beautiful that I had come to Sicily to see her, and that she thinks of me often…

I spoke to my parents about her last night. They had initially expressed unbridled joy when I had said I had found someone new. But they've cooled significantly since, as details of her personality have emerged. No surprise there, but I wanted to understand why my dad seemed so uninterested in my time in Italy generally. After all, we are probably the most European family in the whole of Huddersfield. My dad and I are the descendants of Klopfer, the man who came to love this country, and, more to the point, Norman Clipper met a pretty, French woman called Fabienne during his own adventurous six months as a young man. He passionately identifies as European, and after the Brexit referendum he told his wife that, as far as he was concerned, it had not happened. So his lack of enthusiasm about anything to do with my experiences in Italy left me perplexed.

Last night's conversation cleared things up. The indifference is nothing personal, just a symptom of his mental state. He told me that, exciting as new foreign places are at first, 'they all lose their magic after a while'.

My mother told me to ignore my dad in relation to Italy (but not in relation to Aurora). She reminded me that he used to adore going back with her to Lille to visit her family, and that it was only after the breakdown that he had decided that he 'would not go again'.

Of course, neither of them approved of Aurora's politics. My dad said that we must cling to the centre-left; that populism and extremism and madness were on the rise once more. My mother told me that she knew what the communists in France and Italy were like. And reminded me that my name was Lomax and that I was a Scrivener *Notaire*.

The bell has just rung. Julian has risen from his desk with a pensive expression, and is tightening his tie. I don't know why, but occasionally I get the urge to walk over to him, look him squarely in the eyes, and then pinch the fleshy part of his arm, really hard, just to see what he would do. What WOULD he do, in your view?

I will tell you the exciting news about the novel after luncheon.

A brief editorial intervention. It was suggested by some, during the editorial process, that by this point in the correspondence the reader may be finding the material rather light, and inconsistent with the notion of a 'countdown' to a 'killing'; or perhaps may have already become absorbed in the vicissitudes of certain characters' daily lives and thereby distracted from the bigger picture. Accordingly, we think it reasonable to urge all readers to keep their eye on the ball – this all ends with somebody murdered.

WhatsApp messages from Wen to Hannah,
Friday, 26 August 2016

Wen

Continues to be super fucked up here. The writer gazes
out of the window for hours on end

12:31

He tells me that he finds it calming and 'conducive to
creative thought' to count the black cabs that pass by, and
the City workers who refuse to use an umbrella

12:31

Tried to speak to him earlier. He turned to me and put
finger to his lips! WTF?!

12:32

He's not an actual writer, of course… never published
anything, or indeed written much, so far as I can make
out

12:32

But he keeps telling me that the novel he's working on
must be kept secret from our boss

12:32

> Yeah! I must admit he does make me laugh, though, and he's definitely a good person. There's something kind of cute about him, in a weird way!
>
> 12:42

> Also, nobody seems any good at the job here. I think if I put my head down I could make partner in a few years. Maybe getting ahead of myself, but the work is really not that hard!
>
> 12:43

From: Lomax Clipper
Sent: Friday, 26 August 2016 14:05
To: Katie Wetherden
Subject: Re: Aurora and the novel

Wen's luncheon included Squirrelfish, a fish I've never tried, and which I hope sounds more appetising in Chinese. Profoundly unhappy juxtaposition in the English, isn't it?

The good news is that she is beginning to appreciate my humour. Until today she had resisted joining me in mocking our boss, but when I noted to her that Julian's hair was so black that it brought to mind the occult, and referred to him as the rat-witch, she finally broke.

She has such a lovely smile!

Now, the novel. My new idea doesn't quite involve starting afresh. Instead, my plan involves a reformulation of my original idea, retaining its working title, *And Earlier There Were Ten*.

As that title implies, the original idea had been to reverse the chronology of Agatha Christie's classic. So that instead of starting with ten people stranded on an island, and having someone killed at regular intervals, you begin with the final murder on the island (in my case, it will be Easter Island), without identifying murderer or victim, and work backwards.

Professor Melanie Nithercott's most demoralising comment on the opening chapters that I completed in Italy was that she had found the novel's first line hilarious, before realising that it was not intended to be. But, irony of ironies, it was this very comment that ended up giving me the new idea.

'"That's for me to know," (s)he said, before pulling the trigger.'

While I was on Ustica I kept thinking about that first line, particularly the '(s)' preventing identification. I began to wonder whether the novel couldn't be turned into a piece of comic fiction: a sort of pastiche of itself. It is fun writing crime fiction, I thought… but it might be even more fun taking the piss out of it…

As the idea grew, I realised that I might have had a bona fide stroke of genius. And that all I needed to do was make the novel even worse. Make it as bad as a novel could be. And perhaps imply that the narrator himself hated the story, and had been compelled to tell it. After reworking the first few pages last weekend, I found them to be laugh-out-loud funny. But I couldn't discount the possibility of hysteria, so I sent them to Melanie and have been anxiously awaiting her response.

She replied yesterday. I am pasting the key part below.

'I laughed and laughed, Lomax. I think you may be on to something. The narrator is so wonderfully bitter.'

I told you that I could write! I'm going to go for this now. My plan is to rework the first three chapters, send them to Melanie and, if she still approves, plough on with new material.

I know it's ridiculously early, but just imagine if I got published and it became a bestseller… What would all the partners here say?! A famous writer, just think. It's happened to others, so why not to me? This novel is my way OUT. The way to recover my self-esteem. The path back to Italy!

———

WhatsApp messages from Wen to Hannah
Saturday, 27 August 2016

Wen

Nah, am heading down to Brighton to see my parents today…

10:10

Dad's got himself into a big financial mess with their grocery store. He's super stressed again, so soon after his heart attack. Shouting at my mum a lot, which I hate

10:10

I'm going to review the accounts and see what I can do. It's horrible to be at their age and not have financial security.

10:11

Sorry for opening up like this, I know they'd be devastated if others knew (and obviously it's confidential that the business is in trouble)

10:11

Anyway, hope all good at the school today. That pupil sounds a nightmare!

10:11

Sorry, having one of my little anxious moments here. Shouldn't have told you about the business issues as it's key that customers and others think things are fine. I'd never forgive myself for ruining everything for my parents because of blabbing like that

10:58

And actually I need to clarify, things are not as bad as I'd thought, really. So please forget earlier message!

10:58

_____

From: Wen Li
Sent: Saturday, 27 August 2016 16:36
To: Dominic Corcoran
Subject: Moment of victory

Hi Dominic, just to say that I got the Tube down from Finsbury Park to Victoria and then the train on to Brighton earlier. Piece of cake! :)

_____

WhatsApp message to Hannah
Saturday, 27 August 2016

Wen

Hey, hope you got my messages today! Night, Wen

23:52

_____

From: Lomax Clipper
Sent: Friday, 2 September 2016 14:55
To: Katie Wetherden
Subject: The rat-witch KO'd

Until luncheon today, I had limited material for this Friday's update. Aurora has deigned to speak to me this evening, and I'm going to bite the bullet and invite her to London. Life's too short, and her mood swings are too severe, to make any sense: after each outburst I keep thinking, 'that's my line in the sand', and then she sends a sweet message and my mind becomes a whirlpool of confusion. It's an entirely new psychological experience for me – equivalent to seeing the sun then the rain, the sun then the rain. For instance, the other night she said that she was going out with one of her male friends, who apparently fancies her. I said, a little coldly, that I hoped she'd enjoy herself, and I got message after message of absolute vitriol. She called me pathetic, stupid, aggressive, sick etc… then an hour later sent me a heart emoji!

I'm heading up to Huddersfield tomorrow for the weekend. I've done some good work on the novel, and at times have yelled with laughter. It's coming on almost frighteningly well. The only mildly disturbing thing is that I've become so involved in it that I occasionally fuse what's going on in the book with what's going on outside it – indeed, the novel has now intruded into my dreams. It's set on Easter Island, but last night I dreamt of a murder taking place in central Palermo, under wild moonlight and the starriest of skies. Freaky!

As Google Maps will confirm, our offices are a mere twelve-minute walk apart. Isn't it such a uniquely London thing that you can be so physically close to someone yet not feel physically close at all? Anyway, I'm sorry you'll be working all weekend. Here is a story that may help you through it.

The rat-witch's tie was very tight when he arrived this morning. Later, he cut short luncheon in the Partners' Room and came rushing back to his desk while Wen was still eating. I asked him if everything was OK.

'No,' he said, gazing very anxiously at his screen. 'SOME of us have responsibilities.'

He then turned to look at Wen. Apologising to us both, he explained that he had a major client coming in shortly and a number of problems to fix, so he would have to demand silence.

'No problem,' said Wen, before returning to her soup. She seemed quite oblivious to Julian's glances. Once she had finished the soup, she opened a little plastic box. My heart skipped a beat.

'Chicken feet,' she whispered, a little too loudly, shrugging her shoulders in her very sweet way. She also brought into play a jar full of an intriguing black substance. With everything set, she lifted a chicken foot from the box with her chopsticks, took a big bite and began to chew…

'For fuck's sake!' Julian yelled, suddenly. The outburst came and went in a flash – he fell silent immediately, his face reddening.

Oh dear, Mr Chairman of the Inclusion Committee. I saw that Wen had understood everything re the red cheeks, so I goaded her on with a wink. She apologised to Julian, murmuring that this sort of lunch was normal in China. Quite superbly, she dabbed her eyes. Inspired, I sought to exacerbate things by saying, 'don't cry, Wen' – a sort of voice of solidarity against oppressors all over the world.

'Hang on, there's been a misunderstanding here!' the oppressor exclaimed, jumping to his feet. 'I wasn't referring to your…

your Chinese lunch! It's any sound of eating. It's an issue I have, a psychological issue...' He hurried over to Wen's desk and asked her – with a face of intense cultural interest now – what the black substance in the jar was.

Wen said that it was squid ink. As Julian became very still, I suggested that he should try it. Before he could reply, Wen said not to worry if it grossed him out.

'Why would it "gross me out"?' the rat-witch asked, his voice wild.

'I have a spare plastic spoon, from the café,' I said – according to Wen, very solemnly.

'Great!' yelled the rat-witch.

He put a spoonful of squid ink straight into his mouth, then turned very quickly indeed, managing only an unusual 'mmm'. Shortly afterwards, Wen headed off to some medical appointment. The rat-witch smiled at her indulgently as she passed his desk. Once the door had closed behind her, I asked him if he fancied another spoonful.

'Fuck off, Lomax!' he hissed, revealing a black tongue. Christ, this man needs a good woman.

―――――

From: Julian Pickering
Sent: Friday, 2 September 2016 15:01
To: Toby Enslin
Subject:

Toby, sorry, terrible afternoon here in the office. I wanted to say that I love you with all my soul, and would never dream

32

of judging the alcoholism. I hate myself if that's how you interpreted my flippant comment last night. I was tired, and I guess am weak at times. You're a lovely brave man and I am the luckiest man in the world. I appreciate that this is partly my fault, and that my reticence about our fully coming out as a couple, as you call it, has caused tension, and is probably one of the factors at the root of the relapse. I agree that, given that we are two men in their fifties, my position is absurd. And who would NOT be proud of being with a crazily beautiful person like you?!

But I have struggled all my life with making my sexuality common knowledge. Even with my own father, it's something understood but not really spoken about. I am a walking anachronism, I know, and this makes me so ashamed of myself. But my sexuality remains an intensely private thing for me. I appreciate it's something I need to work through – and I will. Anyway, things are very stressful at present, work is intense, rumours of an imminent reshuffling of the partnership continue, and if they kick me out the flat goes, your psychiatrist goes, everything goes. It's all reliant on my partnership drawings.

I love you so much that to tell you properly would take a thousand hours.

WhatsApp messages from Wen to Mum
Friday, 2 September 2016

Translation from the original Chinese

Wen

Hi. Yes, week nearly over!

15:03

Actually, I'm a bit upset

15:03

A few jokes about my food this afternoon. I joined in but actually feel quite sad now

15:03

The only funny bit was, you remember that Spanish thing you hate, which I got obsessed with during my black food fad?

15:04

Yes, the squid ink! :)

15:05

So, I brought some into the office and my colleagues are so stupid, they thought it was a Chinese speciality!

15:07

Haha! I know, right? Sooo ignorant...

15:07

Anyway, will call later when am back in flat. Tell Dad that at 4 he's got to go upstairs and rest. That's what the doctor said

15:09

By the way, would it be nice if I came down again tomorrow for the weekend?

15:10

I promise it wouldn't be a problem. I would love to.
London can be so depressing in the rain

15:10

Wen

Hi Dominic, sorry but I'm running about 5 mins late. Good
news is I managed to brave the Tube :)

15:17

From: Lomax Clipper
Sent: Friday, 2 September 2016 21:11
To: Katie Wetherden
Subject: Aurora

Good evening.

Sorry if a second email today is a bit much, but I couldn't resist
letting you know how this evening's call with Aurora went!

Our first chat since I've been back in London. I do love speaking
in Italian. Have I mentioned that Aurora speaks almost no
English, and that my Italian is now very good indeed?

Anyway, the bottom line: she's coming to London. My instinct
that a bit of mad spontaneity might work was spot on. We did
have to jump through a couple of hoops. Her initial response
was that Sicily missed me. I said that I missed Sicily too, to
which she replied that she was confused: was I inviting her
to London or not? I had the sense of drifting, so was relieved

35

when she eventually said that she would be happy to come. But she added that she felt conflicted about me paying for her flight. (I hadn't yet suggested that I would – I had been holding back the offer as a surprise!) I said perhaps the best thing was not to talk about it. She laughed and called me sweet.

The rest of the conversation was enlightening. I learnt more than during the heady Italy days. For example, I now know that she works in a musical instrument shop (capitalist, you might say). Aurora emphasised that it was '*Addiopizzo*', which is to say that it refuses to pay the Mafia 'tax'.

Which brings me to the point that all is not well in the La Rosa household. Aurora is into the *Addiopizzo* movement, which seems a very worthy thing, but she mentioned that her family are against her involvement, just as they are against her politics and everything else about her. She described her parents as stupid and small and mean, and ranted about them for some time.

It came as no surprise to learn that her dad is not a communist. In the photo I've seen on Facebook, Gigi looks like a spiv, his white hair slicked back and his shirt unbuttoned, revealing a stunningly hairy chest. When Aurora told me of his displeasure at her involvement in *Addiopizzo*, for a second I even feared the worst, and pictured Norman Clipper meeting a member of *Cosa Nostra* at a wedding in central Palermo. Shameful, of course. Gigi will just be worried about her.

I haven't seen a picture of her mother, who apparently is both complicit and enslaved. I HAVE seen a photo of her big brother Mommo, and when it comes to him it is legitimate to be concerned. He has gold chains around his neck!

––––––––––

WhatsApp messages from Wen to Hannah
Saturday, 3 September 2016

Wen

Hey. Yeah, back in Brighton again with the folks. Main worry is my dad straining so much. He's problematically proud

18:05

This business has been his life's work since arriving in England nearly twenty years ago. And my mum's. I've decided to put in some savings of my own to help out. I owe them, after all

18:05

So, I disagree

18:09

They gave everything to make sure I had a good education

18:09

Fought like mad to build this business

18:09

Anyway, Pete sounds gutted you dumped him. Hope you were kind!

18:10

From: Lomax Clipper
Sent: Friday, 9 September 2016 16:47
To: Katie Wetherden
Subject: Huddersfield and the rest

Katie,

I've been thinking about your email while gazing out of the window here on Gresham Street, counting the already-pissed City professionals who pass by. Four red-faced buffoons in formal raincoats not made for men of their young age have staggered past already and it's not even 5 p.m. Separately I've been counting the number of ciggies a middle-aged fat man in a pinstripe suit – definitely a lawyer or banker – has had outside that posh French place, Cabotte. Six in half an hour, and still going.

Anyway, your email: I find it hard not to take Ross's side. I know I wouldn't want to be married to a lawyer who collapsed into bed at 4 every morning. Is money so important to you?

Aurora is due in London in three weeks' time. I've been tempted to tell Wen all about it, but details of my love life strike me as being too much info for her, for now. Incidentally, earlier today, Wen invited me for a drink after work. She suggested that dreadful pub I've gone on to you about before, behind the office on Love Lane. I agreed, trying my best to give no hint of how much I despise it. But just now, for no apparent reason, she's turned all cold and said that actually she has plans!

The novel is soaring. It's just annoying that all these murders in it have triggered what is now a recurring dream about someone being killed on a summer's night in Palermo, on a street drenched in moonlight, under a star-spangled sky. It's the strangest thing, and I can't even work out who's being murdered in the dream. Anyway, Melanie has told me to stop sending her new pages and to keep to my original plan of sending the amended chapters only when they are all ready.

The rat-witch has announced that he has now received the feedback from Milan, and that I'll be having my annual appraisal next week. It will be rubbish, of course, but little does he know I have rather grander plans for my life.

Huddersfield last weekend was just as my sister had warned. On the way up on the train, after changing at Manchester, I was struck by the familiar, heady sense of release, that rush of euphoria at the sight of the vast open countryside rolling out into the infinite, fresh and lovely under the rain. The moment gave rise to the usual philosophical reflections on identity and the soul: whether somewhere distant on a beautiful moor the real Lomax Clipper, pure and happy, walked alone.

Of course, the views of limitless nature dwindle as the train approaches its end destination, but then there's the high induced by the ever-surprising grandeur of Huddersfield station itself. Do you get that buzz too, on arrival? Stepping out onto St George's Square, standing for a moment under the Corinthian Portico and feeling the usual glow, I soon spotted the man who knows how to put out that glow. The Son of Klopfer was standing behind the Renault, running his hand through his comb-over. He stared at me for some time, before asking if I would drive the short distance back.

I do feel for him. The stare is now beyond language.

I definitely get my chippiness from him, by the way. Caroline's husband, Will – the banker from Manchester – has become pretty successful and they've just bought a big, modern house in Stockport. Norman Clipper cannot deal with it. As I started the car, he told me that 'Mr Bullshitter' had come round recently with Caroline and the kids.

With a sinking feeling, I asked him how my brother-in-law was doing.

'Who really knows?' he said.

Mr Bullshitter chat dominated the journey back home. I got the usual wave of nostalgia when we arrived at the line of drab terraced houses which, as you know, if picked up by a tornado and set down in North London, would probably go for about a million quid each. Not so, of course, on Longwood Road. Entering the house, I had vivid confirmation of my mother's new hobby. She was dressed in Lycra and squatting on the sitting room floor, her dark hair pulled back in a bun, her eyes closed. Squatting beside her, holding her waist, was a muscular young man.

My dad began to stare at the wall.

In the evening I interrogated my mother. I said that yoga was great, but that I'd like to understand better what New Yoga entailed. She told me to stop picking on her. She explained that New Yoga was about accessing your core and rediscovering your passion. Re-connecting with the real you. That it was about learning to thrive, not just survive.

'Fabienne,' a voice called. 'Tap's leaking.'

She shouted back that he knew how to fix it.

'Nope,' came the voice. It seemed to echo around the room.

———

WhatsApp messages from Wen to Hannah
Friday, 9 September 2016

Wen

Actually, are you still available tonight? Would be good to chat through something

17:09

I've realised there is someone I do really like, but my head's a complete mess about it. He's so distant... can't work out if he's playing hard to get

17:09

Cool! So, you won't believe this, but actually it's the Writer!

17:13

———

From: Lomax Clipper
Sent: Friday, 16 September 2016 10:45
To: Katie Wetherden
Subject: Congratulations – and my annual appraisal

I imagine that you've felt fresher than you do this morning. No idea how you do these all-nighters in the office! I hope that you're heading home to bed now and that house-hubby is not too cross. I can see you, sitting in a black cab speeding away from the City, following the course of the Thames. Crossing Parliament Square, racing onwards towards the white castles, the land of magic...

I've just read about your deal on the BBC news website. Your name is mentioned! (Surely untrue that you make a million pounds a year? Please tell me that's not true!)

41

The BBC made no mention of the man who arrived at a pub in Leadenhall Market last night with some key supplies for your all-nighter. It was impressive that you managed to fit in a glass of wine. Our catch-up was the highlight of my week – a week otherwise dominated by my novel. Of course, it was unusual to have to bring a dear friend a pair of newly bought tights. And to see her rush away after fifteen minutes. But you must take what you can get in this world.

I appreciate that you might not have time for this today, but I've just had my annual appraisal. The rat-witch kept pushing it back this week, pretending to be too busy. This morning he sprang it on me, telling me to accompany him to the meeting room 'immediately'. I raised my eyebrows at Wen, who looked away. Still giving me the cold shoulder!

Anyway, if I'd needed a final push on the novel front, Julian delivered it. I was rated 'Sufficient', so not only below 'Partnership Track' but also below 'Good'. It means that I won't get my £500 bonus this year. The rat-witch said that the feedback from Italy had been fine. The issue was the nihilistic humour and the 'low-level wind-ups'. They had not gone away.

He reminded me that I was thirty-three years old. He told me that if I was suffering from depression, the firm was there to help. But he said that he had been dismayed by what I had done to him with the squid ink. He added that the 'consistently bad jokes', which I clearly didn't even find funny myself, wore him down and distracted hardworking junior notaries like Wen.

Enough was enough, he said. Mr Curtain was a fine man.

I said that I had never suggested otherwise.

'Then why mock the name?' Julian shouted.

I replied that I hadn't made any curtain jokes since my return, mindful as I was of our discussion back in January.

'Yes, you have,' he said. He was seething. 'You sneak them in, here and there.'

Then we were back to what had happened in January, which he will not let go. I repeated for the hundredth time that I'd been told Mr Curtain's wife's name was Annette.

'Liar!' Julian yelled. 'I relied on you when I made that damn speech!'

––––––––

From: Julian Pickering
Sent: Friday, 16 September 2016 15:04
To: Martin Pickering
Subject: Tomorrow

Hi Dad,

I've just received an email from Victoria and understand that she failed to visit you this week as she had promised, and therefore has not checked on the state of this plumbing job. If you don't mind, I will arrive a little earlier tomorrow – around midday – and make you some lunch before we head off to the match. I'd like to inspect the work with my own eyes!

See you tomorrow.

Julian

––––––––

From: Julian Pickering
Sent: Friday, 16 September 2016 16:03
To: Victoria Pickering
Subject: Re: Oops

Hi Vicky,

Not to worry about the plumbing – although it would have been nice to have someone there while the men were still in the house, as in my experience it's much harder to get people back to redo a job if badly done.

But do try to see Dad when you promise to. It means the world to him, spending time with us.

Julian

WhatsApp messages from Wen to Hannah
Friday, 16 September 2016

Wen

I bottled it all week

17:38

Annoyed with myself

17:38

We live about 30 secs away from each other here in F Park! Would be so easy to ask if he fancied a quiet drink at the Bank of Friendship, that pub I took you to near mine

17:39

But he wouldn't have been available tonight for sure (writing!)

17:39

And to be fair he seems to spend every evening writing!

17:39

Yeah! Think I mentioned he's too embarrassed to bring up his novel in front of our boss?

17:43

Julian is such a dick. Bigoted, repressed, angry man! Can't believe he heads up our inclusion committee!

17:43

I know, having him join me on my jog to or from the office would have been perfect

17:53

It's less than an hour from here to Gresham Street even at a super slow pace and it's such a great run, especially on the way in

17:53

I go through Highbury Fields, then Islington, with the big glass buildings of the City getting closer and closer

17:53

But he told me he could never do what I do as he wakes last minute in the morning and in the evening hurries back for writing

17:54

Cool, say hello from me! Night of TV alone tonight for me in the damp dungeon of this house, watching stain grow on ceiling!

17:57

Yeah, but this Chinese series my mum has got me watching is mega addictive. And neverending! She's coming up to see me btw, bringing some pea shoots. Ever tried?

17:59

————

From: Julian Pickering
Sent: Friday, 16 September 2016 19:45
To: Toby Enslin
Subject: Back soon

Toby, I can't speak as I'm with the Chairman in an interminable meeting. Plus this bloody team of mine appear to have vanished, leaving me to finish everything off. I've been impressed with the new notary, but suspect I need to be clearer to her that she's to stay at her desk until I've reviewed her work, and not to be influenced by bloody Lomax.

How about a long walk on Sunday on Hampstead Heath? You used to love our long walks there – would do us good?

————

From: Lomax Clipper
Sent: Friday, 16 September 2016 23:52
To: Katie Wetherden
Subject: Re: Congratulations – and my annual appraisal

What an incredible evening on *And Earlier There Were Ten*. I thought I would wind down by sending you a supplement to this morning's email. You'll be sleeping now, no doubt!

The novel has moments of real brilliance, I believe. A verve and intense hilarity that I have only encountered previously in Wodehouse, or *The Diary of a Nobody*. I have the narrator's sulkiness down to a tee. I thought I'd attach just a page. Could you let me have your thoughts when you get a chance?

Am now going to lie back and fantasise about running around the office one fine morning with a publishing offer in my hand. The fantasy has now extended to drenching all of the partners in squid ink. Regardless, it's far more pleasant than the recurring dream about a murder under the Palermitan moonlight!

Incidentally, I booked Aurora's flight this afternoon. Her visit is now only a fortnight away. It was very annoying, actually, because I wrote to her that I'd done so and she replied that she'd thought we'd agreed that we wouldn't discuss 'vulgar' things! Direct translation!

Apparently, her (still stupid) family must not know about the visit. She hasn't explained why, but my guess is that it's because her dad and elder brother are rather protective. Gigi the spiv, Mommo the killer and Luisa the unseen have been told that she's visiting a friend in Milan.

I told her that the plan will fail if they call her phone, because the sound they'll hear will be different. She said to stop worrying – but emphasised she was making a big sacrifice for me. Difficult to enjoy being told that in such dramatic terms...

I've just been looking at big brother Mommo again on Facebook, worrying. It's not actually the gold chains or the black leather jacket. It's not even the size (he's a big boy). It's the expression on his face.

———————

From: Lomax Clipper
Sent: Saturday, 17 September 2016 10:37
To: Katie Wetherden
Subject: Charming

Dear Katie,

Thanks for the email about me, intended for Ross. I've told you before that working through the night is dangerous.

I was surprised to learn that my email of last night was 'exhausting to have to read'. My emails are not sent with any obligation attached. Anyway, I had assumed you were sleeping.

Despite the subject line 'Lomax', I did wonder whether I should be reading an email intended for your husband. I skipped over the private bits but it was impossible not to pick up on the tension at home. Surely this way of life is no good for David.

Presumably you thought that some distraction was in order – and that I was your man. I have now deleted the email but before doing so I copied and pasted some highlights:

'Non-stop emails today.' (NOTE: Two emails, actually. In August, you specifically requested the resumption of the Friday updates.)

'He's at it again, about the book. Now asking me to review an excerpt. With all I've got to do here!' (NOTE: Consider the request withdrawn.)

'It's becoming close to pathological, his desperation to prove himself. I'm really not sure he's even any good at writing. I hope I haven't played a part in causing this. It must be very irritating for him to have to listen to his dad go on about this ridiculous career of mine.' (NOTE: What arrogance! In terms of my ability, I would refer you to Professor Melanie Nithercott.)

'He's so lonely.' (NOTE: Thank you.)

'Aurora sounds insane and deeply unpleasant. How can he believe it will ever work? The real problem is that Lisa shattered his confidence when she left him.' (NOTE: Possibly true about Lisa. Harsh about Aurora, and you ignore entirely the multi-faceted and absolutely captivating nature of her personality.)

'This recurring dream he has about someone being murdered in Palermo – surely it's his mind telling him something about the unhealthiness of this thing with Aurora?' (NOTE: I will defer to you on that, given your vast psychoanalytical experience.)

'I suppose it can't be easy still being single, alone in a little flat in Finsbury Park with a permanently leaky roof. Must be grim seeing everyone around him settled down and happy – like me, with my lovely husband and our gorgeous baby!' (NOTE: A very unconvincing little clarification there, at the end. I would also note that I deliberately chose Finsbury Park as an area to live, and still adore it, because of its amazing diversity and cultural richness. You've admitted several times that you like the area yourself – although you've still not visited my flat and thus seen how quaint my street and those around it are. The area as a whole is cool and inclusive, words that cannot be applied to Pimlico. And, for completeness: there have been no new roof leaks since my return.)

So, Mrs Wetherden. We have known each other since the age of nine. It's been a good quarter-century. Keep well, and my best to Ross and David.

Suspension of all communication from Lomax Clipper to Katie Wetherden. Katie's calls and emails of apology go unanswered throughout the remainder of September and the entirety of October. Towards the end of October, the apologies turn into accusation, with Katie noting that Lomax has no idea how difficult it is for a mother to work the hours she does.

In the meantime...

WhatsApp messages from Wen to Hannah
Monday, 19 September 2016

Wen

Asked the Writer if he fancied a drink at some point this week. He's exhausting himself at the moment on his book and seems spaced out!

12:18

He gazed at me very strangely for a long time, before declaring that, sadly, his working day starts when he gets home

12:18

Maybe revenge for me changing my mind last time? Who knows?! Anyway, sod him!

12:19

Friday, 23 September 2016

OK, you know what, I'll come

09:34

Will plaster on some heavy duty makeup to hide the inevitable crimson flush

09:34

Cool! Feels appropriate to join for drinks tonight. Week has been dull but I've got a reason to celebrate!

09:36

The rat-witch has given me an early review. Had some constructive criticism, but told me that generally he's pleased with my performance so far!

09:36

Saturday, 24 September 2016

Yuk. Sorry! Was I that bad? Remember trying a cartwheel or something in Covent Garden?! Definitely not drinking again

09:34

You're very good at being reassuring Hannah! Obviously I'm sorry if I embarrassed you. Tequila shots not for Wen. Surely you can see the funny side?

09:56

Tuesday, 27 September 2016

Hello! So sorry again for last weekend. Bumble date tomorrow. That app is so weird. A lot of men seem to have a bit of fetish for Chinese girls, which makes me feel, well, not great. This guy seems OK though. American, looks quite a hottie but nice!

11:20

Wednesday, 28 September 2016

So, last night was shit

09:31

I arrived at the (completely pretentious) bar in Chelsea as agreed, and he was there with his motorbike

09:31

Said he would drive us down the Kings Road to an even better bar he knew. I'm terrified of motorbikes so procrastinated and suddenly he looked at me and said, you know what, this isn't going to work. And just left! :(

09:32

Haha, good luck with yours. I'm chatting with three, all seem OK, but am a bit wary after the Disaster. Anyone who talks only about China I quickly delete

09:34

From: Julian Pickering
Sent: Wednesday, 28 September 2016 10:45
To: Toby Enslin
Subject: All sorted with the Priory

Toby, I have sorted everything on the financial front. It is going to be very painful saying a temporary goodbye to you on Friday, but I fully agree that we are at intervention time once more. Last night your behaviour was not safe for either of us. I counted five empty bottles of wine in the kitchen this morning and, as you well know, this amount will end up killing you.

WhatsApp messages from Wen to Hannah
Thursday, 29 September 2016

Wen

Hey, many congrats indeed! Deputy Head is incredible at your age! Not so good down in Brighton. Dad's had a funny turn again and had to be taken to hospital in an ambulance

12:59

Am in an Uber to Victoria now to get the train. Think he is stable

12:59

My mum is in a state, though. Both of them are worrying about who's going to man the shop. This bloody business is killing them

13:00

You know that Lomax (the Writer) is just the sweetest man I've ever met? He was so kind this morning when I got the news. Lovely, lovely boy! My boss was OK too, to be fair

13:01

Cheers Hannah. Dad's staying overnight but back tomorrow. You and Lomax have been great today

23:04

Bumble chats meanwhile, wow! One guy said, so sorry to hear, assume we're not on for this weekend then? And then deleted me!

23:04

Yeah, exactly. Of course your parents were always going to be chuffed about the promotion! Sorry I can't celebrate it with you

23:53

I agree about the shop, but my parents' generation in China have massive pride about money

23:53

It's like totally unthinkable for them that they could go bankrupt or something. (They won't! As I say, it's not as bad as I'd feared)

23:54

No, I can't, because as I said I'll be here this weekend

23:56

I said he was coming home tomorrow. I didn't say it was all fine. There's a difference!

23:56

Tuesday, 4 October 2016

Glad the party went well. Definitely deserved. Nice pics too. Paul is very handsome! Sorry again I couldn't make it

08:08

Friday, 14 October 2016

Hello. How's stuff with you? Thought I'd let you know that my parents might be selling up! Thank God. They might even be considering finding somewhere in London nearer to me if they do sell. How's it going with Paul?

10:00

Moody! Was only an update

10:04

From: Julian Pickering
Sent: Wednesday, 26 October 2016 23:45
To: Toby Enslin
Subject: Hope this gets through Alcatraz

Very moving seeing you today. We're going to get through this, Toby. I love you.

Communication between Lomax Clipper and Katie Wetherden resumes on Wednesday, 9 November.

Incidentally, lest the reader be overly caught up in our characters' mini-dramas, how about reminding ourselves of the impending murder? How about jumping ahead ten months, for a moment, to underscore our point about keeping one's eye on the ball?

Palermo. Saturday, 2 September 2017. Excerpt from an article buried on page eight of *Giornale di Sicilia*, Sicily's leading newspaper. Translation from the original Italian.

'There was blood everywhere. Rivers of blood. And the screaming. The horror. My God, this will haunt me for the rest of my days,' sobbed a local resident, dressed in black, who has lived in the *palazzo* on Via Lungarini all her life – but who refused to give her name.

From: Lomax Clipper
Sent: Wednesday, 9 November 2016 11:56
To: Katie Wetherden
Subject: Your husband

I tried to call earlier. I have received an email from Ross. I was very sorry to read that you've had to take some time off due to anxiety.

He said that you woke late one morning, after minimal sleep, couldn't find your laptop and suddenly lost your mind. He said he's never been so frightened in all his life for you. He added that he loved you more than anybody had the right to love someone, that you and David were his whole life, and that this job was killing you.

He begged me to drop you a line. He said you were terribly upset about the email you had mistakenly sent to me. Out of his love for you he forwarded three other emails that you've sent him about me in the past.

They nearly made me cry. I suppose deep down I've always known what you thought of me. Oh, Katie, what have you got yourself into with this stupid law firm? The wheels have come off, haven't they?

Ross also asked me to consider whether we don't all betray each other from time to time in what we say to others. Whether it isn't cruel how these days our words are too often written, and unthinkingly given permanence.

To test the theory, I tried to recall any unpleasant emails I'd written about you over the years. I did find a couple I'd sent to Lisa. Reading the snide remarks, noting the portrait of a person who was not really you, I didn't like the man who wrote those emails.

Let me know if you're free this evening and I'll come down to Pim and fill you in on Aurora's visit. And we must discuss the news from America! Wen, who is my friend again after her odd little cool period, was in stitches earlier. I pretended that I hadn't heard about Trump's victory. When the rat-witch realised that I was winding him up, he said that he 'could not do this any more'.

———

WhatsApp messages from Wen to Hannah
Wednesday, 9 November 2016

Wen

Luncheon time here! Fucked-up word, right? Ha!

12:35

Last night was just wonderful for me

12:35

Feel so light and free today

12:35

Until last night I'd not told anybody, not even my parents

12:35

Yeah, being diagnosed was such a relief itself...

12:38

> Everything slotted into place
>
> 12:38

> I realised I wasn't actually a potential serial killer with an overriding desire to push people in front of trains, or off cliff edges!
>
> 12:39

> Anyway, thanks again for listening
>
> 12:39

From: Lomax Clipper
Sent: Wednesday, 9 November 2016 17:29
To: Katie Wetherden
Subject: Re: Your husband

Katie, it has nothing to do with your being a woman, or a mother. I would say precisely the same to a man with no children – your law firm is idiotic! I have no doubt that it is harder for a woman to reach your position, but I don't see the logic of you setting about ruining your life out of some misplaced pride. You could do a thousand more worthy jobs!

No worries about this evening. Saturday it is. Delighted to hear that about the Friday updates. Are you sure you're being honest? And where would you like me to start? Aurora's visit, the status of the novel or events in Huddersfield?

Re Wen, yes, she's single (most surprisingly) but, no, she definitely doesn't fancy me. Anyway, she knows all about Aurora now and the... interesting weekend I had with her.

Wen

Yeah, it's so hard to get people to understand the cruel irony of it… I mean, that the very terror of doing something makes you fixate on it

17:31

And it takes a very special person, like you, not to judge

17:31

I wouldn't wish an OCD spike on anyone and I guess I've reached the point in my life when I just had to tell someone other than my psychologist. And now I'm so glad I did!

17:32

From: Lomax Clipper
Sent: Friday, 11 November 2016 12:29
To: Katie Wetherden
Subject: Aurora's visit – Part 1

Looking forward to seeing you and Ross tomorrow!

Now, Aurora. I felt my jaw drop when I met her at Stansted airport. Was that impossibly beautiful young woman with the slender arms and Latin curves and big brown eyes and radiant olive skin really walking towards me, bringing the sun with her, carrying all my dreams like bunches of flowers? Had she really toned down the bedraggled look just for London?

'My writer,' she said sweetly (in Italian).

That was the Friday evening. Let us now fast-forward twenty-four hours to early Saturday evening on Romilly Road. The pluses so far:

- I remain profoundly affected by her beauty, to the extent that I cannot quite think straight (on reflection, not necessarily a plus);

- she has shown at least token enthusiasm re the novel;

- I've had confirmation that she works full-time at that musical instrument shop;

- she has touched me with her fiery earnestness about the *Addiopizzo* movement's goal of eradicating the Mafia tax;

- she has continued to dress like a moderate leftie while in London. No rags; and

- she seems to have been very pleasantly surprised, almost turned on, by the edginess of Finsbury Park Station at night. More so still by the charmless nature of my flat. The hateful roof, which, in mockery of my recent defence of it, had sprung a new leak hours before I left for the airport, has become my best friend. The bucket full of raindrops is a WIN. She is close to accepting that the notarial profession is indeed very different in England. I am wondering why I cleaned the flat at all before her arrival – why I didn't tip the rubbish from the bins all over the floor.

The negatives:

- she has retriggered my Mafia paranoia by complaining ceaselessly about Gigi's disapproval of her commitment to *Addiopizzo*. I keep saying: 'I'm sure he's just concerned?'

- she has had a mild stomach complaint since late Friday night, which she blames on my 'disgusting' paella;

- there have been monologues/diatribes about Gigi, Luisa and Mommo not having the moral courage for radical politics;

- there have been insinuations that I do not have the moral courage for radical politics. She is in strong disagreement with me that hope lies in the centre-left;

- she has gone to change, so there is a possibility the rags will reappear;

- sometimes she's just not very nice. For example, my mother rang at one point in the day, just for two minutes, but Aurora became so irritated that she decided to then spend an hour emailing on my Wifi, telling me not to stress her; and

- we've not yet had sex.

The sole reason for the last point, I keep reminding myself, is just as she said: the paella. But MY stomach has been fine.

Anyway, all in all, not a disaster so far. Yet it is on Saturday night that things take a turn. For details, you will have to wait for Part 2. It's time for luncheon.

———

WhatsApp messages from Wen to Hannah
Friday, 11 November 2016

Wen

Well, the Writer's diet is spesh!

13:31

> But he's still being his lovely absentminded self here
>
> 13:31

> He seems to have had a shit time the other weekend with his psycho Sicilian ex, and I'm pretty confident it now really is all over. I'm letting things flow naturally, and (brace yourself!) I think he's about to invite me round to his for a Sunday lunch!
>
> 13:31

From: Lomax Clipper
Sent: Friday, 11 November 2016 14:41
To: Katie Wetherden
Subject: Aurora's visit – Part 2

Wen's just had a rather delicious-smelling luncheon. Fish spring rolls, pea shoots and what is known as sugar porridge, which is like a rice pudding but with brown sugar and red bean paste. Imagine the planet Mars in a snowstorm. She's still badgering me about my vegetable intake, and forced some pea shoots down me to complement my sandwich. Incidentally, do you know she's never had a Sunday roast? How can she have lived in this country since the age of eleven without having had a Sunday roast?

Back to the Saturday evening in Finsbury Park. Aurora and I are about to risk her stomach by going out for dinner and I've yet to realise that I've made a terrible mistake. I do not know it, but the Ethiopian restaurant on Seven Sisters Road will be everything Aurora hates. How is this possible? She has already said that she would love to try Ethiopian food, has she not? You yourself have been before to this restaurant, have you not? Seven Sisters Road is authentic and multi-ethnic and cool and, yes, a little edgy in places, is it not? So, what can go wrong?

Well, unbeknown to me, the restaurant has changed greatly since I last visited. It's been a year since I went and I did not think to check. Its quality has made it famous in the area – it has been 'found' by the prats from Angel, made a fortune, done itself up. A little haven of pretentiousness on the otherwise unpretentious Seven Sisters Road. Taxis unload lawyer and banker types directly outside it as Aurora and I approach, a sense of doom building inside me, my anxiety preventing clear thought. Aurora enters gleaming Injera in rags. She gazes at the clientele, the elegant Scandinavian waitress, the ornate ceiling. She turns towards me, her face asking: *Et tu, Brute*?

Once seated, Aurora says she is not interested in the menu; she says that I should order for her. A couple who resemble ever so slightly David and Samantha Cameron glance at her and Aurora mouths, '*Vaffanculo.*' She changes her mind, takes the menu, stares in disgust at the high prices. She asks how an open-minded writer could like this sort of place.

I explain that it has changed beyond recognition. From the menu, I note that the place now sells wine, not just beer. In a weird and perverse form of panic, I end up buying an expensive bottle of wine, thereby compounding matters. Aurora has only one glass. I have nearly finished off the rest of it before the food arrives – the service is appallingly slow. Later, while we are eating, I order a further glass. It never comes.

The mood is better by the time we leave. I have become witty after the wine, and part of Aurora has begun to see the funny side of my own earlier surprise. Vicious jibes do continue on the way back to Romilly Road, but I vanquish them with my humour. (Honestly, her hypersensitivity – when it comes to herself – is unique. Her feelings just seem so raw: it takes her ten times longer than the rest of us to get over anything negative).

When we get home, I stand under the drips coming through the bedroom ceiling and say that I'm just having a quick shower to freshen up. And now, finally, Aurora REALLY laughs. She draws me close and with a wink says that her stomach ache has gone away…

I do the moonwalk in my bedroom in celebration, while she takes a real shower. Yet, a short time later, the unthinkable happens. After over forty long nights of dreaming, the sight of her naked on my bed proves too much. I am simply too anxious.

Aurora does nothing to help or reassure. She just looks so terribly offended. I kiss her cheek and whisper my apologies. She asks me what the matter is. All good, just nerves, I assure her, as she tuts. I close my eyes and fall asleep listening to the rain dropping gently into the bucket. Minutes later I wake screaming, on account of my recurring dream.

A bleak story, isn't it? Anyway, the next day she hardly spoke to me, except to declare that I must have some serious problems and that men are queuing up to date her – which struck me as an extraordinarily weird and insecure thing to say! At Stansted I said that I hoped we would see each other soon, and that I would be happy to join any queue. She replied that there was a lot to think about. Then off she went, back to Sicily.

Oh, your email has just come through – no worries about tomorrow!

From: Julian Pickering
Sent: Friday, 11 November 2016 15:10
To: Martin Pickering
Subject: Charlton tomorrow

Hi Dad,

It's freezing cold outside so I absolutely insist that tomorrow you wear the Parka.

I had forgotten that it was a midday kick-off again, so wanted to warn you that if the traffic is as bad as usual, there's an outside chance that I'll be a little late picking you up. I'll aim for eleven but it may be half past, which means at worst we'll miss the first five minutes of the match. I'm so sorry about that, but my friend Toby has been unwell and I need to visit him in the hospital.

Also, I've over-ordered some stuff from Waitrose so will be coming with some food and other supplies – whether you like it or not!

Julian

From: Julian Pickering
Sent: Friday, 11 November 2016 17:59
To: Martin Pickering
Subject: Re: Charlton tomorrow

Hi Dad,

I'll do my best to be there for eleven, as I say. And yes, Toby is indeed the same friend I've mentioned before. You didn't bother to ask, but I'm delighted to add that it's nothing too serious – he's having a small operation.

Julian

Morning, beautiful man! Yes, I left money on the kitchen table for the cleaner this morning. I'm watering the plants each night.

It was so emotional seeing you on Saturday morning that I left only semi-understanding the revised plan. Will it be three weeks from today that you're out? I can't wait to have you back in this flat. So sorry again that I had to rush off towards the end. Couldn't be late for my old man!

I love the idea of you taking up a Master's. With respect to the financials, I remain hopeful that there'll be a reasonable pool this year for partner drawings and that I'll end up making around £200k for the year. That would, of course, be ample for us in our current living arrangements. However, the partnership reshuffle has been confirmed – we'll be informed of the details in the Annual Partners' Meeting at the very end of December. The associates aren't to know anything. It is causing me sleepless nights. Please keep your fingers crossed.

Love you to bits. You looked a new person on Saturday. We just need to ensure that, once you're back, you find your place in the world – there's so much you can do.

About my previous reluctance to 'present' you to work colleagues and my family – it's not about you, of course. It's always been like this for me. But I want to let you know that, once you're back, I intend to do just that. These stuffy notaries don't even know I'm gay! It'll be such a release,

69

finally, being open with everyone. Can't believe I'm saying that at fifty-five.

As for the drinking, there's no doubt you can do this – we had two excellent years before this latest slip.

WhatsApp messages from Wen to Hannah
Monday, 14 November 2016

> **Wen**
>
> I'm so pleased about Paul. You got lucky with him, I think! Regarding OCD, yes I'm on medication. And sure, but what else do you wanna know?!
>
> 09:49

> Well, what if I told you that once when I was in a restaurant with you in Camden, that Argentinian place, I was too scared to pick up the ridiculously sharp steak knife? Has that freaked you out enough?! Haha!
>
> 10:22

> I see that the last example was too much info. Sorry if it disturbed
>
> 10:31

> I would emphasise that this is the whole point of OCD… I'm actually, literally, the least likely person to stab a person with a steak knife. A bit like someone with vertigo is the least likely person to jump!
>
> 10:31

Forget it, then. I see now that it was a bad idea to open up about this. Excruciatingly embarrassing. I overplayed it anyway, partly for humour

10:40

From: Lomax Clipper
Sent: Monday, 14 November 2016 10:51
To: Katie Wetherden
Subject: Eliminating the backlog

Good morning.

Hope weekend was restful. The question I have for you this week, Mrs Wetherden, is whether you have the courage to leave your law firm. Ross strikes me as being overly diplomatic on this front, so it falls to me to say it.

I thought I'd complete the backlog before this coming Friday's update – for who knows what unforeseen events may occur between now and then?

First, it's not officially over – indeed Aurora wrote recently to say that she'd been thinking about Ustica. But whenever I steer the conversation towards the status of things, she changes the subject and tells me not to stress her. When I could no longer repress my indignation at being spoken to in that way, she escalated things rapidly, and told me to stop stalking her (which, needless to say, makes no sense, given that I now only reply to her messages)!! I take your point on her, and am perhaps close to coming round to agreeing with it.

As for the novel, back in October I realised I was going off on tangents, overdeveloping certain characters inspired by people I knew. I've been working Katie Wetherden hours to fix things. The opening chapters are nearly ready for Melanie!

Wen says she can't wait to read the novel, but I've explained there's a long way to go. Talk about positive reinforcement – she said she had a sixth sense that she was talking to a future famous writer! That sugar porridge really is something else, by the way. In exchange I've just invited her to come round to mine this weekend for her first Sunday roast. I've realised I've never actually cooked one!

On the Huddersfield front, last month Norman Clipper set out for a drive in the countryside, thought better of it and returned home to find the New Yoga teacher pressing his face against Fabienne Clipper's bare midriff, stimulating her spiritual core. Once Norman Clipper had regained consciousness, he took to his bed. He has barely emerged since.

My mother tried to gaslight him, insisting that her midriff had not been bare. But apparently he said: 'I know what I saw, Fabienne. And it shook me to my own core.' (A pretty good joke, on paper, but not when told to you over the phone by a weeping man.)

My mother now sleeps in my bedroom and leaves my dad's meals at their bedroom door. She has quit New Yoga. She tells me that the fear of divorce has made her understand how much she loves her husband after all.

Incidentally, I summarised the Aurora visit to my parents by saying that, despite all my hopes, things did not go well. My mother seemed relieved. My dad had a different take.

'Christ, that's a sad story,' he said. 'You had high hopes, didn't you?'

I told him quickly that it was quite sad, but that I was OK

because my mind was on the novel, and I was feeling rather positive and excited about that.

'No, no. Go back to the girl for a minute. It's a hell of a story, that. I confess it's got to me.'

I told him not to let it.

'Too late – you've told me now.' A long pause. Then: 'I don't know how your grandad kept going as a Prisoner of War, do you?'

————

Wen

Hey, still speaking to your serial killer friend?! Just to say, yesterday the Writer finally asked me round to his on Sunday! OMG, can't believe it!

16:40

————

From: Lomax Clipper
Sent: Friday, 18 November 2016 16:16
To: Katie Wetherden
Subject: Bound feet

Happy Friday!

I've reflected on what you said about Aurora. You're right, I'm going to ask her for clarity. It's an embarrassing thing to admit, but my thoughts are not quite rational when it comes to her. Perhaps it's memories of Italy, or her beauty, or the flaming

73

sincerity of her emotions, the vulnerability that emerges when she's at her nastiest…

I'm still amused that you, of all people, are worried about my hours on the novel. How about my question to you, which remains unanswered? Are you going to leave the firm? Please do at least reflect seriously on the possibility.

Re the novel, the good news is that tomorrow Melanie's getting hit with the chapters! I want to send them tomorrow so that I can celebrate on Sunday with Wen – I think I mentioned she's ambling over from Ambler Road for Sunday lunch. My good friend count might be increasing to three!

Wen's a funny one, actually. Very coy about her personal life. As I told you, when I first met her I would have bet that, at twenty-nine, and being so stunningly attractive herself, and so likeable, she'd be boyfriended (or girlfriended) at the least. I've not yet managed to get to the bottom of why that is not the case, and whether she's dating…

The rat-witch hasn't realised that Wen is my partner in crime. Yesterday, Wen just happened to mention that her grandmother had had bound feet. The rat-witch, affecting that soul-destroying earnestness of his, asked her what that meant.

Wen explained that bound feet used to be a status symbol for girls in China, and that the custom involved altering the foot's shape so that it followed the line of the leg. She told us how the feet were first left to soak in animal blood, to soften them. How the arch was then smashed, the foot folded down and the binding cloth sewn around it.

'Truly fascinating,' Julian murmured, his mouth hanging open a little. Wen said that she would find him a picture online. He told her not to try that on her computer because the firm had a strict IT policy. Wen replied that her grandmother had been very proud of her feet. Julian went pink. He said that he hadn't meant that it would be blocked for obscenity – it was just that the policy discouraged any personal use.

I said that perhaps Wen could look it up on her iPhone instead.

'Just STAY OUT OF IT, Lomax!' he shouted, quite needlessly. Think he's close to the edge. I do wish people – you included – could get work into perspective. To be a rich bachelor and partner of Curtain & Curtain without a real care in the world, and still be close to the edge!

———

WhatsApp messages from Wen to Hannah
Sunday 20 November, 2016

Wen

Cheers. A little strange that Paul's still in touch with his ex, but wouldn't say a deal breaker for you at this point?

11:40

I'm just off on my own love adventure… the one minute walk to the Writer's place! Unusual first date, I must say, but there you go

11:40

Just bought two bottles of Rioja from the off licence on the corner. Risking the crimson tide again but there's no way my anxiety will cope without a glass or two!

11:41

So, I will say that Lomax is a very good person. I can be myself with him. He's a bit messed up for sure, and his desperation to do something amazing with this novel is so obvious and so touching, as well as sometimes a little cringe TBH

11:44

But he'd be so hurt if he knew I thought that

11:44

Might tell him about the OCD thing actually, now that the dam is broken (although as I say, please do not tell anyone else)!

11:45

Yeah, parents may have found a buyer for the grocers, but he's offering them a crap deal

11:55

They may end up at mine here in F Park for short term if they do sell… the buyer would hold on to proceeds of sale for a year, as it would be a multiple of first year's takings, or something

11:55

I'd love having them close of course, but it's going to be fucking cramped. Just like the old days in Suzhou!

11:56

Well, no, the shop and flat come all in one. They live above it. With sea views, I might add! :) Will miss those! There's a mortgage on the flat itself. All a little complicated. But it's not all bad, would have my mum's cooking to look forward to!

12:00

Agreed about the OCD. All in good time. Won't bring up the steak knife!

12:01

From: Lomax Clipper
Sent: Monday, 21 November 2016 10:59
To: Katie Wetherden
Subject: Horrible Sunday

Morning. Your request for a sabbatical is a smart move. It won't resolve things in the long term, but will give you time to think.

I had a horrible day yesterday, which is ironic because it was supposed to have been the first pleasant and relaxing day in a good while, with the damn roof finally 'fixed' again, no doubt only temporarily, by another charmer (absolute peach of a fellow, as they used to say), and the novel also temporarily out of my hands. There's no point starting new chapters until I get Melanie's verdict. The joy when I pressed Send on Saturday! I can't imagine the euphoria that must come with finishing a whole novel.

But then I had a very upsetting experience – and I cannot bring myself to forgive Wen.

In short, she was astonishingly insulting yesterday. Very sad – and to think that the day had started off in such a nice and entertaining way, with the combination of her inexperience of Sunday roasts and my cooking skills. We had a fun time on my balcony too, sipping our G&Ts, comparing our favourites from the tens of little back yards and gardens stretching out into the distance below us, seeing who could name the most churches and mosques, laughing

77

as I confused once again the Emirates with Arsenal's old stadium...

Back inside, we were a good way through our first bottle of wine with the beef still in the oven, and all seemed to be going fine, save for the fact that Wen had turned a shade of red for which there are no words. She was drinking the wine very fast. Then, suddenly, I realised that something was a little 'off' after all; that she had something on her mind.

So I tried to change the vibe by encouraging her to tell me more about herself (and by saying we should both slow down with the wine). She opened up for the first time. She told me that she'd been bullied at school in Brighton – interestingly, the Indian kids had been the most racist towards her, she said, but the whites had had a go too. She told me that whenever Mr Curtain mistakenly calls her Win, it brings it all back.

She mumbled fairly incoherently for a while about her parents – her dad has been sick and, from what I gathered, they're in dire financial straits. Then, changing topic quite abruptly, she told me that she hadn't had a boyfriend until uni in Exeter. When I asked her whether there were currently any guys on the horizon, she went painfully shy, and mentioned a handsome management consultant with whom there may or may not be something.

I said to her that the problem with management consultants is that nobody really knows what they do to make their money. I began to refer to him as Gatsby, a joke she didn't really get. She's not so literary...

Anyway, by this stage, and despite my increasingly less subtle comments, she was once again hammering the red wine. It all became a little confused and drunken on her side, and when we saw the smoke coming out of the oven, she howled so violently that she had to lie down on my sofa.

Having failed to save the beef, to my horror I turned to see that Wen's eyes were beginning to close. I sought to revive her by teasing her – very gently – about Gatsby. Suddenly, she jumped up from the sofa, lost her balance and fell into my arms. Bringing her face close, she whispered: 'Don't you understand? Gatsby doesn't exist! I like YOU!'

What a ridiculously inattentive girl. The number of times I've spoken to her about Aurora. And she's crazy, because whatever she may currently think, she can do infinitely better than me. She'd realise it soon enough if we ever did try. Anyway, I told her that I was very sorry, but she was barking up the wrong tree; that I was still very much sentimentally entangled.

She looked at me for a while, then said: 'You don't mean that Sicilian who messed you around?' I said, yes, and that I had made this clear on several occasions.

Do you know what she said next? She looked me in the eyes and slurred: 'Oh my God, you've been leading me on! You're a weirdo!'

With that, she staggered out of my flat, without saying goodbye. Leaving me standing seething and humiliated by the oven.

I received a couple of messages from her early this morning before work, which together formed the least charming apology I've ever read. There followed an intensely boring, and unnecessary, little disclosure about how she suffers from anxiety. Real snowflake-style, self-pitying, and no doubt self-diagnosed, stuff!

She even went on about what she may or may not have disclosed about her parents when she was drunk, with the most transparent attempt at retraction! I replied that she had told me EVERYTHING. Hope it rattled her. I told her that if there's one thing I can't stand, it's self-pity.

The only positive is that she hasn't had the courage to make it into the office this morning, after my response.

WhatsApp messages from Wen to Hannah
Monday, 21 November 2016

Wen

Random one, but fancy popping round to mine this evening for a catch up? Food on offer…

18:03

Cool, no worries. Say hello to Paul from me! Yeah, all good. Yesterday was nice, think he does like me, but I may have had second thoughts. Will keep you updated though!

18:08

Yeah, I know it sounds weird. But that's me!

18:17

A brief editorial intervention. This is a reminder to the reader that the Selected Correspondence does not end lightly. Things will begin to take shape soon enough. The characters do not yet know it, but an accident will lead to a good part of the action shifting to Palermo. Subsequently, ten months from now, the headline of the previously cited Giornale di Sicilia *article will read as follows (translation from the original Italian):*

Stabbed to death on Via Lungarini

From: Lomax Clipper
Sent: Friday, 25 November 2016 17:02
To: Katie Wetherden
Subject: Terrible news on the novel

This Friday update is not the most cheerful. Professor Melanie Nithercott has emailed her feedback on the novel, way earlier than expected. Would you believe that she's had 'a little thought', which is that there's no need to have time going backwards?

Will she have realised what a crushing blow this is? Does she understand how much work will be involved in re-reversing time?

The worst thing is that she's right. I see it now – time going backwards adds almost nothing except confusion. But why the hell didn't Melanie think of this earlier?

I'm going to have work like mad again. I'm certainly not giving up. I do believe that my drive, my ambition – and, yes, my talent – mean that this saga is going to end in glory. It better had: the dreams I have for the novel are the only thing stopping me from developing the Norman Clipper stare.

To exacerbate matters, Julian has got wind of my setback and is reveling in it, while pretending to be supportive. I was telling my dad on the phone, thinking I was alone in the office, when he snuck in behind me.

'Fancy that!' he exclaimed when I'd finished. He said that he was pleasantly surprised to hear that I had a little hobby.

I explained that it was not just a little hobby. And that I was quietly confident my novel would be published one day.

He said, well, good for me, and that we all must have our dreams – and gave me the most triggering little wink.

Finally, I'll confess I'm feeling bad about Wen. She's actually been off all week and I don't know why (the rat-witch clearly does, but isn't telling) – I can only assume now that she's ill and it's not got anything to do with last Sunday, and my response to her on Monday morning. I bloody hope not, anyway! Regardless, I'm beginning to think that I may have gone a little too far with that response. I've sent her quite a few messages this week, and emphasised that I can get her any supplies she needs if she's unwell, but nothing back from her. Thinking about going round and buzzing her at the flat but perhaps best not.

Will let you know how tonight's call with Aurora goes.

From: Lomax Clipper
Sent: Friday, 25 November 2016 22:32
To: Katie Wetherden
Subject: Over with Aurora

Asked Aurora for clarity. Got it. She's seeing someone else. I expressed disappointment, but acceptance. In response, she warned me not to text again or she would report me to the authorities (loose translation). Nice and normal. Happy days.

From: Lomax Clipper
Sent: Friday, 25 November 2016 23:18
To: Katie Wetherden
Subject: Re: Over with Aurora

Following my call with Aurora tonight, the usual non-stop text messages have now come through, reeking of pathology as always. Obviously, I have not replied, given her overriding threat that any response will result in a police report! I thought I'd translate the last two for you so that you get a sense of her style:

'You tell me you are "disappointed", because of your own sick, egotistical expectations and demands, which have nothing to do with me! You make me vomit, little man. I warn you – do NOT respond to this message or you will have big problems. Now DISAPPEAR forever, sad little man :)'

'PS now I will block you. By the way, Lisa was right, you are a big LOSER hahaha'

———

From: Lomax Clipper
Sent: Tuesday, 29 November 2016 15:20
To: Katie Wetherden
Subject: Signing off

Lovely to see you all at the weekend. Do keep me posted on the sabbatical. It's so weird, isn't it, the emotional part of the brain? Despite that last message from Aurora, and despite everything the rational part of my brain says, I can't stop thinking about her and the special moments we shared. No doubt about it, part of me is still in love with her and pining for her, mad as that is.

Anyway, there will be no Friday update this week, and indeed you will be hearing a little less from me for a while. I need to get Melanie this revised draft and receive her feedback before she goes off on her travels in February. It's crucial that I break the back of it before Christmas – I intend to use all of my spare time in the office.

Wen's still off sick, you know – the rat-witch has confirmed she's been in touch and is unwell, but is not elaborating. I've sent her several more messages, apologising for any confusion and for my mean message, and wishing her a prompt recovery from whatever it is. I can see that she reads them, but she generally doesn't reply. In fact, the only reply I've received from her came after I went round and dropped off a bag of treats from Sainsbury's, ranging from paracetamol and toothpaste to Milky Bars and Coke! Nobody answered any of the buzzers so I left the bag outside the front door. Half an hour later, after a bit of badgering on my part, she wrote that she was so sorry, but that the bag was no longer there.

I thought I'd sign off on a lighter note, with a tale of revenge. At luncheon today, Mr Curtain apparently approved the introduction of agile working for employees, the rat-witch's pet cause. He was on fire when he came back from luncheon and announced the news to me. He began to rhapsodise, saying that Change was about to come to these offices. I fought back hard, agreeing with him that it would be oh, barmy, to allow our minds to be Barack-aded against new ideas.

The rat-witch was not biting. He explained that agile working would involve working from home once a fortnight and changing desks every week. I said that swapping desks would be bizarre in my and Wen's case as there were only two of us.

'It's the principle of it,' Julian said, frowning at me. He turned his back and walked to the window, ranting about the importance of moving with the times.

As Julian was speaking with his back still turned, the diminutive Mr Curtain came suddenly into the room, his red braces on and his white hairs standing dismally each side of his pate.

Reacting quickly, I called over to Julian, asking him whether he would be swapping desks every week too. The rat-witch swivelled around in a fury, yelling that he was a PARTNER.

'For God's sake, Julian!' Mr Curtain cried.

———————

From: Lomax Clipper
Sent: Tuesday, 29 November 2016 15:25
To: Katie Wetherden
Subject: Re: Signing off

PS I forgot to mention that I have a spare ticket to the National Literacy Trust Christmas dinner on 20th December. Yes, really – Mr Curtain paid for several out of his own pocket and offered them up on a first come first served basis in a firm-wide email, by way of this year's Christmas surprise. Dinner is at Simpson's in the Strand, no less! You or Ross fancy being my guest (I'm imagining Ross, as you'll probably be busy)? It's the one evening I'm allowing myself off before going back to Huddersfield for Christmas.

———————

You'll be sleeping now, my love, but I wanted to get something through to you in Alcatraz for when you wake.

All evening I've been re-writing this email in my head, to the sound of the rain. Unable to hear your voice, I spoke to your sister, so that she would talk to me about you, and at least I could hear your name. I went down onto Upper Street, ate at our usual table at Ottolenghi. I've been looking around this sitting room for hours, finding YOU everywhere.

A case of hypocrisy tonight, as your sensible partner decided to be a little reckless himself, and enjoy a whole bottle of Chianti Classico. A little prop, let's say.

I have no idea what's going to come of the reshuffle at the year end – none of us do, except for Mr Curtain and his henchmen. It seems to me that, no matter how hard I try, there is always humiliation. Today I had a little win – the flexible working I've campaigned so hard for was approved by the partnership. But then that little shit Lomax decided to embarrass me in front of the Chairman.

It would be pathetic to suggest that Lomax is actually bullying me now – but he's coming mighty close. I am so insulted and disgusted by the way he constantly implies that I'm small-minded. There's nothing I can do about it – nothing I can say which he won't raise his eyebrows at, or take the piss out of.

If I were feeling generous, I'd note that he has no idea that soon I might be without a job, if the worst happens. But I struggle to believe that such news would elicit in him anything but glee.

Our lives, Toby, have been a struggle, but the struggle is not in vain. We will see ourselves through this shitty period one way or another, and find our own little share of happiness. That is all this sorry struggle can really be about.

God, what a self-pitying email! I blame the wine...

WhatsApp messages from Wen to Hannah
Tuesday, 29 November 2016

Wen

Hey, sorry but I've not been well

23:43

Last week the OCD really exploded on me. Couldn't leave flat to go anywhere further than the bins outside my front door

23:43

For some reason I had to keep checking windows were properly shut. Aaargh!

23:44

And that's the least of it

23:44

Been back to the psych in Marylebone this week and changing dose. Doing some exposure therapy as well

23:44

Basically it means the psych continuing to confront you with images of your worst fears until you become numb

23:44

Can be very effective, but not the most enjoyable experience!

23:44

On you, I'd say no need to mention the little Madrid 'slip' to Paul. If it was a mistake, then telling him about it is selfish as it's only getting it off your chest. If you're confident you won't do it again, no need to mention, I'd say

23:46

On the shop front, looks like they may be going ahead shortly after Christmas

23:46

Dad seems haunted by it all. Plus as I say their money will be tied up for a year

23:46

Sofa beds being looked at on Amazon as I write!

23:46

———

From: Julian Pickering
Sent: Saturday, 3 December 2016 23:02
To: Toby Enslin
Subject: Final message to Alcatraz

I cannot sleep here for joy at the thought of you being back in this bed tomorrow! Nothing makes sense without you here. I swear I'll be a better partner, a better support to you from tomorrow – a notary's own solemn promise!

An interlude, during which Toby Enslin returns home to the flat on Upper Street, Lomax Clipper works frantically on fixing the opening chapters of his novel, now entitled And Later on Easter Island, *and Wen Li returns to work while continuing to undergo Exposure Response Prevention. The therapy is supervised by the psychologist Dominic Corcoran, whose considerable fees are covered by Curtain & Curtain's private health insurance.*

Much of the seemingly diabolical yet ingenious work involved in the therapy falls to Wen to perform outside of Dominic Corcoran's warm and exquisitely appointed consulting rooms. Wen is instructed to leave her flat without checking whether her windows are closed, accepting that one might be open. She is instructed to join the queue for the Victoria Line at rush hour at Finsbury Park tube station. She is even told to purchase a penknife and to grip it inside her handbag while talking to colleagues.

Each night, Wen crawls into bed and weeps and weeps. But then, one morning, she begins to feel a change...

Communication from Lomax to Katie Wetherden resumes on Tuesday, 20 December. Wen's communications to Hannah resume on Christmas Day. But, before then...

From: Julian Pickering
Sent: Monday, 12 December 2016 10:02
To: Martin Pickering
Subject: RE: Christmas plans

Hi Dad,

I was sorry to read this. Sorry for you, that is. As you know, Victoria is a funny one. Since the arrival of the fourth child, she and Chris seem to have side-lined both you and me. Little Anna is wonderful, of course, and I appreciate that any grandfather would want to see his grandchildren at Christmas, but the idea that you go all the way to Cobham for lunch and then have to make yourself scarce in the afternoon! I assume the suggestion is they will be driving you back to London?

Anyway, this is nonsense and you must come here to the flat instead. It's made my day, actually, as there's nobody I'd prefer to spend Christmas with and I confess I was feeling a little melancholy myself at the thought of not seeing you over the festive period. You can stay as long as you want!

I should add that my friend Toby will be here this year, but I assume that's OK.

Julian

————

From: Julian Pickering
Sent: Monday, 12 December 2016 10:51
To: Toby Enslin
Subject: This Christmas

Hi Toby,

I wanted to mention straight away that it looks like Dad will be with us this Christmas – he's been messed around by my sister. I hope this is OK. Appreciate that it means less me and you time, and I know that you declined your own sister's invitation this year in order to spend time with me, but it's also potentially a very important development. In a way, coincidentally, my dad spending Christmas with us is in line with my promise to you to be a better and more supportive partner. It feels the right time for me to stop being so ridiculous about things. And time for my dad to really accept that you're part of my life, and maybe even for him to know that we live together. Enough with this elephant in the room!

Obviously I intend to treat him like a king. I would be very grateful if I could call on the Enslin culinary expertise this year. Only the best. No turkey, let's go for the goose!

I confess I'm rather excited. As excited as I've been in years. Fancy a bite to eat in Le Mercury later?

Love you,

Julian

––––––––

From: Julian Pickering
Sent: Monday, 12 December 2016 17:03
To: Martin Pickering
Subject: RE: Christmas plans

Hi Dad,

Understood. I think it's madness, personally, but it's your choice, of course. I'll also be speaking to Victoria about this as I think it's outrageous that they're not inviting you to stay the night.

I do hope that this really is only because you want to see the kids, but I can't help thinking it's also because you didn't want to spend it here. I can guess at the reason. A rather abrupt change of tone from you, which is very saddening.

Julian

From: Julian Pickering
Sent: Monday, 12 December 2016 17:12
To: Toby Enslin
Subject: RE: This Christmas

Toby,

I confess that I had hoped for a little more enthusiasm on your part. Anyway, you can relax because Dad's not coming – he's decided to go to Vicky's after all.

And I emerge from three weeks of madness! I've been averaging four hours' sleep a night due to this Masterpiece of a novel! And not even four straight hours – I am now PLAGUED by this nightmare about an unidentified person being beaten and stabbed to death, in the distance, on a picturesque Palermitan street. The weird thing is I can never work out who is doing the killing, either, or indeed whether it's one person or several people – a crowd gathers, then scatters, gathers again, scatters, strange smiles and strange eyes flashing bright under the palest of moons. The sooner this novel is completed the better, as regards my psychological wellbeing!

The emotional/sentimental side of my mind is still tormenting me too, writing its own sad and beautiful poem entitled Dreaming Aurora. I'm aware that, in a way, the frantic work on the novel is a distraction, a crutch.

Yes, of course it's on tonight at Simpson's in the Strand! I confirmed to Ross earlier. He and I will let you know how this goes! There's going to be a raft of best-selling authors there. Joanna Trollope, Joanne Harris, Zadie Smith, William Boyd, Claire Tomalin, Michael Frayn… Lomax Clipper (haha)…

Turns out that Wen really was unwell, you know – some kind of kidney complication, poor thing. She's back at work now and we've made up, sort of, with further apologies from both sides. Things are at least now civil again.

Congratulations on the sabbatical, by the way!

PS there's now a rodent in my novel, inspired by Julian. It scurries about the island eavesdropping for the narrator. The narrator secretly distrusts and despises it.

———————

From: Lomax Clipper
Sent: Wednesday, 21 December 2016 12:17
To: Katie Wetherden
Subject: Re: I hear you surpassed yourself!

Morning. I can confirm that Ross's account of last night's events on the Strand, amid silver carving trolleys and champagne flutes, in an oak-panelled London of a distant past, is reasonably accurate, but I had a few quibbles. You know how OCD I can be when it comes to details! See below the Master's version. It is actually set during the mingling session before people took their seats for dinner – all the famous writers were doing the obligatory rounds of the circles of guests.

*****

Joanna Trollope OBE: So, your friend tells me you're a writer?

Lomax Clipper: Oh, well... let's say an aspiring writer. I'm working very hard on my first novel at the moment. It's a piece of comic fiction that –

Mr Curtain: Hmm? You're not working on a novel!

Ross Wetherden: I can assure you that he is.

Joanna Trollope OBE: The very best of luck with it! Your friend says it's bound to be good – he says he's never met anyone so passionate about literature.

Lomax Clipper: Well, Ross is very kind. But my novel's got rather a long way to go before it sells like *Chocolat*!

Ross Wetherden: Ugh.

National Literacy Trust lady: You know, Joanne Harris is here this evening too. We're terribly lucky –

Mr Curtain [sotto voce]: This is Trollope, you fool.

Joanna Trollope OBE: I must say, the champagne is quite heavenly.

*****

To set the record straight: I did not say *Chocolat* in a creepy voice.

Anyway, Merry Christmas.

———

WhatsApp messages from Wen to Hannah
Sunday, 25 December 2016

Wen

Merry Christmas, Hannah! Hope you're having a lovely day with your folks. No celebrations here, but we're all about to go for a nice bracing walk along the prom!

10:08

How's Paul?

10:08

Don't worry, I know it's a busy time! Hope Christmas was lovely

14:55

From: Julian Pickering
Sent: Thursday, December 29, 2016 13:20
To: Toby Enslin
Subject: News

It's not good news, Toby. I'm being demoted to the lowest rung of equity, which is actually worse than being a salaried partner in terms of how much I will earn. So I retain the facade of being an equity partner to the outside world, but the reality is we've been screwed. I'm not out on the street, but the bastards are saying the demotion has immediate effect, with the result that I get a mere quarter of the bonus drawings I had expected and deserved from a whole damn year's hard work. To clarify the maths: in an instant, we have seen our total income shrink in half.

I am sorry, I've failed us here. Incidentally, we are not to tell anyone – the firm doesn't want to let on to our staff or the outside world that we are, at best, struggling.

They say that if I can bring in half a million of fees next year, I might be catapulted back up. But I can't work any damn harder than I am working at present! I think that I'll have to start looking elsewhere. But where?!

Happy 2017 to you all from Longwood Road, the greatest road in Huddersfield. If not the world. Many people say that (Trump impression there).

Outside it's bracing and thrilling, an icy mist drifting in from the moors. The winter of Huddersfield. The winter of kings. Inside the fire burns bright, as does the fire inside of me. Hope all well with you, far away over the night, there in the insipid Cotswolds.

I'm a bit drunk, and have just ended the longest and most SPECTACULAR exchange with Wen. Nobody else is awake here, so I thought I'd provide you with an update on things.

I've been writing like a wild man, emerging only at mealtimes or to unwrap presents and help with chores. My mother says I am distant and is worried I'm going the same way as my dad. He had apparently made great strides in December and shown glimpses of his old self. But my sister and her family were over until the 27th and Mr Bullshitter got him down terribly.

The gloom and resentment began when the family arrived in Mr B's new Lexus, and deepened over Christmas lunch when their kids complained about having to sleep on the sofas. On Boxing Day, my dad came into my room and asked whether my novel was a love story. I said, no, it was a piece of comic fiction. He asked me again why I hadn't considered writing the love story of Klopfer and my grandmother – the story of the German Prisoner of War being marched through Huddersfield in 1945 and spotting the most beautiful woman he'd ever seen in the crowd. And Rachel gazing at him and thinking, but he doesn't look like a bad man. Rachel smiling at him through the rain. Klopfer thinking about that smile throughout his internment at Stirley Hill. The war ending, Klopfer requesting leave, then fate intervening, a chance meeting in church. Klopfer falling hard for Rachel. Klopfer falling for Huddersfield too, falling for this country. Rachel's father outraged but then softening slowly, warming to Klopfer...

I said it was a great story but he'd told me it so many times that he had broken me. That I felt only tremendous anxiety whenever he began to tell me it again.

My dad tutted, walked to my window and stared down at the Lexus. He said that he'd been very sorry to hear about Aurora and could see I was still beaten up about how it had ended. He said he appreciated that I'd had a very special time in Italy. His gentle words brought a lump to my throat and for a moment I even thought I was going to burst into tears! Just when I'd pulled myself together, he turned and motioned to be silent. Someone was coming up the stairs.

'Mr Bullshitter,' he whispered.

Yesterday I returned to London for just under two hours. When I arrived at King's Cross the fact that I'd be spending New Year's Eve on my tod hit me. My panic led to me thinking about Wen, forgiving her instantly and being rather reckless about any feelings she may still have for me. I texted her, saying that I hoped she was better, and that I wondered if she was around to keep me from wallowing in alcohol.

She replied instantly, with remarkably good banter! She said she was indeed better, but in Brighton with her folks. She added that there might just have been a whiff of self-pity in my text message. And that, if there was one thing she hated more than racism, it was self-pity.

Boom! I necked a couple of shots of whiskey in a shithole of a pub near the station, bought my ticket back to Huddersfield, and replied by saying that I couldn't stand skivers. She wrote back that she bet Aurora's new boyfriend was ripped and handsome as hell! And maybe he was even a successful writer!

That got me laughing out loud, possibly a little hysterically, and it turned out to be the most intense New Year's Eve ever! I bought a bottle of wine for my second long train journey of the day and wrote some mad stuff on the novel while continuing to indulge in the most inappropriate, yet somehow warming banter with Wen. If anyone ever read that thread, we'd both be done for harassment!

It was weird, actually, because when the train was approaching Huddersfield station I realised that I had tears running down my cheeks. Tears that I could not ascribe solely to laughter, nor to sadness.

I got a taxi from the station, as I wanted to give my parents a surprise. When I came in, my dad looked up and shook his head. He said he'd read that London was the loneliest place in the world.

But I wasn't feeling lonely at all! I was busy thinking of a reply to the latest message, which said, 'Have a nice time with your parents, LOSER AND STALKER! PS Did they ever find Lisa?!'

'Many thanks, Anxious Snowflake!' I eventually replied. 'Be brave again this coming year!'

Wen

Happy New Year! Getting engaged is a punchy resolution!

11:07

Although my main one is men-related too :)

11:07

The return of Wen Li to Bumble is about to happen. As soon as I get back to London!

11:07

Sale should be completed by end of January. Crazily fast. Horrible time for all concerned, but my second resolution this year is no self pity!

11:08

No, decided against anything with Lomax. We're great friends though. We've made a joint commitment to get back on with dating this year. Think he's still a bit beaten up about this horrendous Sicilian

11:09

———

From: Lomax Clipper
Sent: Friday, 6 January 2017 19:38
To: Katie Wetherden
Subject: A Friday update

Your first Friday update of 2017. I can't promise a resumption of regular service until I've completed these revisions. I am running out of time. Melanie is off to Spain at the end of the month!

Which reminds me that there's only a month to go until your sabbatical. Although I'm more interested to hear about the long-term plan!

Last night I worked till 5 a.m. here in the flat, woke up screaming an hour later, then could not get back to sleep. I was so drained that I treated myself to an Uber to work. I had a meeting with Julian and a client scheduled for nine. Julian is already unbelievably tense this week – he appears to be starting 2017 as he means to proceed. By five to nine, having already been held up by traffic and a brief altercation with a cyclist, the Uber was on Gresham Street, about fifty metres from the office. But then the traffic stopped moving.

I realised that my door wasn't locked and in my dazed state I disobeyed the driver. After a quick look out of the window, I opened the door only to hear a CRACK (the most sickening noise I've ever heard), and to see a cyclist shoot into the air.

He had been whizzing down the narrow space between the kerb and the stationary cars, and had been in my blind spot. His handlebars, to which – thank God – he had attached a sturdy bag, had slammed into the door. He landed on his backside on the bonnet.

He was a banker of around our age. Miraculously, he was OK, except for shock and scratched hands. He actually sought to reassure ME in the end. I was in a terrible state, apologising hysterically. Not least because, surreal as this sounds, this wasn't any old cyclist. It was the cyclist we had just had an altercation with ten minutes before! Same guy! So it suddenly dawned on me that the driver might think I was a psychopath who had had a moment of insane vengeful rage. As if I, of all people, have it in me to try to kill someone.

The whole thing's costing me a fortune. Thanks to the bag, the bike suffered limited damage, but the Uber needs work. After we'd swapped names and numbers, to my horror the cyclist hopped back on his bike. I urged him not to cycle, explaining that he might suffer a delayed psychological reaction.

'Just leave it now,' he said. But throughout the morning I had images of his face turning strange as he cycled. During luncheon I texted him saying that I did think he should go to A&E.

'STOP!' he wrote back.

I told him not to be so proud. And that he had better not cycle home!

'NOT YOUR CALL!' was his defiant final text, before he blocked me.

I said to Wen, the awful thing is that I'll never know for sure whether he gets home OK tonight. Wen said not to get her started on things like that – apparently she's a bit OCD too. I said that didn't surprise me – what Snowflake these days ISN'T a little OCD?!

Of course, I was reprimanded for arriving late. After the telling-off I walked into Julian and nearly knocked him to the floor. I am exceptionally tired.

———

Wen

Reason first date of 2017 hasn't happened yet is Lomax. He keeps offering to review Bumble conversations and I foolishly keep taking him up on it!

11:06

Last guy 'clearly had nothing to say'. Another one was 'trying far too hard, and failing'. Think I might have to stop involving him…

11:06

Oh no, he's definitely still in love with this Aurora girl. Have made my views on her clear to him. Think the batshit crazy hours on his novel are partly a way of trying to forget about her

11:10

Intrigued that you've read up on exposure therapy btw. I'm having a follow up this month. Really does work! If you've got an obsession with germs, try sticking your hand down a toilet and then forcing yourself not to wash it all day! You'd see!

11:10

So you're all interested in this again now? Not sure I want to dive deeper, given your previous reaction?!

11:15

But yeah, rituals don't have to be visible, like washing your hands. Mine are mental. So, I end up going over and over in my mind how I feel about something, or whether I nearly did something, or whether I wanted to do something. Anyway, not in the mood today, sorry!

11:15

Where's this going, Hannah?

11:27

Looks like you've actually understood nothing (silly me!)

11:27

It's the exact opposite of what you think, as I keep telling you. In my case it's all down to an absolute terror of harming anyone or anything

11:28

So basically, because of your reading, you want to know whether I've ever had an obsessive fear of killing a kitten? You know what, I'll be honest and say, weirdly enough, that did indeed happen once. Enjoy!

11:33

Whoa!

11:39

That's the most offensive thing anyone has ever said to me

11:39

And as if I even wanted to come to your sister's party!
11:39

Hope the kittens grow up to be less ignorant than you!
11:39

Cessation of all communication between Wen Li and her friend Hannah Richards. Subsequently, to her dismay, Wen discovers that Hannah has betrayed her by telling their mutual acquaintances about Wen's anxiety disorder. She swears to herself that she will never speak to Hannah again.

Meanwhile...

From: Lomax Clipper
Sent: Friday, 13 January 2017 04:56
To: Katie Wetherden
Subject: Temporary escape from Easter Island

I've somehow managed to time things so that you receive my big news on your usual Friday. It's nearly 5 a.m. again here at the desk where the magic happens, rain pattering on a roof that is to me the Sword of Damocles, but I've just sent the opening chapters of *And Later on Easter Island* back to Professor Melanie Nithercott. She doesn't know that she's going to encounter herself in the form of Detective Carla.

Today will be a challenge in the office but I see a new world opening up while Melanie reviews the chapters. With my mind away from murder for a while, hopefully the recurring nightmare should cease. And, as for real life, troubled Aurora is the past – Bumble dating app the rosy future.

———————

From: Lomax Clipper
Sent: Friday, 13 January 2017 19:05
To: Katie Wetherden
Subject: Drama

(Email dictated by Lomax Clipper and written by Wen Li.)

It is funny to think that I wrote to you so triumphantly in the early hours of this morning. Much has happened since. Wen and I have worked hard on this account of today's events, which I have found therapeutic.

I have spent most of the day in A&E at Moorfields Eye Hospital. I have a corneal abrasion, the result of trauma to the central part of the cornea. The story is set out below.

It is around 11 this morning. I am at my desk at Curtain & Curtain, playing with a pencil, exhausted after my night's work completing the revisions and a subsequent, particularly vivid recurrence of the Palermitan nightmare. Meanwhile, Mr Curtain has popped down for a chat with the rat-witch. The Chairman, who has a badly burnt pate, has recently returned from ten days in South Africa.

'A spectacular beast, the lion,' the little man has just said.

Wen, we now know, has been glancing at me, concerned that I might have gone into one of my trances. I continue to play with the pencil while Mr Curtain asks Julian whether he has heard of 'the so-called Lion Whisperer'.

Instead of simply replying that he hasn't, Julian waffles inanely. He is saved by Wen.

Wen says: 'I've seen the Lion Whisperer's stuff on TV. Terrifying! But the lions do seem to recognise him. They're even affectionate at times.'

Mr Curtain says: 'I'll bet that he never turns his back.'

Wen says: 'Hmm, I'll check next time I watch it.'

Mr Curtain says: 'Something triggers in the lion when it sees a turned back.'

There follows a pause. I have found that I am getting extremely close to being able to spin a pencil around my thumb. The key, I have found, is to propel the pencil with the middle finger.

Mr. Curtain breaks the silence by saying: 'They'd go straight for his neck!'

The image is apparently too vivid for the rat-witch. He begins to cough.

'What is wrong with you, Julian?' Mr Curtain asks.

'Apologies, Charles,' Julian says. 'I'm very...' But he is interrupted by a sharp cry of pain. He turns and gasps, before Mr Curtain lets out a piercing scream.

Wen accompanied me to A&E. The pencil fell out naturally in the end but sight in the right eye remains poor. I'm told that, as long as I apply the ointment carefully, vision should return to normal within forty-eight hours. I must not, under any circumstances, rub the eye.

Dictated but not read.

A brief editorial intervention. The above is a key moment in this Selected Correspondence. Even taking into account Lomax's pining for Aurora, who would have really believed back then that, only three months later, Lomax would be moving into Lina di Mauro's apartment on Via Lungarini, Palermo? And that, five months after that, Via Lungarini would be the scene of such chaos, with shouting and wailing from balconies, crowds of onlookers pushed back by police, sirens blaring, an ambulance speeding away into the night?

From: Lomax Clipper
Sent: Friday, 13 January 2017 20:31
To: Katie Wetherden
Subject: Re: Drama

Hi. Wen has Now left the flat. I didn't include bit about what led to the accidendt. I had just received a tExt from Aurroa! Said she Missed me! Cannot Believe it! Z

_____

WhatsApp messages from Wen to Rob
Friday, 13 January 2017

Wen

Hey Rob, it's Wen! We've taken the next step and are in the scary real world outside of Bumble! Sorry couldn't reply earlier, had to take a friend and colleague to hospital… strange as this sounds, he had managed to stick a pencil in his own eye!
20:44

Fancy a drink tomorrow, then? Very impressed you like Hot Pot!
20:44

Excellent. London Bridge at 7 sounds good to me. Happy to meet directly at whichever bar you prefer, as opposed to station, because I will prob be arriving in Uber. Glam, I know! :) Have a nice evening
20:51

_____

From: Lomax Clipper
Sent: Saturday, 14 January 2017 15:06
To: Katie Wetherden
Subject: Thanks

I woke up screaming this lovely Saturday morning to find that the vision has fully recovered in the right eye, as promised by the delightful guys at Moorfields A&E!

Very annoyed that the nightmare hasn't stopped. It's so kind of you and Ross to offer to visit, but there's really no need to leave Zone One for this. I had to have further conversations with my mother yesterday to assure her that I am OK. My dad made some good jokes this morning when I phoned. He seems in better form at the moment.

You and Wen MUST stop being so negative about Aurora – you're both saying that this is dangerously unhealthy and I'm living in my head, but where else do we live, dear Katie, other than in our heads and hearts? She might be a bit troubled, but I do believe that deep down HER heart is in the right place. Remember that she is from a much more dramatic culture. She wears her passion on her sleeve, and in a weird way the temperamental nature is sort of liberating for an Englishman. Nothing is held back, and even when she becomes Angry Aurora there's an essential honesty that transcends the toxic river of words that foams from her lovely mouth. When I called Happy Aurora back last night and got confirmation that she had broken up with the Sicilian guy, and that she'd realised she still missed the man I'd been in Italy, the lights of the world began to shine. Happy Aurora's enchanting voice transported me to a distant island of sun and lemon trees. I felt that sun on my shoulders, reviving me, as I floated blissfully in the Tyrrhenian sea. I saw the sun dipping below the horizon, the sky an endless variety of colour. I tasted the heady red wine of Ustica, the capers, the aubergines, the ravioli. I heard the waves lapping that old sea wall after dinner, remembered my euphoria, the sense of escape and freedom in otherness. I breathed in that intoxicating sea air, gazed at Aurora's bewitching beauty under the wild moonlight…

I'm going out to Palermo to visit her as soon as I can. This is worth another shot! I AM a different man in London, broken by the anxiety and aggression that pervade the place. The bullying roofers who couldn't care less about my eye, and who insisted on walking me up the Blackstock Road to the bank in the freezing cold for immediate cash payment. The grimness of then seeking refuge in one of Finsbury Park's old boozers, listening to the chat of men seemingly auditioning for a role in a Guy Ritchie film. Realising I wasn't up for a pint after all and being called a fackin' kant by the landlord. Reflecting on how I'm stuck in my miserable job, with all the juniors, including even Wen already, threatening to overtake me. Thank God for the escape route of the novel. Professor Melanie Nithercott had better like those amended chapters!

———

WhatsApp message from Wen to Rob
Saturday, 14 January 2017

Wen

Hi, this is honestly not my style, but I'm going to have to pull out at appallingly late notice. The friend I mentioned has had a relapse or something in his eye and has had to go back to hospital. I need to go check on him. I promise you I'm not a flake like so many people on Bumble and was really looking forward to meeting you. If everything is OK, I could possibly make later? So sorry

17:50

———

From: Lomax Clipper
Sent: Saturday, 14 January 2017 20:30
To: Katie Wetherden
Subject: A Twist

(Email dictated by Lomax Clipper and written by Wen Li.)

What a roller-coaster. An hour or so after my email to you this afternoon, the eye became extremely painful, my sight became blurred and then I saw only mist.

I rushed back to A&E. On the way, as if the Gods were in disagreement as to how this day should go, I received a call from Professor Melanie Nithercott. The loyal soldier had spent two solid days on the chapters. She said that she would write with more detailed thoughts, but wanted to let me know that the revised draft was exquisitely funny! That, if I kept to that standard, she reckoned the novel would be a hit! I almost cried with joy, momentarily forgetting the pain and the mist!

Anyway, apparently I now have a corneal ulcer, which is more serious than an abrasion. Darkly, there can be no absolute certainty that I will regain full sight in the eye – but I remain optimistic. The ulcer has been caused by a bacterial infection, most likely a result of rubbing the eye. What an idiot!

I am on hourly antibiotic drops. I've bought a patch but I cannot wear it until the infection settles.

My parents are down tomorrow. Wen picked me up from A&E and has just made me her incredible sugar porridge. She is the kindest person, even if she does write so herself.

Still can't believe it about the novel!!!

Dictated but not read.

Wen

Sorry Rob, I've been totally distracted getting my friend back home from the hospital

21:02

It's really quite serious and he might have lost sight in his eye

21:02

I'm popping over to his again tomorrow to look after him (he lives super close by). So I think in the week will work better for me, if you're still OK to bear with me?

21:02

Sorry, realise I've been totally shit here. But I've got myself into a bit of a tizz

21:03

No, no! Don't worry, he's most definitely not my type! :)
21:10

117

All email communication from Lomax Clipper ceases for a fortnight while he rests in his flat. The corneal ulcer is eventually brought under control by the antibiotic drops. However, sight in Lomax's right eye recovers only partially. The ophthalmologist finally approves use of the patch.

Lomax's visitors during this period are Katie and Ross Wetherden, Norman and Fabienne Clipper, and Wen Li. Being shy, Wen does not meet the other visitors.

Whenever alone, Lomax furtively continues to speak to Aurora La Rosa. Lomax does not tell Aurora of the corneal ulcer, for fear of dampening the mood. Instead he tells her that his eye has recovered fully from the accident and his sight is perfect. He adds that his debut novel is on track to being published soon.

Once use of the eye patch is approved, Lomax resumes written correspondence too. His words to Aurora become passionately romantic, spurred on by the occasional sweet emoji response from Aurora, and not deterred by the continuation of his recurring nightmare. In a stroke of good fortune, Aurora tells him that she is unable to meet until the final weekend of February – the preceding weekends she will be marching with her friends. This, Lomax believes, gives him sufficient time to master the fully-sighted look.

To his mother's displeasure, towards the end of the interlude Lomax informs her of his and Aurora's reconciliation. Her alarm at her son's choices increases when Lomax decides that it is time to re-engage with work on his novel, and increases further still when Lomax yields to Julian's continued questions over the telephone and considers attempting a return to the office.

But, before we get to that, Julian and Wen...

From: Julian Pickering
Sent: Thursday, 19 January 2017 10:20
To: Toby Enslin
Subject: Ultimatum

What the hell has happened, Toby? Everything was fine until last night. I appreciate I've been grumpy this week, but I'm under tremendous stress here at work. I'm also now a team member down, as poor Lomax seems to be in the wars. Of course, he thinks the worst of every question I have for him. He hates me nearly as much as you do, judging by last night.

Anyway, there is no more money for the Priory or any of that nonsense this time – it clearly just gives you a little expensive holiday before you slip again. It is now up to you to decide how you see things going forward. I simply do not accept coming home late and seeing you pissed as a fart again, and then listening to you mock me. I am mocked in the office and mocked and taunted at home by my drunken partner, and I'm completely sick of it!

History teaches that you'll likely now be drinking again in the kitchen this morning, while waiting for the King's Head to open. If that's true, I'm no longer interested. I CANNOT DO THIS ANY MORE, do you understand? I want someone who contributes, even at a minimum level, to our lives. I'm done. You'd promised!

———

Wen

Haha! Cool, the Southwark Tavern it is. You've been so patient about my drama. Hope meeting me doesn't end in a bit of an anticlimax for you after all this messing about!

09:00

Thanks for such a lovely time. Best of luck with the big meeting tomorrow, Mr High Powered! I'll be thinking about you while stamping docs

23:02

PS you DEFINITELY look a bit like Hugh Grant in his younger days!

23:02

Friday, 20 January 2017

Ooh, he emerges!

22:14

Had been worried you were in the process of politely disappearing after our first meet-up :)

22:14

Was super happy to see your messages pop up! Hope your famous meeting went OK?

22:14

Absolutely available on Saturday. Who wouldn't want to stroll around the Tate Modern pretending to understand the paintings of an unknown Frenchman? Joking, would be great! Maybe we could go for a walk along the South Bank afterwards too. Full on, two dates in three days :)

22:15

From: Julian Pickering
Sent: Tuesday, 24 January 2017 11:32
To: Toby Enslin
Subject: Please read

I cannot keep answering my phone or replying to frantic bursts of text messages while busy here in the office.

I'm glad you think the problem is me, and that you can't wait to see the back of me. Call me cruel, but from my side there will be little to miss of you too, on the basis of this month.

Of course, I am stupid and soft, so am willing to support the detox – indeed I insist on it, as it's not safe for you to just stop drinking and go cold turkey immediately. Call it a last gesture of goodwill. In the meantime I'll begin looking for a second, temporary flat for myself in order to give you time to transition from our – or rather, MY – current one.

You probably won't recall this, but you spat in my face last night outside Ottolenghi, while calling me a loser. It was the final straw.

Wen

Oh, trust me, there are plenty of skeletons in the Wen Li cupboard too! :)

17:02

Tomorrow I'm checking on Lomax, but then free for rest of weekend. Fancy Chinatown, so I can introduce you to Suzhou cuisine?! See, girls can ask too!

17:02

I just love that you're jealous of Lomax, it's so silly! :)

17:19

And yeah, the Wen Li recipes are the greatest of all, but a bit punchy to invite you round to mine on only the third date

17:20

However, provided you continue to behave, perhaps you'll get to try my cooking soon?

17:20

It will need to be fairly soon as next month I will have some lodgers, in the shape of my parents!

17:20

Yes, really! I know, a little challenging given the size of my flat. Will explain tomorrow over some… Coke Zero

17:25

123

WhatsApp messages from Wen to Hannah
Thursday, 26 January 2017

Wen

Stacey has just written asking me if I'm OK as she's heard
I'm 'struggling with some mental health issues'. WTF?!
That's now four uni friends who know I'm 'nuts' (to quote
Anna). Many thanks!

17:39

Apology NOT accepted

17:41

WhatsApp message from Wen to Rob
Sunday, 29 January 2017

Wen

Morning, Mr High Powered. I woke up this morning feeling
very happy. A good kisser too, what more could a girl
want?!

09:19

While Wen Li's love life blossoms and Julian Pickering's falls apart, Lomax Clipper makes a half-hearted attempt to return to work on Monday, 30 January.

From: Lomax Clipper
Sent: Monday, 30 January 2017 13:48
To: Katie Wetherden
Subject: Re: Let me know it goes!

Ahoy, matey.

Captain Clipper 'ere. Fabienne Clipper furious that I went in this morning: she wouldn't listen to my explanation that the best way to get more time off work was to show I CAN'T work.

A very productive morning, in which I achieved what I set out to achieve: the rat-witch has raised the possibility of an unpaid sabbatical.

I confess my performance was a tad melodramatic but it was true that I couldn't manage – am already back home. While the eye patch works fine for writing, problems arise when I have to keep shifting my gaze, as one must in the office. I am going to spend the afternoon wallowing in Melanie's more detailed feedback, which is exhilaratingly positive.

Mr Curtain came down to see me first thing. He gazed at me for some time while I worked on the agonised look. He was still there when Julian returned from his meeting. Julian said in a cheerful voice: 'Captain Hook is back, you see!' Mr Curtain asked Julian what made him think Captain Hook had ever worn a patch. The rat-witch replied that it was well known.

'No,' Mr Curtain stated.

Julian then made a really awkward and inappropriate crack about Wen and yours truly being the walking wounded – if it wasn't one thing, he joked, it was another. We all stared at him until he went red.

It's very cool, I must say, how Wen has adapted to being friends and apparently let all previous feelings fall away. But she does remain grumpy with me because of Aurora. During our 'coffee break' (you know she never drinks coffee?) I took off the patch and asked her whether she could tell that the eye was partially sighted. I explained that I was working on a look that masked the problem before my weekend in Palermo. She said that I was crazy, and that the very fact I felt the need to do this said a lot about this 'relationship' of mine.

A little irritated, I turned the conversation to her new boyf, a man named Rob. He's only 29, like her, but apparently already a Business Development Director at an asset management company. Sounds a definite Mr Bullshitter to me, and I told her as much.

Later, when my lowing like a cow finally cracked him, the rat-witch asked Wen to leave the room and then interrogated me. He said that it was pretty apparent I was struggling. I reiterated that the ophthalmologists had said that they couldn't promise that sight in the eye would return to what it was, but that we were all aiming for that and, actually, I'd seen improvements in the past days. That it might be a matter of months.

Then he dangled the offer. Hmm, I thought. Imagine a sabbatical in a place where I could finish a novel and resume a love story. Ideally it would be a sunny place, by the sea.

A brief editorial intervention. Sunny places by the sea and scenes of violent murder are, of course, not mutually exclusive.

WhatsApp messages from Wen to Rob
Thursday, 2 February 2017

Wen

Lovely waking up next to you

08:49

Must say, your Barbican flat is sooooo cool! Quite a luxury having a 10 min walk to work this morning. I felt like a bit of a City slicker myself!

08:49

From: Lomax Clipper
Sent: Friday, 3 February 2017 12:07
To: Katie Wetherden
Subject: Pondering

Time back in Huddersfield sounds great. The idea of a medium-sized law firm in Manchester is intriguing.

My sabbatical would be longer than yours, I think. I'd like six months for mine. Of course, it will be extended to forever if the novel works out. I must say that it feels like destiny, this chance to head off to the Queen of the Islands!

My idea went down like a cup of cold sick in Huddersfield. I'm not discounting your reaction either. Your point about the recurring nightmare, however, is weak: it's a consequence only of the novel. During daylight hours my mind yearns for Sicily.

Given that the sabbatical would be unpaid, I would have to sublet the flat without letting the landlord know, and also get an overdraft. Although, possibly, I could teach English out in Palermo.

The obstacle of the eye has been surmounted. Yesterday the ophthalmologist told me (under persistent questioning) that although Palermo was not what she had had in mind – and I would have to return to Moorfields if complications arose – a monthly check-up in Palermo should hopefully suffice.

She gave me the number of a former colleague, now in Rome. He put me in touch with a magically-named ophthalmologist in Palermo. Carmela Rapisarda's Italian was beautiful, just like Aurora's. She said she'd be happy to send reports to the ophthalmologist here.

Yesterday I wrote to Aurora saying that before I booked my flights for our weekend I wanted to run a bigger idea past her, which might entail having to deal with a few things before we met. She hasn't replied, so I'm calling her tonight.

Wen popped by again yesterday evening. She's not impressed by my plans. But, then again, I'm not particularly impressed that she'd go for a self-important little City boy. I explained that Aurora was a flawed bird of paradise, whereas Rob sounded like a standard pigeon and Wen could do so much better.

She said she was staggered that I would contemplate disappearing to Palermo for six months with my bad eye. I replied that the eye continued to get a bit better each day. To prove it, I put the patch over the good one and asked Wen to move around the room.

After a while I thought I had spotted her. But it was my suit, on a clothes hanger.

<hr>

WhatsApp message from Wen to Mum
Friday, 10 February 2017

Translation from the original Chinese

Wen

Mum, what is it? I missed four calls and now you're not answering! Please answer

11:19

<hr>

WhatsApp messages from Wen to Rob
Friday, 10 February 2017

Wen

Hi Rob, not ignoring you. I just tried to call. Don't worry if you can't call back straight away. My dad's died. Massive heart attack. On my way down to Brighton

11:36

Thanks, very sweet. Love you, Wen

11:39

Sorry, didn't mean love you. Head's all over place

11:40

<hr>

Happy Friday to you!

My Friday would be almost perfect, were it not for the vague sense that Wen is beginning to ignore me. No doubt her Mr Bullshitter has something to do with it. This morning I texted her asking for the usual updates on the rat-witch, and she has failed to deliver! The selfishness!

But, ah, the luxury of writing a Friday update from bed under a newly fixed roof, instead of the office! Hope Huddersfield is going well. The pictures of your little break in Azores made me think of Easter Island. Incidentally, I have tentatively begun an outline of chapter four this week.

I've written to Julian saying I need another week before making my decision. However, the eye continues to make small strides, and deep down I know what I must do. If it weren't for you, my mother and Wen all filling my head with worries, I would have probably already informed Julian.

Aurora seemed pleasantly surprised by the idea, although not as invested in it as I had hoped. She said I was like an Italian in my impulsiveness, and that she LOVED that. But then she emphasised that I should not think we were a couple, and anyway what did that mean? I assume she was just trying to say that we should let things develop naturally. So I assured her that I wouldn't be bothering her every day as I would be working hard on my novel!

I asked Aurora for any tips on apartments in Palermo, and

what the rental market was like, but she said she didn't believe in markets and that the conversation was getting a little heavy! Fine for her, still living with Gigi the spiv, Luisa the unseen and Mommo the killer!

The idea of meeting her comrades is not so enticing, by the way. I have seen photos on Facebook of tremendous beards, groups of people all dressed in rags. They're very into the Mazurka, which apparently involves finding a square in one of the dodgier parts of Palermo and performing a folk dance, changing partners. A horror show!

But all of this falls away when she speaks in her achingly lyrical Italian about life in Palermo. We only spent a morning there before taking the ferry to Ustica, yet how I remember the ancient men leaning against Gothic palaces with cigarettes stuck in their mouths, the women necking espresso, their voices rising and falling in a rhythmic flow that was like song, the dandy embracing his mamma before an Arabesque dome. And in the distance Mount Pellegrino, the most beautiful promontory in the world (according to Goethe).

———

WhatsApp messages from Wen to Rob
Monday, 13 February 2017

Wen

Thanks Rob, and of course I didn't expect you to come all the way down to Brighton, don't worry

19:19

Completely appreciate how busy you are

19:19

133

_____

From: Lomax Clipper
Sent: Friday, 17 February 2017 10:03
To: Katie Wetherden
Subject: Your message

Not been ignoring your email about Aurora. It's just been a bit of a hectic week – have spent most of it in a Travelodge in Brighton. Long story.

I'm touched by your vehemence but you're going to have to let this go, Katie. I feel destiny calling. You're either with me on this or we will have to avoid the subject. I MAY delay my departure for a little while, but that is for the entirely separate reason that Wen has just lost her father, and might need my support. The boyfriend seems to have an EQ the size of the rat-witch's, but I am treading carefully as the girl is clearly very much in love.

PS nice Valentine's pics on Facebook. I think they mustn't celebrate it in Italy. But Aurora liked my card.

_____

From: Julian Pickering
Sent: Friday, 17 February 2017 13:02
To: Charles Curtain
Subject: Our conversation

Dear Charles,

I refer to our conversation of this morning, which I thought would be helpful to set down in writing.

As discussed, until recently my allocated team comprised the most senior of our associates, Lomax Clipper, and the junior associate Wen Li. That was considerably smaller a team than that of any of my fellow partners. Recently, I have lost the services of Lomax for what will likely be a number of months, should he take my offer of an unpaid sabbatical – an offer you described as overly generous, but which I thought was deserved on account of his long service to the firm.

More recently still, I have had to do without the services of Wen too – her father passed away this week. I have told her not to rush back, and while she has ignored this and tells me she will be back in the office on Tuesday, this event underlines that I do not have sufficient support to build my practice. I am very clear on my targets for the year, but it will be almost impossible to meet them if I am supported by only one diligent but very junior notary – and when my support consists of one, it only takes an unforeseen event to reduce that to zero, as has happened this week.

Accordingly, I politely repeat my request for a further senior associate to be allocated to my team in Lomax's absence.

Best

Julian

———

WhatsApp messages from Wen to Rob
Friday, 17 February 2017

Wen

Hey, no worries. We're holding up, just about

14:19

Will be commuting up and down from here next week, after the funeral

14:19

Not great, as I struggle with trains (I'm a bit weird)

14:19

But I had time off sick before Christmas and only been in the job five months so am worried will get sacked if I keep having absences

14:20

Let me know if free later for a chat? Got to go speak to my mum now

14:20

WhatsApp message from Wen to Hannah
Saturday, 18 February 2017

Wen

Thanks Hannah, appreciated. Hope all OK with you

16:19

WhatsApp messages from Wen to Rob
Wednesday, 22 February 2017

Wen

Hey, Mr High Powered!

12:07

> Thanks again for your words. Your messages have kept me going
>
> 12:07

> Should be back in London this weekend for good, to give my mum a bit of breathing space
>
> 12:07

> Especially as soon she'll be living here with me!
>
> 12:07

> Free to meet Sunday?
>
> 12:07

———

From: Lomax Clipper
Sent: Monday, 27 February 2017 14:03
To: Katie Wetherden
Subject: Decision taken

The deed is done – am just back from a meeting with the rat-witch. I would be in a state of elation, were it not for some concerns about Wen. She got back to Finsbury Park last Sunday and was obviously still badly shaken, but also a little lonely. The twat of a Business Development Director had cancelled on her, supposedly because of some urgent preparation for a big meeting.

I went round to hers, where I was presented with the treat that he was missing out on: wild shrimp noodles! She was very tearful and told me a lot of other things about herself that I hadn't realised. She's a lovely vulnerable young woman.

But I put my foot in it regarding the Business Development

Director, saying that he should have made it over. I said that I was under no strict time requirement for Palermo and if she wanted me around for a bit longer that would be absolutely fine.

To my surprise, the last point offended her even more than the first. It was all very sad to see her so defensive and upset with me. She said she has countless good friends (clearly doesn't). Anyway, despite my best efforts, tension remained in the air. And when we were half-way through dinner, who should finally come round to give her a big surprise but the Business Development Director! He was a little tipsy, in my view. Wen's face lit up in an instant upon seeing him (she really is beautiful, you know. I think I've mentioned this before, but the dickhead has massively lucked out, as in any logical world she would be totally out of his league, and he doesn't even seem to appreciate it). He seemed far from happy at seeing ME, and I soon felt a little surplus to requirements. And then embarrassed – they clearly could not wait for me to go.

I do hope he doesn't piss her around. Regardless, later that night she followed up on WhatsApp, insisting that, while she thought it was madness, I should not delay Palermo on her account. At which point it hit me: it was time to take the leap.

When I went into the office this morning, Mr Curtain came to wish me all the best for the sabbatical. He's a shit but, I suspect, a less evil one than the rat-witch. He asked whether there was a key Sicilian novel he should know about. I mentioned *The Leopard*. After a pause he remarked that it was a terribly solitary animal. I agreed, but noted that the novel wasn't about a real leopard.

Mr Curtain replied that he had never said it was.

PS a colleague of mine, not Wen but someone else, has got bad OCD. Actual OCD, not the sort of thing I sometimes claim to have (somewhat lazily and disrespectfully). Just been reading about it on Mind.org. Sounds horrendous. Do you know anything about it?

————

WhatsApp messages from Wen to Rob
Thursday, 2 March 2017

Wen

Yeah, Mum's not arriving till early April now, I think

12:43

Ah, don't say that about Lomax. He's lovely really. And he likes you!

12:46

Sorry again about tonight. Horrible dose of flu. Work being very patient (as are you)

12:46

————

From: Julian Pickering
Sent: Friday, 3 March 2017 13:22
To: Charles Curtain
Subject: Re: Our conversation

Dear Charles,

I refer to my email of 17 February. Have you come to a decision with respect to the question of associate support?

Best

Julian

————

From: Julian Pickering
Sent: Monday, 6 March 2017 16:22
To: Toby Enslin
Subject: Your email

Toby, I am glad the detox was successful. I have found myself comfortable but rather modest lodgings not far from home – a tiny place on a short rent in Clerkenwell. As I have said numerous times, there is no immediate pressure on you to do anything – you can have the flat to yourself for a couple of months until you find somewhere else.

I would reiterate, however, that the flat is mine (and that obviously I can't maintain two London properties indefinitely). You have paid nothing whatsoever towards it, nor towards our common expenses. You have not worked since I met you.

This is all most unnecessary and foolish, threatening to get lawyers involved. I would be angry about some of the defamatory allegations, if they hadn't made me laugh on account of their absurdity. Lawyers will get us both into a financial mess.

Oh, Toby, I can't bring myself to write more cold messages. Can't we just meet and talk this through?

––––––––––

From: Lomax Clipper
Sent: Friday, 10 March 2017 17:09
To: Katie Wetherden
Subject: Re: You've disappeared

Sorry, sorry. I've been so busy sorting stuff. I am free now until I leave on the 25th. Very keen to hear more about this idea of the gentler law firm in Manchester.

Aurora seems to be looking forward to seeing me too, although she's still showing no interest in my accommodation. I'm going to stay in a cheap hotel for the first fortnight and then find a flat once I'm there. Really hoping that once I get to Palermo, and immerse myself in the reality of it, my strange nightmare will finally stop! Not least because I'm beginning to suspect that the unidentified victim of the Murder in the Moonlight is actually me!

Ironically, I'm subletting my flat to two Italian waiters. I've told them that the landlord must not find out or we'll all be in trouble.

Melanie is back from Spain. She thinks Sicily is an excellent place to finish the novel. She repeated that the only thing to watch was the narrator's hatred of the story, which was threatening to go too far.

Sight in the eye inches forward. I can only practise for so long each day though, so do still rely on the patch.

I fear that we were in Huddersfield at the same time. I had completely forgotten that you were there! When my mother picked me up from the station, the first thing she said was that a Palermitan communist for a daughter-in-law was her worst nightmare! (If only she knew MY worst!)

She also told me that my dad's mood had dipped again. When we arrived, he was sitting on the roof under a light rain. I climbed the ladder and sat down next to him. I told him that I had tremendous experience with leaky roofs; and that a plastic sheet was not a long-term solution.

Staring at the grey sky, he said at least there'd be sun in Palermo. Minutes later, the Lexus pulled up outside the house and he said that he hadn't remembered to tell Caroline I'd be here. I was struck by an idea for a little practical joke.

My dad shook his head at first, saying that Mr Bullshitter wouldn't fall for it. But the lights were back on in his eyes.

'Get up here, lad, help me hold him!' he was yelling a minute later, pinning me down, and barely concealing his joy.

By the time he eventually climbed the ladder, Mr Bullshitter was incandescent. He shouted that only Norman Clipper could catch a burglar on a roof. His face when he saw me! My dad roared! Once we were back inside, he gave my mother a hug and told her to get her coat.

My mother asked him where we were going. She had tears standing in her eyes.

'The pub!' he said.

———

WhatsApp messages from Wen to Mum
Friday, 10 March 2017

Translation from the original Chinese

Wen

Oh, Mum. Don't say that. I'm calling you now

19:03

I loved chatting too! Love you so much

20:05

I'll be down tomorrow. Soon you'll be here living with me

20:07

If you feel very low this evening just call any time, OK? Might not see messages immediately but I have it on loud ring

20:08

Hi Mum, assume all OK now and you're sleeping. Good night. Will be with you tomorrow

23:58

WhatsApp messages from Wen to Rob
Saturday, 11 March 2017

Wen

Yeah, last night was magical

12:43

You've been very sweet, not only about this sad time for me but also about the sex thing

12:43

As I said, for me making love is a psychological as well as physical thing. That makes me sound precious, but it's not, I've just got a hypersensitive mind, I guess

12:43

And last night I just felt so full of love for you. There, I'll say it again :)

12:44

You've been a wonderful support to me these last few weeks. I'm still in a bit of shock about my dad. But you're a very special man. I find it difficult to open up to people, and tell them all about my life, but with you I really feel I want to. Maybe one day I will…

12:44

Ha, no, nothing terrible! :) No particular secret

12:52

From: Julian Pickering
Sent: Monday, 13 March 2017 13:22
To: Charles Curtain
Subject: Re: Our conversation

Dear Charles,

That is understood. Naturally, I am disappointed. Wen has had a further couple of absences since my original email, both of them attributable to the matter we discussed, and I am full of empathy for her. But that does not diminish the difficulty for me of having days when I work with no team.

However, you know this already so I suspect any further words on this matter from me are redundant.

Julian

From: Lomax Clipper
Sent: Friday, 17 March 2017 10:04
To: Katie Wetherden
Subject: Re: Patron of the Arts

Katie, I had thought your email was a joke. But this morning I saw that you had indeed transferred £5k to my bank account! I've just sent it back, mildly offended. I suggest we don't discuss it further.

See you all tomorrow for lunch – looking forward to it!

––––––––––

WhatsApp messages from Wen to Rob
Saturday, 18 March 2017

Wen

Hey, back home in F Park

11:34

Lovely night last night. Loved Sushisamba

11:34

You're great at taking my mind off stuff

11:34

Have a nice time tonight with the other City Boys! :) And no worries about Sunday lunch. Just let me know when works in week xxx

11:34

––––––––––

From: Lomax Clipper
Sent: Friday, 24 March 2017 22:36
To: Katie Wetherden
Subject: Re: Arrivederci

Yes, lunch was superb last weekend. My god, David has his mother's face! I can't get over how similar!

No idea where the week went and how it's already late Friday evening. Thanks so much, but no need for tomorrow. Wen's coming round to help – she said there'd no doubt be Clipper chaos with the suitcases and she'd like to give me a hand!

Have just had to remind Aurora AGAIN that I'm arriving tomorrow! She's not free during the day but hopefully we're meeting for a pizza in the evening. Will let you know how this goes!

———

WhatsApp messages from Wen to Rob
Friday, 24 March 2017

> **Wen**
>
> Hi, I'm back home. I wasn't melodramatic walking out like that, and I'm not a snooper, Rob!
>
> 22:48

> The message appeared on your phone and it was right next to me on the bed! Like, WTF?! You told me you'd been working late all week??
>
> 22:48

Amazing to think you were moaning earlier about my 'weird' attachment to my friend Lomax. And now this!

22:49

Just tell me the truth. All of it. I'm a big girl

22:49

Wow. Silly me. Actually, the worst part for me is that you met her on Bumble too. Addicted to the app?!

23:06

From: Lomax Clipper
Sent: Saturday, 25 March 2017 11:37
To: Katie Wetherden
Subject:

Farewell, Mrs Wetherden. I am about to board here.

Wen accompanied me all the way to the airport. Particularly touching given how much she seems to hate trains and the Tube. I said that I would actually prefer an Uber but she saw through it and insisted.

She says that it's still going well with the boyfriend, which is a relief – I do think she could do way better, but hopefully it'll turn out that I did indeed leave her in safe hands.

It was a strange journey, actually. She opened up about her dad and cried. Everything she says about her mother, and her concern for her, is so utterly beautiful. Listening, it struck me again that there's something infinitely golden about Wen Li. I felt as if I were coming home, not going away.

As we were approaching security I reiterated that I would always be on the other end of the phone, and reminded her of our deal to Skype regularly. After the briefest of hugs, she told me I needed to hurry on through. She gave me a card and then turned and darted away. Inside the card, she'd urged me to look after myself, and to eat enough vegetables, and said that she'd be keeping her fingers crossed every night that Aurora would not let me down. She finished with an oddly literary line, telling me not to care about truth, when all everyone wants is some happiness.

PS found it! It's (sort of) from F. Scott Fitzgerald.

————————

From: Wen Li
Sent: Saturday, 25 March 2017 12:01
To: Dominic Corcoran
Subject: Next week's session

Hi Dominic,

Just to confirm, Friday at midday works for our next session. But I'd also be very happy to do earlier in the week if you had any slots available?

I am just in an Uber coming back from the airport, after seeing my friend Lomax off. Lomax has been so wonderful about dad, you know, which is why I'm feeling so emotional right now. He was unbelievably warm and gentle on the way to the airport. I had thought that the guy, Rob, I've been dating (now over!) was being good about it, but I realise he wasn't really. At least, not in comparison.

Lomax is a mess himself, but he's such a sensitive man.

Nobody outside my family has ever looked out for me like he does. It's just such a shame to see him flying off to Sicily. This ridiculous Sicilian better not upset him again, or she'll have me to answer to!

Well, sorry for this ramble. And thanks again for everything, Dominic. I'm speaking to my mum this afternoon about the sale of the grocers. So I can't promise that you won't get another email.

Wen

3

The Moonlight

*Sicily and England, from March 2017 until the night of the
murder on 1 September 2017. We are getting closer, dear reader.*

*This section includes the correspondence of a new character: a
Sicilian man named Fifi de Angelis. During the period covered
by this section, both Lomax Clipper's and Fifi de Angelis's
communications are sent from the historic quarter of Palermo
named La Kalsa, which is one of four neighbourhoods that
together form the Sicilian capital's Old City.*

*After returning from seeing Lomax off at the airport on
Saturday, 25 March 2017, Wen Li is informed by her mother
that the sale of the grocers in Brighton is now close to
completion. As feared, the sale will bring in minimal proceeds.
Later that weekend, Wen Li suffers another bad relapse of
her OCD, which, despite her best efforts, leads to a further
absence from the office on the Monday.*

*The same weekend, Toby Enslin returns from his latest detox
and begins to drink again immediately. Julian visits him at
the flat on Upper Street, where they engage in a bitter row
that turns violent. The next day, they decide to expedite their
split, with Julian agreeing to a small financial settlement. It
is decided that for two months Toby will remain in the flat,*

while Julian lives in the rented Clerkenwell studio apartment nearby. Julian soon begins to regret how this has ended and is eaten up with concern about Toby and his alcoholism. But best to leave further discussions for the moment, he decides – after all, things might still blow over.

From: Lomax Clipper
Sent: Monday, 27 March 2017 19:02
To: Katie Wetherden
Subject: The Watchdog: Part 1

I had considered taking the title of Lampedusa's famous novel for the subject line of my email update. But I have not yet met a Leopard. I HAVE met a Watchdog.

On Saturday evening I took Aurora to 'Pizzeria Frida'. The menu offered a dazzling range of toppings – pistachio, mint, spicy mushrooms, ricotta cheese. I ordered a *'vulcanotto'*, without realising that they make their pizzas in a range of shapes. Mine looked like Mount Etna!

A bit of fun, you might think. Yet my dinner companion, who had elicited tremendous emotion in me when I first spotted her waiting outside, was in a funny mood, and declared herself conflicted. Much worse, she was not my only dinner companion: she had invited along her comrade Diego, who is clearly besotted with her.

They'd come directly from the march. Fresh from the fight, as it were. Aurora in her rags looked like an earnest and beautiful Sicilian revolutionary. Diego did not have the same soldierly quality, for he was stoned. And nor was Diego beautiful. He was a beard wearing an Italian man. The hair on his head was dreadlocked, and pulled back into a ponytail that swished as he moved. He wore khaki pants and a stained T-shirt emblazoned with angry Italian words I cannot remember.

Presently, with Diego passed out at the table, I told Aurora that I was sorry she was disappointed by the pizzeria, but that it was nevertheless so exciting to see her here in Palermo. I asked her whether afterwards we might wander around the square, alone. She asked me why I was squinting, and I explained that my right eye was tired after the long journey. She said that she too was tired, and it was better if we both got an early night. Her brother Mommo had made Diego promise to get her home safely from the march.

Charming, I thought. We went our different ways after the meal, for the historic quarters were to the right, and Via Bari, the street where her family lives, to the left. Diego did not even look at me as I said good night. Nor did he thank me for the pizza he hadn't eaten!

It took me an hour to get back to my ramshackle hotel – Google Maps does not like the historic quarters. The sinister little alleys are too narrow for it. At one point I realised I was being hunted by an army of stray cats, and wondered whether I was about to experience a real-life variation on my recurring nightmare. But I made it back safely and woke on Sunday morning in a cheerful mood – Spring was streaming in through my hotel window; looking out of it, I saw the sea.

I am popping out now for a beer and a couple of arancini. Deep-fried rice balls, filled with meat sauce! Two Euros a pop!

_____

The introduction of Fifi de Angelis
Translation from the original Italian

From: Fifi de Angelis
Sent: Monday, 27 March 2017 19:09
To: Ignazio de Angelis; Rosaria de Angelis; Elisabetta de Angelis; Saveria de Angelis
Subject: This silence must end

My dear family,

It has been six months since the scandal. I see that you all continue to block my number. I'm going to write you a long email this week. Please read it when it arrives.

Fifi

———

From: Lomax Clipper
Sent: Monday, 27 March 2017 20:30
To: Katie Wetherden
Subject: The Watchdog: Part 2

I'm back. I ate three arancini in the end – and then burped, like a manly Sicilian.

Now, a bit of colour about the area I'm staying in. When Goethe arrived in Palermo in the year 1787, he found lodgings in an area of the Old City named La Kalsa. There are four distinct areas that make up the Old City – La Kalsa, Albergheria, Vucciria and Il Capo. While some bits have undergone regeneration, they remain the areas where Palermo's poor – and the odd faded aristocrat – live flanked by its historical treasures.

I decided to follow Goethe, and so found a 'hotel' in La Kalsa. I think La Kalsa is actually the most inspiring of the historic quarters – although this remains only a hunch. 'La Kalsa', incidentally, derives from the area's original Arabic name, which meant 'the chosen' – rather fitting, I thought.

It is edgy as hell by night, but enchanting by day, time-warped and resplendent with heady colour. Imagine psychedelic tapestries of Byzantine mosaics, teeming bazaars, crumbling Norman grandeur, cupolas and domes. Gardens of citrus trees shading World War II ruins. African hair salons side-by-side with baroque churches. Date palms and frescoes!

I had read that it was 'an area of poverty', but the story today is a bit more complicated than that. The buildings and alleys and squares that have been recently done up are exquisite. A serene, old-world charm pervades these parts, and combines gorgeously with the arty bars that are just MADE for a writer. Yet La Kalsa is an area of extremes: you step out of these bohemian havens onto a leafy *piazza*, turn right down a quaint street – and find yourself arrived suddenly in a land of horror. A land of no street lights, of spilled rubbish and broken pavements, stray cats and dogs, eerie Italian men loitering on street corners...

Situated amid all this beauty and damnation are some of Palermo's gems: Palazzo Mirto, for several hundred years a home of wild opulence for Sicilian nobility, now silent and set out of time; the Museo dell'Inquisizione, its cells bearing graffitied maps of Sicily that are like pirate treasure maps; Palazzo Abatellis, housing art that ranks among the finest in Sicily.

Life is lived outdoors – locals spend their days shopping at street markets, hollering from balconies, or resting motionless on chairs placed just outside their doors. Couples whizz up and down nonchalantly on scooters; street vendors set out their goods, glancing left and right in case they have to run. Stunning, hard-eyed women in Jimmy Choo heels navigate the stone-paved streets with dexterity.

And always there is the breeze from the Tyrrhenian Sea.

Next I will tell you what happened today when I went flat-hunting. First, though, I am popping down for another rice ball.

WhatsApp message from Wen to Rob
Monday, 27 March 2017

Wen

Hi Rob. I agree everything was a bit abrupt. OK, let's meet to talk

21:06

From: Lomax Clipper
Sent: Monday, 27 March 2017 23:30
To: Katie Wetherden
Subject: The Watchdog: Part 3

Part 3. This morning I tracked down an estate agency. I explained that I sought a flat here in the Old City. The cocky young estate agent asked me why. I put my eye patch on, and said I sought authenticity. He looked at me with a face of fear.

He had no flats in La Kalsa. But he did have one in another

historical quarter, Albergheria. If the name looks like a challenge to pronounce, you should try the challenge of being taken around the place on a scooter! Emaciated cats jumped overhead, from one World War II-bombed building to another, eyeing the garbage below. Fat men in string vests spat from their balconies. Putrid water spilled from broken pipes. I've no idea how the place can be put in the same league as La Kalsa. The worst parts of La Kalsa may be worse than any area of any other city I've ever seen, but they are Monte Carlo compared to Albergheria.

Incidentally, the Italians go on about African immigration in the Old City, but from what I saw the immigrant population are the only ones saving Albergheria from total collapse! The only acceptable-looking shops and bars I saw were African. The only nice-looking people I saw were African!

When we came to a stop, I remarked to the agent that the building in front of us looked ready to fall. The agent replied that this was the place. An unshaven, middle-aged landlord let us in to the building. He too wore a string vest, and he too spat while he walked. He didn't give a damn about my patch. He took us across the courtyard and then, to my distress, through a metal gate at the back of it. Beyond the metal gate was a wretched little patio, bordered on its other side by a high crumbling wall. There was a hole in the wall, through which I could see onto the street.

Extending out into the patio was a weird and illegally built living unit. I was about to check it out when a stray Alsatian wandered in, through the hole in the wall. The landlord panicked, and said the watchdog came free.

———

Wen

Hi Hannah, I do miss your company too. You don't need to keep apologising. You've been kind, checking in on me since dad passed away. Happy to meet for a quiet drink

17:55

Wow, considering moving in is a big step. You'd be on course to achieve your new year resolution! Yeah, my new flatmate arrives next week! :)

18:20

———

More from Fifi de Angelis
Translation from the original Italian

From: Fifi de Angelis
Sent: Wednesday, 29 March 2017 20:19
To: Ignazio de Angelis; Rosaria de Angelis; Elisabetta de Angelis; Saveria de Angelis
Subject: My message to you all

My dear family,

As I say: six months since the scandal. And it has taken this long – six months, without a word from any of you – for this psychopathic dwarf (my own sister's words) to put aside his fury, his hurt and his shame, and to write to you all.

First of all, I am happy here in Palermo. I never want to come back to live in Agrigento. But I speak to Nonna every day, the best grandmother in the world, and the only person whose

158

love for me is unwavering, and I know from her that you are not well again, papà. I insist on coming to the hospital when they operate.

You all did a very wicked thing, taking the side of others against me. Believing that absolute bastard, Damiano, and his friends. Telling me that I must leave the only home I had ever known, that I had disgraced you. But I have found it within myself to forgive you. So I ask you: let's make peace, finally, and forever.

You know my greatest fear of all during the past six months? That the scandal served as a good excuse for you all to get me out of your lives. After all, I've been a source of embarrassment all my life, haven't I? But, in truth, I can't believe that even you would take advantage of the situation.

I want to tell my side of the scandal one final time, and I ask you to believe me. It is true, certainly, that I behaved very badly in biting Damiano – biting him repeatedly, and very hard indeed, causing him to have to go to the hospital. A twenty-eight-year-old man should not be biting people. But a man standing at 130 cm, when defending himself against a group of normal-sized men, does not have so many choices. Damiano was a bad person. He gave me his friendship and then one day he took it away.

He was also a coward. The truth is that HE had invited me to the bar to meet his other friends. Only when they began to make jokes about his dwarf friend did he look ashamed, and then he began to make jokes too, and finally changed his story, to save face. Can you imagine my hurt, when he turned to ask me why I had come, and how I had known he would be there? When he added that my following him around had begun to scare him?

159

Even then, I kept my calm. My first friend, the materialisation of a lifetime's hope, was disintegrating before my eyes. But I would not cry. Would not show hurt. At a certain point, he left the bar to have a cigarette outside, I followed him out and told him what I thought of him. My plan had been to walk away, once I'd told him. But we had a nasty argument, which became worse and worse, and suddenly all his friends were surrounding me and taunting me, pushing me around in a circle, kicking me, swatting my head. I managed to kick Damiano in the shin, he got angry and tried to pick me up to throw me, and yes, when he had me in his arms, I bit him and bit him until I could bite no more.

And then there is a police report against me, and it's everyone's word against the word of the crazy dwarf, and Uncle Antonio has to get involved to stop a court case, and it's in the local newspaper and it's so much shame for you all. And behind closed doors you make clear to me that you don't believe my version of events.

I am not saying that the story reflects well on me. But it is very different from me following him to the bar, insisting I join the table and then later attacking him like a madman, unprovoked.

This is the truth. And I want to be part of this family again, even if from afar. We must do this for Nonna. She is ninety years old, and this story has broken her.

Yours

Fifi

A brief editorial intervention. The reader will doubtless agree that Fifi de Angelis seems, at a minimum, a little troubled. Might he be the character who, in six months' time, commits murder? And what about the other characters whom we have met thus far?

So far, the sole character who can be discounted as a potential murderer is, of course, Wen Li. People with OCD are among the safest categories of human being. Wen's type of anxiety is at the opposite end of the spectrum to psychopathy. If the reader has not understood that by this point, it is saddening.

Psychopaths, on the other hand, do not spend their time worrying whether they might be capable of murder...

WhatsApp messages from Wen to Rob
Friday, 31 March 2017

Wen

Well, I'm also happy about last night

14:09

And willing to pick up where we left off

14:09

But no more surprises please!

14:09

———

From: Lomax Clipper
Sent: Friday, 31 March 2017 14:11
To: Katie Wetherden
Subject: A Randy Miss Havisham

That photo of you and Ross standing in front of Royds Hall brought back memories! If you pass by Longwood Road and see the former headmaster of that school on a roof, tell him to get down!

A week in, and this hotel is breaking me. It is weird and disgusting. The couple who manage it are aggressive and mean. Thank God I won't have to endure the place for much longer.

The only plus here is the Wifi. The negatives include the general filth, and the absence of an acceptable toilet – there is just a black hole in my bathroom floor, with a rubber flush button next to it. You have to stamp down hard with your foot. I nearly lost my phone down the hole last night while squatting.

On my foldable desk is a plastic plant that screams depression. Each morning the woman hands me a towel folded in the shape of a swan. There was a scene on Wednesday night, when I tried to smuggle in Aurora after our first pleasant evening together. The woman shouted at me that the place was not a brothel. Aurora screamed at me that I had shamed her. We left the so-called lobby in a shared fury, only to find the communist with the mega beard standing in the dark alley outside. I was disgusted to see Diego in front of my hotel, and asked Aurora what was going on.

Aurora claimed not to know either. It turned out that Diego had been following us around the *piazza* all night, under the moonlight (I know, I know). Aurora was not happy about that, and I was glad to hear her tell him so. I thought that would be the end of it, but then he got out a joint and they began to smoke it together. And then they began to flirt, and then she agreed to him walking her home! I was so angry when they left that I pummelled the pillows on my bed for about a quarter of an hour!

I wish I could just focus on the rest of the experience here in Palermo, which is so exciting. But the very fact it's exciting adds to my sadness that Aurora does not really give a damn, and that I am living it alone, like a buffoon.

At least I've now found new accommodation. Right here, in La Kalsa! I am moving in one week's time. It is on Via Lungarini, which is the whole area summed up in one street. A homage to nostalgia. Restored beauty and eerie abandonment standing together, side-by-side! It is a narrow street of ancient *palazzi*, lined with balconies. Some of the *palazzi* are derelict, standing graffitied and wretched in gloomy shade. And yet, metres on, as the sun (or moon) comes slanting down through the alleys, you see that others are elegant, returned to their former grandeur with leafy balconies and polished facades!

Christ, I can write, can't I?

Will resume shortly: someone is calling me repeatedly on the new mobile!

———

Wen

Haha! :) Well, I guess I'm flattered if I'm the chosen one! :)

15:20

———

From: Lomax Clipper
Sent: Friday, 31 March 2017 15:26
To: Katie Wetherden
Subject: Re: A Randy Miss Havisham

Sorry, that was a truly unpleasant, sinister young man named Enzo who was calling. I am not sure I've ever mentioned him. He's a Sicilian guy from the firm of notaries I worked at in Milan. He's from Palermo, so I had thought I would put aside the vague dread he inspires in me, and reach out for advice. A foolish mistake – God, does he give me the creeps! To paint a picture: he is tall, thin and sports a sort of 1940s hairstyle – seemingly Brylcreemed and with a dramatic side parting, which is particularly odd for a man in his late twenties. He has unkind, unblinking eyes. I remember him as impeccably dressed, but somehow in a very hostile way. He labours under the usual misapprehension about English notaries being as important as Italian notaries. And he adores trying to speak in English. So he was very happy to call.

He asked where I was staying and laughed and laughed when I said La Kalsa, remarking that he loved British humour. I said I wasn't joking and he laughed and laughed some more. His laugh is unreal and horrible. Anyway, he asked me why I'd chosen Palermo for my sabbatical, and I explained that I was trying to rekindle a love affair. He seemed to approve, made a misogynistic joke (standard) and then spoke haughtily of the importance of trusting your 'goat'. I decided not to correct him.

I was telling you about the room I'm going to be renting, in an apartment on Via Lungarini. The *palazzo* in which the apartment is located is like a lost world: the former home of Sicilian nobility, falling slowly into ruin. Neither wretched nor restored, it falls somewhere in the middle of the street's two extremes.

I entered through its grand but graffitied doors to find myself in a cobbled courtyard. There I encountered a Latin bear, who was gazing at me from within a glass cabin. The bear was smoking and wore an old navy suit and tie. He was the porter of the building, and said his name was Nino.

Growling at me as I removed my patch, Nino guided me to a lift with cage-like doors and a seat with cushion inside. The lift took me up to the top floor where an ornate wooden door opened at my touch, and a low, husky voice said to enter.

165

I obeyed, crossing a theatre of war between Splendour and Time. Cracks ran the length of the *salotto*'s high ceiling. Antique furniture was damaged and worn. The air was still, and sunlight revealed the dust coating an old grand piano.

Reclining on a faded chaise longue, wearing a black silk kimono, was Lina di Mauro. The live-in landlady, Nino had told me in the lift, was celebrating her sixtieth birthday. She had long dark hair and was slender and beautiful. She blew smoke as she asked me my name.

The room she was letting was large, with a decadent charm. Its bunk bed, however, had no bottom bunk. I saw I'd have to climb a ladder to get into it.

Lina, moving languidly about the *salotto*, offered to do me a deal on the price. I had questions but suddenly she yawned, reached for a black cigarette and returned to her chaise longue. She told me we could follow up on details tomorrow.

PS DAMN! Damn the world! Only finishing this account have I realised that a flat-share is probably not ideal if I want Aurora to stay over. Stupid idiot! Have just flung two arancini across the room.

———

Translation from the original Italian

From: Fifi de Angelis
Sent: Sunday, 2 April 2017 12:00
To: Ignazio de Angelis; Rosaria de Angelis; Elisabetta de Angelis; Saveria de Angelis
Subject: Re: My message to you all

Can it honestly be true that my email does not even deserve

a response or an acknowledgment? Are we doing this for life, then? You want nothing more to do with me, ever?

————

WhatsApp messages from Wen to Hannah
Sunday, 2 April 2017

Wen

Yeah, have taken him back

16:03

Agree a risk but worth another shot, really like him

16:03

Actually, was thinking, you and I could change our meet up on Wednesday into a double date?! What do you reckon? Would Paul be up for that?

16:03

And good call about the Chinese restaurant. Will be harder to stab you with chopsticks! :)

16:03

Great! Yeah, my mum's OK. She's just having a nap in the sole bedroom!

16:15

————

Wen

Yeah, got back safe. Thanks for coming, was a lovely evening. We all got on so well. Hannah thinks you're great, as does Paul. Can't remember having such an easy, nice time in a group!

23:59

From: Julian Pickering
Sent: Thursday, 6 April 2017 03:02
To: Charles Curtain
Subject: An update

Dear Charles,

You'll note from the time of this email that things are becoming far too stretched here. Wen is an excellent young notary, but given her grade, the recent upset in her life and her issues, which we've discussed, I cannot bring myself to make her work late into the night with me. Thus, while I am being asked to work harder than last year, I am now having to cover tasks which any partner should expect to be able to delegate to a team of three or four notaries.

I would like a meeting with you, please. The current situation is not sustainable, and in my darker moments I wonder whether this isn't a plan to have me leave of my own accord.

Please let me know when you have a slot free in your diary.

Julian

From: Lomax Clipper
Sent: Friday, 7 April 2017 19:01
To: Katie Wetherden
Subject: Friday weekly update

Best of luck with the covert interview.

My parents have said they plan to come and visit in July. I have told them that it will be very hot by then, and that – if the last fortnight is anything to go by – there is no certainty I will still be here. My dad told me not to be so miserable! It's incredible, the change that's come over him!

Aurora has invited me to dance the Mazurka with her friends. She has not yet told me the date. It seems like a test, and I am having intense anxiety about it. The right eye continues to improve slowly, but I have no idea how I'll cope with the Mazurka without the patch.

We've seen each other twice this week, each encounter involving little more than a late-night walk around a *piazza* under the most astonishing moonlight (I know, I know), eating a pistachio ice cream. She falls into long silences that are absolutely impossible to know how to deal with – it's as if she's silently screaming at me that I bore her. The only positive is that Diego seems to have disappeared. (And no, I haven't killed him!)

I moved into Lina's place this morning. I'm cross with myself for being impulsive and ending up in a bizarre flat-share with her as opposed to having my own place. But I had to get out of that hotel – and nothing else I've found in the Old City is habitable.

Aurora put the knife in during our last walk, saying it was a shame

I would not have privacy. She also asked why I was so fixated with La Kalsa when she didn't live in the Old City and I was clearly not relaxed here. I noted that it would have been helpful to have received her opinion prior to transferring the money to Lina. It's about the first time I've dared to be confrontational, and I learnt my lesson. She threw her ice cream down onto the ground! There is tremendous tension between us.

Moving in was also tense. Only when I arrived with my stuff did it occur to me that Via Lungarini could well be the beautiful street I see in my recurring nightmare. The suited Latin bear, Nino, then grilled me. He smokes incessantly inside that porter's cabin, monitoring everything and sticking his chin out at residents as they pass. I believe he seeks Absolute Power within the *palazzo*.

Lina too smokes incessantly on her chaise longue. Her home is full of smoke, and is covered with dust. I intend to do something about the dust.

I've done nothing on the novel since I've arrived, which makes me feel sick with frustration – my future hinges entirely on it! The problem is noise. There is nowhere quiet in this city, including my new accommodation – a neighbour hollers constantly from the balcony next to my dusty, dusty window.

––––––––––

WhatsApp messages from Wen to Rob
Friday, 14 April 2017

Wen

Hey, imagine you're out on a Bumble date? Joking!

20:03

> Sorry about this week. Still in shock about my dad and it just hits me sometimes
>
> 20:03

> Plus, having my mum here in this flat is very intense
>
> 20:03

> And there's something else I guess I should tell you about myself at this point
>
> 20:03

Translation from the original Italian

From: Fifi de Angelis
Sent: Friday, 14 April 2017 20:23
To: Ignazio de Angelis; Rosaria de Angelis; Elisabetta de Angelis; Saveria de Angelis
Subject: Re: I miss you all

Betta, thank you for FINALLY sending through your response 'on behalf of the family'. I tried to call each one of you after it, but see nothing has changed. It seems that our correspondence must remain written for now.

I did not properly understand the overall message. Are you all letting me back into the family or not? At a certain point you seem to imply that I'm a sort of menace. That all my life I have been bothering people, trying to be their friend and then becoming angry when it doesn't happen. It's so ridiculous and unfair. So hurtful. Don't we all search for friendship? I've never harmed anyone, except Damiano. And none of you could imagine how it is to be a man of 130 centimetres, living in Agrigento. The loneliness. The jokes.

171

I never had a friend in Agrigento, male or female, until Damiano, who betrayed me. And then, let's be honest, all of you too could be mean from time to time. That Christmas when papà joked to his friends, in front of all our family, that he would put me in his pocket and go for a walk. The time on the beach when Betta and Vera's boyfriends had the stupid competition to see how far they could throw me into the waves. And me playing along, trying to smile, while weeping inside at the degradation, the humiliation, my sisters' failure to support or protect or defend. Who would not feel a growing anger at human beings? There were so many of these episodes, too many to remember.

But I have no more anger in me now. I am living a happy phase of my life here in Palermo. I live in La Kalsa, in a clean, if very small, studio apartment.

The apartment does not get much light, but the arrangement is informal and flexible and good – I am only tied in for a month's rent, with an option to renew at each month's end. I'm working at a tobacconist in the beautiful New City here, and my colleagues are OK, mostly. I've found a famous *focacceria* nearby where the waiters treat me very well and the food is exceptional. It's a place popular with young guys, and I spend many evenings there, watching people come and go. In short, life is better than in Agrigento.

… ah, enough. Probably none of you care about this and anyway, I am digressing. The fact is, I do not really understand your email. It just seems a long, vague criticism of me. You've not even responded clearly to my point that I will be coming to the hospital to see papà. This coldness, from one's whole family, is simply unbearable. Please respond with more clarity: what is your position with regard to me?

Fifi

Wen

Ha! Cool, so say hello to Maria from me and have a lovely romantic time babe! :)

20:26

No need for the selfie as proof you're in the office, btw. Although you're looking hot and ever so important! :)

20:26

Well, it's just that I have an anxiety disorder. OCD. Am on medication for it. When it hits I find it difficult to face the world

20:27

Thanks Rob. And yes, don't worry… am not going to go loopy on you! :)

20:40

And yeah, my boss knows. He's pretty reasonable about it, although so cold and formal all the time. Such a comically awkward Englishman!

20:40

I do think they are getting pissed off with my absences, but it's only been a couple of further days off

20:40

My mum is also getting worried and I reckon a little suspicious

20:41

She said that before coming to live with me she hadn't known I had such regular migraines!

20:41

No way, Mum doesn't know anything about the OCD

20:55

I just go with the migraine thing

20:55

TBH sometimes she really does bring on a migraine! :)

20:55

We are stressing each other out a bit here in flat

20:55

Feel so sorry for her, but it's such a small space for both of us

20:55

Anyway, glad you're done for the evening. Chat later?

20:56

Oi, I've told you not to call him that! Lomax is not having an ideal time. But careful what you say about his writing, Mr High Powered!

21:33

He may well just surprise you and publish a bestseller. And then wouldn't you feel silly??!

21:33

———

From: Lomax Clipper
Sent: Friday, 14 April 2017 22:40
To: Katie Wetherden
Subject: Serious problems now in the flat

Another week passes, a mere page of the novel done. This coming week there's the Mazurka with the communists. As if I didn't have enough on my mind. Extraordinary goings-on here in the land of lost luxury.

I had not known that Lina had a son of about my age. His name is Roberto, and he is a large and bad-tempered man. He lives with his girlfriend two floors below. He wears a black leather jacket and has black spiky hair. He does not have anything of his mother's dissipated aristocrat look. Instead he looks like a guy who could punch you in the face – or indeed kill you on a Palermitan street, under the stars. He was here arguing with Lina on Tuesday evening when I returned from a very unsatisfying walk and pistachio ice cream with Aurora. He seemed furious that I had come to live with his mother.

Since then, Lina has not helped matters. She lies on that chaise longue dressed in her silk kimono, chain-smoking her black cigarettes and gazing into my left eye, telling me how she loves my English accent, how she found the patch such a quaint surprise, and how she hopes I will remember her when I'm a rich and famous author. All in the presence of spiky-haired Roberto!

Her monologues move on to repeated, bitter declarations that she is from a 'good family', but that her husband frittered away her inheritance, before leaving her for another woman. And that this guy – here she points at Roberto – takes after his terrible father.

On around the tenth telling of her story, while averting my eye from the sight of her playing with the loosely tied belt of her kimono, I noted that one of the dusty antique clocks behind Lina had stopped at five minutes to midnight. For a moment I found myself wondering whether the "husband" hadn't actually left her at the altar; whether this wasn't all just another strange dream, in which Miss Havisham had become confused with Mrs Robinson.

Anyway, everything got much, much worse this evening. Basically, I had finally got round to doing the dusting.

I must stop. Roberto is knocking at my door. Not safe.

———

Further WhatsApp message from Wen to Rob
Friday, 14 April 2017

Wen

No worries. So sorry you're working so hard. Chat tomorrow?

22:50

———

From: Lomax Clipper
Sent: Friday, 14 April 2017 23:55
To: Katie Wetherden
Subject: Re: Serious problems now in the flat

Jesus Christ. Am OK. But suffice it to say that Roberto told me he did not know what was going on between me and his mother, but that it had better stop. An implied threat of physical violence!

I told him that all that had been going on was dusting. This was quite true! The dust in the flat had become intolerable, so this afternoon I bought a large, white ostrich feather duster, and with that I dusted my bedroom. To avoid boredom I put Elton John on full blast on my iPod while I worked. I did a terrific job, even dusting the ceiling – I took the ladder from the bed to do that. By the time I had finished with the bedroom I was so fired up that I asked for Lina's permission to dust the rest of the apartment.

She croaked: '*Si*'. So I got the feather duster, put the earphones back in my ears and began to dust again. I don't know whether it was frustration over Aurora, or bitterness at the noise in Palermo, or shame at having certain feelings about a sixty-year-old woman, but I went MANIC with the dusting.

I dusted the piano, the lamps, the mahogany desk. I dusted below the chaise longue while Lina reclined on it. I got my ladder and dusted the *salotto*'s ceiling. Then I dusted the kitchen, and the bathroom. Finally, there remained only her bedroom left to dust, and again Lina gave me her permission. She was far away there on the chaise longue, and entering her bedroom seemed safe.

So I went in with my duster. I dusted her walls, all her shelves. Then I went to her bedside table, in order to dust that. Apparently, it was at this point that Lina came in and said that I was NOT to touch the Bible on her bedside table. But, obviously, with the iPod on so loud, I did not hear her. I picked up the Bible from the bedside table in order to dust below it, and then screamed in horror at the sight of Lina flying at me across the bed in her kimono.

And who should come in, just as Lina is lying face down on the bed, her dishevelled kimono revealing a bare arse, with me standing above her, eye patch on and feather duster raised high above my head, as if I were about to spank the hell out of her?!

Translation from the original Italian

From: Fifi de Angelis
Sent: Friday, 14 April 2017 23:56
To: Ignazio de Angelis; Rosaria de Angelis; Elisabetta de Angelis; Saveria de Angelis
Subject: Re: I miss you all

I just wanted to add something. All I want is to be loved.

Fifi

From: Julian Pickering
Sent: Thursday, 20 April 17:01
To: Martin Pickering
Subject: Re: Match

Hi Dad,

Absolutely no way I'm taking you to the match on Saturday if you've still got a bad cold. I will come round and make us lunch and we can watch some TV. Also, I know this will annoy you, but I've massively over-ordered from Waitrose again – an online cock-up – so I'll have to bring you some stuff, including some microwavable meals. Mad to throw them out, and I can assure you some of them are very tasty indeed.

I can tell you all about work too, and all the rest. Having a terrible time.

Julian

––––––––

From: Julian Pickering
Sent: Thursday, 20 April 19:05
To: Martin Pickering
Subject: Re: Match

Hi Dad,

Actually, yes, 'all the rest' did refer to my friend Toby.

'Love affair dramas' was a slightly hurtful way of putting it. I don't know what Victoria has told you, but never mind. I know that this side of me is far too much for you to handle in any detail. Let's just keep the talk to football and work, safer that way.

Julian

––––––––

WhatsApp messages from Wen to Hannah
Thursday, 20 April 2017

Wen

Yes, definitely up for another gathering of the fab four tomorrow. You guys OK with Vinoteca in Farringdon? A Rob suggestion…

12:33

So jealous of your moving-in plans!

12:33

Yes, had long chat with boss today about absences

17:41

Haven't been that many, but I did have another day off this week

17:41

Am very ashamed about it. Julian was kind of OK about it, but something ominous in his tone

17:42

Clearly dicey ground for a relatively new joiner

17:42

Not told Rob as don't want to freak him out. Wish I could get Lomax's opinion TBH

17:42

Yeah, but I don't want to mention it to Lomax because any reference to Julian gets him so fired up

18:28

And definitely don't want to trigger him at the moment, just when things finally seem to be looking up for him out there!

18:28

Take the job, Katie!

I have managed ten pages of *And Later on Easter Island* this week. The noise here, though! However, I have a plan – tomorrow I'm going to go and work in the grand old public library of the city. Surely it must be quiet there.

To my surprise and delight, my right eye is now improving quite significantly. On Monday I have my check-up with Carmela Rapisarda. Her clinic is located in the elegant, belle-époque world that is the New City of Palermo. I went to find it this week and, God, how I love it there. Wide, dreamy avenues of neoclassical buildings and Liberty facades; chic *aperitivo* bars, cleanliness, an unobstructed view of the crystalline sky. Italy's oldest opera house, in Teatro Massimo!

It is not even a long walk from the Old City – you just carry on down to the end of Via Maqueda, and witness Palermo turn into a butterfly before your eyes.

In other news here, Lina di Mauro has a lover. He looks a bit younger than her, in his late forties or early fifties, and is a big Latin bear like Nino the porter. We do not know his name. I say we, because spiky-haired Roberto, Nino the porter and I have formed a secret, and somewhat precarious, alliance against our common enemy. All has been put aside for now re the feather duster, in the interests of the greater good. The lover is my enemy because he is an intruder in my home. He is Roberto's enemy because he is shagging his mother. He is Nino the porter's enemy because Nino believes himself to be

181

King of the *Palazzo*, and does not like scandals within its walls.

The first night the lover came, I arrived in the flat to the sound of Lina screaming inside the bedroom. I thought she might be under attack, so was about to shout and bang at her door when the screaming ended suddenly and Lina came out, with a blissful gaze. Following her came the lover in a red silk dressing gown. They took their places on the antique chair and chaise longue and shared a cigarette, ignoring me. Lina murmured dreamily that he had exhausted her.

Nino now reports to me and Roberto whenever the lover arrives in the courtyard. I report to them when he is about to leave.

————

WhatsApp messages from Wen to Mum
Friday, 21 April 2017

Translation from the original Chinese

Wen

Hi Mum, sorry but I'll be back quite late tonight. Having a lot of fun with Hannah and our two boyfriends. :) Are you OK, having a nice evening? I'll try not to make too much noise

22:19

And some big news… I've invited Rob to come over for Chinese food next Thursday so you can meet! You and I need to make a meal plan! :) Love you

22:20

————

I'm back for Part 2!

On Tuesday, I went folk dancing in the street with twenty-five communists. I was confident going without the patch, given the eye's remarkable recent progress. Naturally, the Mazurka was held in the grimmest place imaginable, Albergheria. The street was Via Letizia. Check it out on Google Street View. Clotheslines and electrical cables hung entangled above my head. Mangy dogs stared hungrily.

When I arrived on Via Apocalypse, scratchy violin music was playing on a cassette player they had brought from their retro-fashion musical instrument shop. I suggested to Aurora, who was looking wildly sexy in her khaki pants and sleeveless top, that I could provide the music through my iPhone, but would need to keep the phone in my hand in order to avoid the risk of theft. She looked so offended that I panicked, and told her I needed to pop to the loo. I entered a foul little bar, where I was served a shot of a mystery liquor.

By the time I came out, the Mazurka had begun. I stood with some stray cats as the circle of couples rotated around each other. I realised that Diego had not disappeared, but multiplied. There were at least fifteen of him, all with the same dreadlocks and beards. All scowling at me with the same hatred.

The dancers clung and they spun, in scenes that conveyed the joy of simple things. Upon Aurora's gesturing, I stepped forward. Imitating the beards, I kept my head high and my torso straight, pulled her in gently and gently flung her away…

183

The cassette player then conked out. Aurora told me to sit down with her in the circle so she could introduce me to her friends. Grim moments these, sitting amid the litter and puffing on a joint, listening to them congratulating themselves for having appropriated the Mazurka. It turned out I was the only one who actually lived in the Old City! When Diego lit a second joint, I excused myself and went back to the bar. There I pissed down a black hole in the bathroom, heard the music playing again and necked three shots of the mystery drink.

Whatever it was, I came back out for round two and began to MOVE. I danced with all the scowling communists in the world! When the Mazurka was over, I saw that Aurora was laughing uncontrollably, her eyes full of something bordering on love. Under Diego's gaze she pulled me close and we kissed.

I wandered with her back to my place, holding her hand and infinitely happy. When we arrived in front of the *palazzo*, we looked into each other's eyes and I was struck by the thought that I was dangerously in love with her and she meant me no good. But she kept staring, transfixing me, her face turned silver by the moonlight that had stolen in through a gap between the *palazzi*, so I waved away my strange thought, deciding that the world was too broken to be taken too seriously. Entering the flat on tiptoe, I saw Lina dragging the lover into her room. We crept into mine, climbed the ladder up into bed and, as Lina wailed, we stepped back in time and returned finally to Ustica.

———

Translation from the original Chinese

Wen

Morning. Feeling OK? Tonight's the big night! Sorry I was back late again last night, but did you see the food I brought back from China town? We have food for a month haha!

09:19

If you fancy cooking, obviously fantastic. No problem if you're not up to it and you want me to

09:19

But do please let me know

09:20

Wonderful! Thank you. In that case, remember that tonight we should only prepare the stuff that I wrote down on the list on the kitchen table. Rob won't like the other things. They're for me and you on a different night :)

09:45

And no, Rob will be coming separately. Later, at seven thirty

09:45

Yeah, the pork will be perfect for him, he'll like it. Not too spicy please... very, very important

16:20

Also, I'm going to be stuck in the office a little later than I'd hoped. May not be back till six thirty or seven

16:20

Please stick to the list I wrote down, am counting on you

16:21

No chicken feet! I told you, the English do not like chicken feet. PLEASE JUST LOOK AT THE LIST

16:44

I don't want to touch the special tea. I bought something cheaper. It's in the cabinet above the hob

16:44

There is no way I can leave earlier. I told you, I need to be careful here. Job situation is delicate because of my absences for my migraines

16:59

And no, there's no need to dress up too formally. Just natural

16:59

His name is Rob, not Lomax!!!

17:40

No, he will not want to see the poems I wrote as a child. He can't read Mandarin, as I told you. Please put them back

17:51

> So sorry, just stressed! :)
>
> 18:02

> See you soon, will be back before seven
>
> 18:02

> This will be a first, your daughter inviting a boyfriend round!
>
> 18:02

> Wonder what Dad would have said :)
>
> 18:02

> No!!! You're going to make me cry. Please, please just KEEP TO THE LIST
>
> 18:12

> OK, OK. It's fine, you and I can have it afterwards when he has gone
>
> 18:21

> Leaving office now. Love you
>
> 18:21

From: Julian Pickering
Sent: Thursday, 27 April 2017 23:04
To: Toby Enslin
Subject: Further letter

Toby, I have received the new letter from your lawyers (who are being retained through money earned by my slaving away till midnight each night, I might add).

Please note that I do not accept that you have any claim to a flat whose mortgage is paid by me alone. I intend to raise your abuse and your alcoholism in my response. If you want to get into the gutter, I will follow you there.

Julian

Wen

Hey, you were such a good sport with my mum tonight. Her cooking's not bad, right?!

23:05

Am so proud that she managed to be on good form

23:05

She's struggling to get out of bed in the morning at the moment

23:05

I've been telling her to see someone, but of course she's refusing to even consider that!

23:06

Wish I was at yours right now. No worries about tomorrow night btw. Saturday it is, for Mr High Powered's birthday dinner!

23:06

WhatsApp messages from Wen to Hannah
Thursday, 27 April 2017

Wen

It went brilliantly here tonight, thanks. Rob and Mum got on well. On Paul, his bad breath doesn't seem a major deal, Hannah! Just tell him but kindly. Plus, sorry I really don't need to know that he's rubbish at sex

23:55

Yeah, but think how hurt he would be if he ever found out you had said that. I also think you could have made the effort to go see his folks this weekend?

23:57

Think I'm Team Paul at the moment ha! :)

23:58

No problem about tomorrow night, looks like I'll be watching soap opera with Mum!

23:58

———

From: Julian Pickering
Sent: Friday, 28 April 2017 09:45
To: Charles Curtain
Subject: Our meeting

Dear Charles,

While I thank you for our earlier meeting, and your agreement to allocate two new notaries to my team, I did want to put into writing my profound disagreement with your proposed

189

treatment of my colleague Wen Li. Given what you have instructed me to do, I wanted to put on record that I find this professionally and morally wrong. As I said, I even think this exposes us to a potential claim, not to mention the possible reputational consequences.

As I confirmed, her absences since joining some eight months ago have indeed been unhelpful. But her father passed away recently, which accounted for certain of those days, and the other days are explained by a mental health disorder which I agree we should have been made aware of, but which should ideally be treated with tact and care. While I have gleaned from my conversations with her that she's relatively financially secure – I understand that her mother is a successful businesswoman – I nevertheless have no idea what this news will do to her.

Julian

––––––––

WhatsApp messages from Wen to Hannah
Friday, 28 April 2017

Wen

I've just been fucking sacked. Can't believe it

10:58

They're happy for me to work through till end of May, how kind of them!

10:59

––––––––

Katie, I got so excited at your email that I whooped and whooped until Lina knocked and blew smoke in my face! She said that it's one thing being woken by screaming each night (she can talk!), but during the day is too much. I said this was very odd, given the man yelling from the balcony next door, and the generally sickeningly high noise levels in the *palazzo*. She seemed to suggest that my English noises trigger her in a different way.

Anyway, the new firm sounds perfect. Your realisation that Huddersfield is home is very moving.

This week I went to see Carmela Rapisarda, who confirmed that there have been no further complications with the eye. It is improving dramatically. Carmela is perhaps the second most beautiful woman the eye has ever seen. She was dressed in a white suit that enhanced her bronze skin. Her clinic is located on Via della Libertà, the New City's most elegant street. She had the balcony doors open, and white voiles were billowing in the breeze. She told me I should throw away the patch, as it might hinder my progress.

I lingered awhile in the New City afterwards, wandering around the Giardino Inglese, having a light 'branch' (lovely misspelling on the menu) in a clean, trendy eatery. Many of the shops had posters with slogans written in wonderfully bad English, such as 'the sky has the limits!' Finally I sighed, stepped out of the strange dream and headed back to authenticity.

Last Saturday I was disappointed to find that the public library, located in the magnificent, sixteenth-century, former 'Collegio

Massimo della Compagnia di Gesù', does not open at weekends. However, I went back on Monday afternoon and upon entering let out a cry of joy: there was a gorgeous silence inside. I've worked at the library each day this week. This novel is getting there, believe me. There are paragraphs, even whole pages now, that are of the stuff that makes a writer famous.

Things are going very well now with Aurora – better than they ever have. Yes, it was a very romantic night, that night of the Mazurka. At least, until around four in the morning in the bunk bed, when the nightmare hit and I nearly perforated her eardrum.

She definitely is vulnerable, by the way. I think that her need to keep writing to lots of other guys, and even to try to get the attention of strangers in bars when she's out with me alone, is borne of an unfathomable insecurity. It's so weird when she tells me in a rushed, slightly manic voice how so-and-so flirted with her, how the bus driver asked her out, how Mommo's friends all fancy her etc. I just want to say to her, Christ, Aurora, you're absolutely stunning, you don't need to keep telling me this.

Anyway, I honestly think that in her own way she is close to committing – and perhaps this weird self-reinforcement is part of the process she is needing to go through. Indeed, to my excitement and horror (a strange cocktail), an invitation to visit the family on Via Bari would appear to be imminent.

Via Bari, incidentally, is half-way up Via Maqueda, so in a sort of no man's land between Old City and New. Spiritually speaking, Aurora turns left down Via Maqueda, in search of rebellion and exhausted Culture. I'm not sure which way Mommo turns. Probably he stays put: gangsta chavs perhaps find home to be somewhere in the middle.

That reminds me, there is one unpleasant footnote to an otherwise relatively happy account of my love life. On Monday night, I walked Aurora back as far as I dared to her place on Via Bari, and came upon a disturbing scene. We had just turned off Via Maqueda when we saw Diego further down the street, loitering in front of her *palazzo*. Suddenly, a huge, homicidal-looking guy in sunglasses and gold chains pulled up on a scooter – and slapped Diego in the face! I retreated, with Aurora's whispered words that Mommo hates stalkers reverberating in my head.

I've run out of time as I have to head down to give an English class. More about that in this evening's follow-up email.

––––––––––

WhatsApp message from Wen to Rob
Friday, 28 April 2017

Wen

Hope you're having fun with the lads. How many pints so far? Let me know if you're around for a chat later. I've got some work 'news'!

21:03

––––––––––

From: Lomax Clipper
Sent: Friday, 28 April 2017 22:04
To: Katie Wetherden
Subject: A Palermitan start-up, continued

Nino and the lover had a row in the courtyard this evening. Nearly a bear fight!

It was about these English lessons I'm giving. The story begins with me meeting a tiny guy named Fifi. Now, everyone is short here, but Fifi really does have restricted growth and is surely no more than four feet tall. He works in a tobacconist in the New City, but lives back here on the dark side, close to Via Lungarini.

I met him on Wednesday evening, while I was eating in a focaccia place near to the flat. To my discomfort, I became gradually aware that a relatively powerful-looking, muscular, incredibly short young man, with smartly-cut, short dark hair and an intense gaze, was staring at me. I realised I'd seen him in the place before. Always alone and always gazing – but never, until now, at me. Suddenly, he jumped down from his seat, walked across very purposefully and asked if he could join me. The poor guy was so friendly, and clearly lonely. In the intensity of his dark brown eyes I saw such insecurity. So I did my very best to be as nice as possible.

Fifi told me that he was twenty-eight, and had moved to Palermo from his hometown of Agrigento, after a big family falling-out – he did not elaborate. Agrigento is some distance from here, on the southern coast of the island – it has always sounded to me like a fantasy city, perched on a hill overlooking the sea and not far from the Valley of the Temples, said to be one of the most outstanding ancient-Greek sites in the world, never mind Sicily. However, Fifi told me that the area of the city his family lived in was several leagues grimmer than Albergheria. A statement that made me start to hiccup. Later we got on to me, and Fifi asked how I was managing financially. I said I was deep into my overdraft, and had considered teaching English only to find that the British Institute required various qualifications. Fifi laughed, saying that I was too English. Do it freelance, he said!

An interesting thought, and when I got back to Via Lungarini that evening, half-distracted by my ruminations over whether it had been a good idea to exchange numbers with Fifi, I mentioned his idea in passing to Nino. To my dismay, Nino's eyes widened and he pulled me into his cabin.

We would undercut everyone in Palermo, he said, and offer lessons for five euros an hour. The key to his plan was '*gruppetti*'. If I taught groups, he enthused, we could make a fortune, in cash!

I asked why he should get a cut, and he growled that he would get the people in. I said I would sleep on it, but by the next morning the news was all over La Kalsa. Roberto texted me that he was in, for a cut. The lover told me to ditch Nino and go with him instead. Nino was WILD by Thursday evening, waving me away while yelling in dialect down his phone.

This morning was the first class. I taught ten of Nino's '*amici*' in the little *salotto* of his and his wife's living quarters, which he has converted into a classroom. He collected the five euros from each of them. The level of English was shocking.

Aurora despises this venture. She says I should be teaching the city's poor for free. But, when she mentioned it to her family, apparently her dad and Mommo paid attention. Indeed, she told me in a disgusted voice, they are both now keen to meet her English friend.

———

WhatsApp messages from Wen to Rob
Saturday, 29 April 2017

Wen

No worries, wasn't trying to pester! :) Glad you had a fun night. See you tomorrow! Also, please note that it's now officially your birthday, so I would like to be the first to say it: HAPPY BIRTHDAY, my lovely Rob!

00:03

Have been thinking about our chat all morning

12:22

Sorry again for giving you my depressing news on your birthday

12:22

What have you done to yourself, getting together with an unemployed nutcase?!

12:22

But at least she'll have her black La Perla on tonight

12:22

While she dines with you at… Phoenix Palace! A Chinese restaurant I believe you once said was on your wish list?!

12:22

Managed to book a table for 8. Hope this meets with your approval :)

12:23

Ah, full of banter are we today, Mr Birthday Boy?

15:20

Anyway, yes, I'm now defo sure oven is off, which has allowed me to go to bedroom to mull over choice of dress :) See you at 8!

15:21

Hey, don't be silly, the OCD banter didn't offend

17:03

Didn't mean to ignore your message

17:03

But ironically your joke was kind of right. I'm so so sorry but have had real episode again. Recurring thoughts about all sorts of things. Bed is only place for me

17:03

I do sincerely apologise. Would have called but can't even bring myself to speak on phone at moment

17:04

Please forgive me

17:04

Well, that was a very noble reply, but please look out your window! Your Chinese sweetheart is here! Tricked you babe! :)

19:00

Haha. Well, you deserved it after your mean joke today! Open up! I've got your present with me and then we'll need to get going (eek, just realised I've been assuming 2 hours didn't give you enough time to make other plans!?)

19:03

Oi, it's raining out here. Let me in! :)

19:09

Humiliated and betrayed. Never contact me again.

22:09

WhatsApp message from Wen to Hannah
Saturday, 29 April 2017

Wen

You sick bitch! I've just told Paul what I came across this evening.

22:28

From: Lomax Clipper
Sent: Friday, 5 May 2017 21:15
To: Katie Wetherden
Subject: La Famiglia and the language school

The partners at your firm must think you've gone mad, leaving them for a regional outfit! While to me it seems as if the world has turned perfect for you.

Roberto, whose black hair is particularly spiky this evening, has just told me that, in his perfect world, he would kill the lover, just as he was entering the *palazzo*. I told him that in my perfect world the language school would have succeeded, and my novel would sell millions of copies, allowing me to buy a villa by the sea. He replied that surely it would be better to be married to Denise Capezza, the actress they're all crazy about here. I said, only if Denise Capezza loved me for the right reasons. He stared at me for a good while after I said this, most confused.

Giving up, he changed the subject by asking how my dwarf was doing – earlier this week he'd come across me and Fifi as we were taking a stroll. I was very strong back on this, not least because I have warmed to Fifi quite considerably this week – we've met up twice and indeed I've only returned a short time ago from an amusing evening with him in the focaccia place. He's a little insistent with his text messages, for sure, but he's certainly the nicest man I've met in this city, and is very good company over a drink – excellent sense of humour, if a little on edge at times. Given the insecurity that pervades him, I'm rapidly becoming protective. So, I told Roberto that he needed to open his mind a little, and I would not have him insulting my friend. Roberto's nostrils quivered when I said this – perhaps I should pick my battles.

Wen, incidentally, has been cheated on by that little shit, the Business Development Director – she caught him with her best friend! And she has lost her job. Another spectacularly bad time for her. She's currently not speaking or writing to me because of the 'interfering' email I sent to the rat-witch about his sacking her. I'm desperately trying to think of some plan that will allow me to redeem myself.

Stopped for a moment there, as I thought the lights were going again. We're having intermittent electricity outages in the *palazzo*. The rumour is that it's Nino the porter's fault – he has been pissing about in the basement. However, nobody in the *palazzo* has dared to confront him. Lina WOULD dare if she gave a damn about the outages, but she does not. She lies smoking in the moonlight.

This is a terribly garrulous email, largely due to three large glasses of wine with Fifi earlier, but the main point of it is to say that I am meeting Aurora's family a week tomorrow. This, together with Wen's news, is what has driven me to drink. My fear shows how screwed up I am about the Aurora situation – surely if I want this to work, I should be ecstatic? Or is all I am really living a dream?

Regardless, I have found myself gazing at photos of Gigi on Facebook, fixating on his slicked-back white hair, open shirts and spectacular chest hair. I've found myself brooding over his and Mommo's displeasure at Aurora joining the *Addiopizzo* movement. I'd previously drawn comfort from the idea that this was just concern, but now I have discovered Gigi's line of work: he owns a tanning salon. A Google search for 'Mafia fronts in Palermo' filled me with nausea.

Finally, the language school. It has gone down in flames. The air in the *palazzo* is thick with recrimination. The school had quite a little journey there, for a week. The first students were so enthused – or so I was led to believe – that applicants multiplied miraculously overnight. I feared that something was not quite right, but Nino said we were shaking up the market.

I did three classes each morning from Saturday to Tuesday, and we made over four hundred euros. Nino had found nearly a hundred students in less than a week! He rebuffed Roberto's request to come in for a cut, and said we were getting '*ricchi ricchi*'. But then…

Yet here I must end, for the lights are flickering. I'll try to send this before the Wifi goes.

———

From: Fifi de Angelis
Sent: Friday, 5 May 2017 21:17
To: Ignazio de Angelis; Rosaria de Angelis; Elisabetta de Angelis; Saveria de Angelis
Subject: Re: I miss you all

No response again, from any of you, for three weeks. I must be such a nuisance?

I had said to myself never to send another email. But perhaps the truth was that all I needed was the inspiration of three glasses of red wine! :) Now I've had them, and I'm completely drunk, and I'm also extremely happy because I have made a REAL friend here in Palermo! A wonderful English guy. He is intelligent, thoughtful, sensitive. In fact, super intelligent: he's a writer. He doesn't judge me, patronise me, he doesn't ever make me feel uncomfortable. We have so much fun, so many laughs together. The friend I've always wanted!

Oh, please reply. Say that you love me. Sometimes I dream that you will surprise me one morning by calling me, all of you together, out of the blue.

Good night,

Fifi

———

WhatsApp messages from Wen to Lomax
Friday, 5 May 2017

Wen

Hello, dear Lomax!

23:50

Sorry for writing those mean things to you

23:50

I know you were only trying to help by writing to the rat-witch

23:50

Can we speak tomorrow? Hope all well with the novel... you will get there!

23:50

A brief editorial intervention. There are now less than four months until the murder.

From: Lomax Clipper
Sent: Saturday, 6 May 2017 09:52
To: Katie Wetherden
Subject: Re: La Famiglia and the language school

Good morning, Mrs Wetherden.

A sore head this morning, but power, thus Wifi, is back. And with it, six new messages from Fifi, reminiscing about last night. As I say, he's somewhat intense when it comes to electronic communications.

Anyway, I was saying that by last Tuesday the language school was flying, but it had suddenly occurred to me that I had not received any money. On Tuesday evening, when I got back from writing at the library, I complimented Nino on his new tie, and asked him to hand over my share of the takings. He refused, explaining that there were people he needed to take care of, and things I didn't need to know.

When I told Aurora this over the phone on Tuesday night, she said that if my business was paying the *pizzo* she would never speak to me again.

So the next morning I did not tell her (but did mention to Fifi, who told me to be careful) that a man wearing a motorcycle helmet had just walked into the courtyard, straight after the lesson, and snatched a brown envelope from Nino's hands. I did not tell her how Nino's fearful expression, and the dragon emblazoned on the man's helmet, had struck dread into my heart.

But I did tell her when I discovered the separate point that Nino was operating a sort of Ponzi scheme. Late on Wednesday night, the lover crept out of Lina's bedroom and disclosed this bombshell to me. The school was a sham, and the lover had proof in the form of text messages. Nino was promising every student that they would get their money back and a hundred per cent profit if they got two new students to come to the lessons.

So, after taking into account the commission owed, we were only earning a third of what I had thought we were earning. And then there was the suspected *pizzo* payment. And the purchase of Nino's new tie. The partners, I realised with dismay, could even be in debt.

Once he had shown me the evidence, the lover nodded gravely to me before returning to Lina's bed. I went to confront Nino the next morning and found him with his head in his hands. The school, he mumbled, had made some bad *investimenti*.

I told him the game was up, and in my agitation ended up disclosing my source. This resulted in scenes of high drama as a short time later the lover made to cross the courtyard, whistling as he went. Nino leapt out of his cabin, bellowing in dialect, and soon faces were appearing at the *palazzo*'s windows. It was about to turn violent when a languorous, beautiful lady in a black silk kimono appeared, and said, in her husky voice: '*Basta.*'

They stopped immediately. It is Lina di Mauro who really rules this *palazzo*.

Speaking to Wen shortly. God, she's in a mess.

———

From: Fifi de Angelis
Sent: Saturday, 6 May 2017 15:59
To: Rosaria de Angelis
Subject: You've destroyed me

Dear Mamma,

You are so skilful at breaking my heart. After your call I walked around my room crying, like a child. Congratulations.

You said that I have frightened you and that you hope I am not bothering the Englishman, just as I bothered people in Agrigento. You implied once more that I am a sort of psychopath. Can I ask just one question: why do I not deserve even one friend, to your mind?

I am not defending myself ever again to anyone. I behaved badly by biting Damiano. That's all I've ever done wrong in twenty-eight years. I am delighted to have a true friend here in Palermo and the idea that you could spit on the beauty of this friendship.

I hate you so much. I hate you nearly as much as I love you.

Fifi

P.S. nobody will be able to stop me from coming to the hospital to see papà. I know the date of the operation. Nonna tells me everything.

During the week that follows, following some feedback from a recruiter, the obvious is confirmed to Wen Li: it will take a while to ascertain interest, let alone to secure a job at another notarial firm, so even in the best case scenario there will likely be a gap in employment of at least a month, once she leaves Curtain & Curtain at the end of May. The failure of her relationship with Rob Davidson, and the betrayal by him and by her friend Hannah Richards, weigh on her heavily. Her OCD spirals again.

Wen's mother also begins to seek work, albeit half-heartedly and in vain. Between the two women they have seven thousand pounds in savings.

Very late at night, Wen thinks of her father. She knows that he would have told his women to fight, to be strong. She whispers her secret to him, imploring him not to judge and to understand that OCD is not her fault. She tells him of a lovely man named Lomax Clipper, a man of whom her father would have disapproved on account of his apparent instability. She tells her father that he would have been quite wrong to disapprove, and through laughter and tears explains that Lomax is now seeking to save her, proposing the wildest and most ridiculous plans that somehow DO save her, suffused as they are with eccentricity and care.

She whispers to her father that, despite all of her and her mother's problems, if there's one thing she really wants now, it's for Lomax's novel to succeed.

Meanwhile, over in Sicily, Lomax Clipper's relationship with Aurora La Rosa and his friendship with Fifi de Angelis continue to flourish. In both cases, Lomax Clipper seeks to put aside some nagging concerns: in the case of Aurora, her mood swings; in the case of Fifi, a certain growing intensity.

From: Lomax Clipper
Sent: Friday, 12 May 2017 20:19
To: Katie Wetherden
Subject: Tomorrow's the big day!

I'm disappointed that you would discount the possibility of Wen working for your new firm. She could have started as a paralegal and, so far as I understand it, she's already passed virtually all the law exams required to be a fully qualified solicitor. I would ask you to rethink – I'm sure she'd be happy to move to Manchester.

The notary firm in Milan and another one in central Palermo weren't interested in her – they only take English notaries on secondment so that they don't have to pay them themselves, which makes sense (incidentally, it's been confirmed that Curtain & Curtain would not support a further secondment for me). The only spark of interest in Wen that I've found is from a little firm on the outskirts of Palermo – but Wen said firmly, no.

I told her not to be so discriminatory.

As for other matters here, tomorrow evening is the biggie: I'm going to Via Bari to have dinner with Aurora, Gigi, Luisa and Mommo.

Partially mitigating the fear is an increasing optimism – at times I find myself daring to believe that things might be coming together here. It has been a golden week, spring giving way to summer, the sun bouncing about Via Lungarini, the writing flowing in the fine quiet of a library steeped in history. Lina now most welcoming to Aurora, making her feel at home. Aurora popping in her earplugs and climbing gracefully up the ladder into bed, calling Gigi to say she is staying at her friend Paola's once more. The eye continuing its recovery. The knowledge that Carmela is always there. Nino, having settled our language school debts (no desire to find out how), now silent, a broken man. The lover AWOL. Roberto away in Rome…

Halcyon mornings walking hand-in-hand with Aurora down Via Lungarini, to the envious stares of local men; balmy evenings alone with her in the Orto Botanico, amid sycamores and coffee trees. Standing beside her before L'Annunciata, gasping as the Virgin Mary's expression transforms; passing a statue of Santa Rosalia, catching Aurora making the sign of the cross.

Listening to her deny that she had made the sign of the cross, her voice captivating and wild. Early-morning jogs alone around La Kalsa, to glances asking me, 'why?' Co-opting Fifi in an attempt to return a Prada suit I had bought in Milan's sales one year ago; Fifi's face straining to remain serious as the haughty shop assistants wave us away. Wallowing in the abandoned luxury of Palazzo Mirto, my favourite place in the world; marvelling inside chapels at the stuccowork of Serpotta, La Kalsa's greatest man. Ah, everything coming together!

And yet: think of the very name 'Serpotta'. Think how the little snake was the master sculptor's symbol, and how the reptile lurks within the florid beauty of his work.

I will leave Part One of this update on that chilling note. I'm going now to my usual place for some focaccia with Fifi. Just the three messages from him this evening, to remind me.

PS wonderful photo of the three of you – you look happier than I've seen you for years!

––––––––––

WhatsApp message from Wen to Lomax
Friday, 12 May 2017

Wen

Do NOT ask Katie that about her firm in Manchester, please. It's an absurd idea and I'll be furious if you do!

20:30

––––––––––

From: Wen Li
Sent: Friday, 12 May 2017 21:46
To: Dominic Corcoran
Subject: Summary

Hi Dominic,

So, the serial killer issue. Here's my best and fullest explanation of what happens to me at night, when I'm in bed. In other words, when there's no obvious situational trigger (e.g. there's nobody standing with their back to me while I'm holding a knife!).

As you predicted, writing it down has been weirdly calming. It's like I'm looking at it from the outside in.

So, basically it begins like this. I lie in bed, sometimes happy,

211

sometimes sad, sometimes reading, sometimes trying to sleep, doesn't matter... and suddenly, out of nowhere, a thought comes to me: are you 100 per cent sure you're not a potential serial killer?

My reaction always seems to follow the same steps:

Immediately laughing it off, often out loud. Sometimes even speaking to myself, saying something like: 'That's mental!'

Really trying to think about something else.

Realising that I can't actually think about anything else. The thought keeps returning, and keeps upsetting me more and more.

Finally, the terrible decision (despite what you've told me) that the best way to 'nip this in the bud' is to look for evidence in support of me NOT being a wannabe serial killer.

The evidence is kind of assembled mentally, as if I were a barrister presenting a case. It is then challenged, undermined and destroyed by the bully inside my head. The evidence is re-assembled, and then destroyed again. Each time, I feel myself getting more desperate.

This goes on for about an hour until in the end I'm so exhausted that I just fall asleep.

FYI, it does not happen every night. The bully in my head comes and goes. Often I have pretty long intervals without it. But when the bully does come for me, it's always the same pattern.

So, there you are. Look forward to our session next week. Sadly, to confirm what we discussed, there really is no way I can continue with you after the end of this month, for financial reasons.

Best,

Wen

————

From: Lomax Clipper
Sent: Friday, 12 May 2017 22:59
To: Katie Wetherden
Subject: To continue

Fifi ended up weeping with laughter again this evening. He can't get over me trying to return that Prada suit to the branch in the New City!

He's planning to go back to Agrigento for a short visit this summer, as his dad will be undergoing a hip operation. Apparently his family are still not keen on him coming. There must have been a terrible argument, but he won't speak about it.

Anyway, I was telling you about *serpottas*. So, yes, there are snakes in my garden here. Obviously, the principal snake is Fear: a ceaseless contemplation of Mommo's Bad Ass Mafia look, and Gigi's open shirts and tanning salon.

Such a shame, these fears, intruding on any trace of positivity about tomorrow's big event! Honestly, Katie, I lie on my bed here, Googling 'Solarium Maqueda', yet nothing comes up. I search for articles about the tanning salon that was raided last week, and put my head in my hands. I text Fifi about it, and he sends me back so many messages, some reassuring, some less so, that I have to switch off my phone. As I drift off, thoughts of Gigi's slicked-back white hair become confused with

213

memories of a dragon emblazoned on a motorcycle helmet, and Nino's frightened face as he passes a brown envelope to a man. I dream of Aurora snogging me at the dinner table, and her father excusing himself, before returning with Diego's head dripping with blood...

And this is all the mere build-up to the Nightmare, which has become somewhat refined artistically. We are on Via Lungarini for sure now, outside the grand main door of my *palazzo*. The night remains bright, alive with shooting stars, the moon high in the sky. The shadow of a stray dog appears in the moonlight and, following the dog, we see the silhouette of a man who has been badly beaten, and who is sinking slowly to his knees. Before he collapses, he stretches out his arms towards the sea, towards Ustica. Behind him a crowd forms and disperses, forms and disperses, but nobody will say what has happened, and nobody seems to care. Then the sparkle of a diamond-encrusted knife... at which point poor Lina receives her nightly wake-up call.

Sorry, got to stop mid-flow. Have to deal with something.

WhatsApp messages from Lomax to Fifi
Friday, 12 May 2017

Translation from the original Italian

Lomax

Hi Fifi, I tried to call back a couple of times. Anything wrong? Saw all your messages, agree it was a great night tonight. Really tired now though, so heading to sleep. Happy to chat tomorrow!

23:05

————

From: Lomax Clipper
Sent: Saturday, 13 May 2017 00:20
To: Katie Wetherden
Subject: To continue once more

Final instalment. Had to stop because Fifi had had an upsetting call with his sister and was in quite a state. She sounds very unpleasant. Hard to advise him though, when he still won't tell me the reason for all the tension. Not sure he should have answered the call after some wine – alcohol hits him hard. Anyway, I calmed him down.

To finish on the other *serpottas*. There's the occasional concern about Fifi's stability, as per above, and the thought that he might be becoming fixated with me. There's the return of the dust in this apartment. There's the grim prospect of meeting up with Enzo, the evil-faced notary with the brylcreemed side parting, from the firm in Milan. He called to say he would be down to see his parents in three weeks' time. He then burst into a rant, heaping abuse on Sicily's asylum seekers, telling me that their boats should be shot out of the water. The viciousness in his voice! He seems to have inside him all the anger in the world.

And, despite the reflowering romance, at times I cannot deny that Aurora makes me gloomy. Yesterday, she agreed to my idea that we walk up to the top of Mount Pellegrino together, to see the patron saint's Sanctuary. Aurora knows the walk well because, when she was a kid, every September Gigi would force the family to join the pilgrimage up to Santa Rosalia's shrine.

215

As we climbed, I marvelled at the views of the city and sea. But unlike Goethe I never got to see the Sanctuary. Twenty minutes in, Aurora declared herself bored. I tried to jolly her along, but to no avail – she reacted badly to my disappointment, and told me that she was beginning to doubt our relationship again.

She always says that, at the smallest thing – she goes immediately for the nuclear option. Terribly destabilising. And it was strange, actually, because as we were walking back down, I received a typical WhatsApp from Wen. She asked how things were going this week, said she was looking forward to Skyping, implored me to keep focussed on the novel. As I read the message, all of a sudden I found myself thinking.

But I must not think of Wen. After my ruthless dispatching of any romantic chance we might have had, it would be self-indulgent to consider trying to rekindle anything beyond our deep friendship now. And this assumes she would be interested herself, which is a rather big 'if'! Anyway, the truth is that she is far too good for me... she's deserving of the very best of men! And, while Aurora is perhaps a damaged person, if I've tried this hard to make things work, it would be crazy to have doubts now. After all, in less than twenty-four hours I'll be inside Gigi's home. Who knows, perhaps the evening will go swimmingly and put an end to my fears. Reminding me that *serpottas* are small and the garden's grass green.

PS I doubt it – more likely I'll get shot. At times I do think that I possess a sort of heroic courage.

———

From: Lomax Clipper
Sent: Saturday, 13 May 2017 20:01
To: Wen Li
Cc: Katie Wetherden
Subject: URGENT: NOT SAFE

AM SENDING THIS ON WHATSAPP AND EMAIL. NOT SAFE HERE.

AM WRITING FROM INSIDE THE BATHROOM.

GIGI'S HELMET HAS PICTURE OF DRAGON. HE COULD BE THE MAN WHO CAME TO COLLECT THE PIZZO PAYMENT.

ACCORDINGLY, THOUGHT SENSIBLE TO RECORD THAT I AM AT VIA BARI 23, PALERMO. THE NAME IS 'LA ROSA'.

———————

From: Lomax Clipper
Sent: Saturday, 13 May 2017 20:15
To: Wen Li
Cc: Katie Wetherden
Subject: RE: URGENT: NOT SAFE

CHECK YOUR DAMN WHATSAPP! ONE OF YOU PLEASE RING MOBILE IMMEDIATELY, TO GIVE ME EXCUSE TO LEAVE. GIGI WANTS TO SPEAK MAN TO MAN.

———————

Translation from the original Italian

Lomax

Fifi, please call my mobile. Not safe here. Also note I am at Via Bari 23 Palermo. The name is 'La Rosa'.

20:16

From: Lomax Clipper
Sent: Saturday, 13 May 2017 20:18
To: Wen Li
Cc: Katie Wetherden
Subject: RE: URGENT: NOT SAFE

IGNORE PREVIOUS MESSAGES. ALL IS FINE. EMBARRASSING MISUNDERSTANDING. PLEASE DO NOT CALL. NO NEED AND I WILL NOT BE ABLE TO ANSWER AS RUDE.

Further WhatsApp messages from Lomax to Fifi
Saturday, 13 May 2017

Translation from the original Italian

Lomax

Please ignore previous message. Big misunderstanding! All fine here. Sorry.

20:21

218

Fifi, please stop calling! All fine, was my mistake! Do NOT under any circumstances come to the apartment!

20:23

From: Julian Pickering
Sent: Saturday, 13 May 2017 21:44
To: Charles Curtain
Subject: Notice

Dear Charles,

Forgive the time of this email, but I've decided it can't wait.

In the past year or so I have seen the foundations of what promised to become a positive period of my life, both personally and professionally, begin to fail. And as the precariously constructed building continues its slow collapse, I have realised that what I have left and what cannot be taken from me is my integrity.

It is not consistent with that integrity to beg you to think again about the sudden reversal of your decision to allocate me new support. But, far more importantly, I have come to the view that it is not consistent with that integrity to continue to work for this firm after what we have done to poor Wen Li. Seeing her reporting to work diligently every morning at nine on the dot, despite being out on her ear at the end of the month, makes me feel very small.

Recently I received an email – it doesn't matter from whom – in which my claim to integrity took a beating. The email led me to reflect on many things, and ultimately to a determination to bring about some change in my life.

Please take this as my notice of resignation from the firm. I will of course see out any required transition period for the sake of clients.

Julian

––––––––––

From: Julian Pickering
Sent: Saturday, 13 May 2017 22:11
To: Toby Enslin
Subject: Re: Leave me alone

Toby, writing to tell me to 'leave you alone' in circumstances where I do nothing BUT leave you alone would be funny were it not for the malice that now lurks in every sentence. As regards anything to do with finances and your new demands, please note that I've just resigned from the firm. And I could not feel better, baby!!! I intend to follow in the path of a man named Lomax, and take a little break for a couple of months. Lomax is writing a novel, you know.

Sorry you're drinking again. I'm drinking too, it must be somewhat contagious.

A brief editorial intervention. It was suggested during the editorial process that it would be helpful to clarify a key point to the reader at this stage. So, to clarify: it is indeed one of our characters who is murdered at the end of this Selected Correspondence. And, without wishing to labour the point: another of the characters commits the murder.

From: Lomax Clipper
Sent: Sunday, 14 May 2017 14:15
To: Katie Wetherden
Subject: A remarkable evening

Sorry again for the false alarm last night, Katie. Things had me going for the first ten minutes there on Via Bari!

Oh God, I feel like such a dick. While Mommo is indeed clearly not a nice person, Luisa and Gigi are the loveliest parents – I don't know why Aurora goes out of her way to try to aggravate them.

When I arrived she was still out so I had to meet the parents without her there! Gigi, the poor git, broke the ice by talking about the language school, and asking, I suspect without really meaning it, whether he could come in on it. Dazed by the sight of the motorcycle helmet, I stammered that the school had collapsed. Then, after he had lit a cigarette, he said he wanted to talk to me about his daughter. I felt my chest getting tight, but after my second quick bathroom escape I then ended up squirming with shame because everything he said was so gentle and charming.

He told me that he knew that Aurora and I weren't just friends, and that I seemed a very nice, polite young man. He said that all he had ever wanted was for her to meet a guy who was a good person. Apparently, he and Luisa stay up worrying about both Aurora and Mommo – in Mommo's case, because

222

of his temper (cue a further tightening of my chest), and in her case, because of her friends, and the cannabis. He told me that they're also very nervous about the *Addiopizzo* movement. Palermo is a relatively safe city, Gigi explained in a sad voice, until you start meddling in things.

It didn't feel like a speech from a Mafioso, and it was at this point that Aurora's big, warm mother picked up what transpired to be HER helmet, which was emblazoned with what, on closer inspection, was a fish, not a dragon. Luisa told me that her daughter was 'complicated, but deep down very good' – something I fully agree with, although I couldn't help but notice that this was a not-so-subtle warning. Then, minutes after Aurora finally showed up, Mommo came in too, and his brutish face softened a little once he'd checked me out (and presumably deemed me zero threat). I felt like crying with relief as I watched the softening happen. Even more so when he made bitter comments about the corruption in Palermo – he told me that to get a good job in this city, you needed to know someone who knew someone, and it all stank.

Again, it didn't seem like Mafioso chat, and he and I soon formed a pleasant-enough, if edgy, connection. Indeed, over dinner Mommo remarked that finally his little sister had invited someone normal into their home. I ROARED with laughter at this, letting out all my nervous energy – this got me an icy stare from Aurora and confused glances from her family.

God, does she give her parents a hard time. I did feel I needed to weigh in at times and (very gently) defend – against the most vicious accusations – their positions on politics, safety, the sourcing of their food from shops that may conceivably pay the *pizzo* etc. The result of this was that the parents became

223

visibly fonder and fonder of me, especially the mother. After the meal, and a crushing handshake and intimidating farewell from Mommo ('Keep treating my sister as you should', or words to that effect), Luisa laughed, seemingly embarrassed, and told him to stop being a clown. She then said she'd be happy to drop me home on her scooter, as she had to pick up some keys from the family's tanning salon (of which she is very proud).

My shame at my previous fears only increased when we arrived back at Via Lungarini. Luisa was so warm, telling me that I was a *bravo ragazzo* (a 'good boy' indeed, at thirty-three!), and advising me on where to go to eat Palermo's best chickpea fritters.

When I entered the courtyard, Nino was in his cabin. I thought I'd finally pluck up the courage to ask him about the man who had snatched the brown envelope. He told me that the man was his cousin, who lives in the *palazzo* next door.

I asked him indignantly why he had looked so scared.

Nino reacted to this perceived slant by bellowing in my face. The lover, just returned from a mysterious trip to the countryside, passed us in the courtyard and said that Nino was always scared, because he had no balls.

It's strange, the Palermitan dialect, because when it is spoken softly, it is lyrical and charming. Yet when it is bellowed…

Must stop – Aurora has just arrived!

From: Wen Li
Sent: Sunday, 14 May 2017 14:22
To: Dominic Corcoran
Subject: Re: Summary

Hi Dominic,

Very nice of you to write back to me so quickly yesterday. You're so non-judgmental, which is a relief given you know my weirdest and darkest thoughts! :)

It's also very reassuring to me that you will help oversee the transition to Samantha after the end of this month. I don't think anyone could be as good as you, but if she trained under you and is your recommendation then I like her already. I sound spoiled now, but I'm going to miss coming to dreamy Cavendish Square. I suspect St Ann's is not going to give me the same feeling when I arrive haha! Of course, I know these things aren't really important.

Thanks again,

Wen

————

From: Lomax Clipper
Sent: Sunday, 14 May 2017 15:25
To: Katie Wetherden
Subject: Re: A remarkable evening

Life is a damn rollercoaster here. Aurora has just been disgustingly rude to me. Her parting words were, loosely translated, that I should fuck off and never contact her again. And if I harass her, she will call the police (what the hell?!).

I had assumed she had come round to thank me for putting in a good performance with the family last night. Yet the fact they all liked me is exactly what has wound her up.

Looking back, I suppose I wasn't sufficiently alert to her insane hypersensitivity last night. I knew she was becoming irritated, but I genuinely thought that it was more directed at the family than at me. And what was wrong with me complimenting Luisa on her cooking, for Christ's sake? Or saying that sometimes practicality probably did mean you'd have to source from shops that paid the *pizzo*? And what was really wrong with admitting, upon Mommo's amused questioning, that Albergheria was not my favourite part of the world?

Aurora told me that my sucking up to them was sick. She wondered aloud what issues I must have with my own family.

I could feel myself going red as she shouted. Aurora said that I looked like I was about to cry like a baby. Then she told me to fuck off.

I wish I was Italian and that I'd been able to yell back theatrically. Instead, my repressed anger has turned into a smouldering hatred, of the type I've not felt since Lisa called me a loser, and it has made me have some rather unpleasant thoughts. In particular I hoped the cow would trip on the dodgy tile in the courtyard on her way out and twist her ankle! Sadly, she spotted it.

I'm genuinely hurt – and anxious too. But, pathetic as it sounds, what will I do if she calls me again and says she's forgiven me? I honestly thing I would forgive her too. There's something wrong with me, and it's not about sex or infatuation or beauty. I feel I've become caught up in her disturbance, her pain, and that I'm enabling her behaviour. It's not right, and for the first time I'll admit I am frightened by this relationship and my own mind in relation to it.

I know this puts me in a pitiful light, and that you must be sick and tired of this story, but nothing similar has ever happened before in my romantic life. I think the only thing for it is to try my best to just put it all aside, forget the real world for a while, and go full out on the novel again. I'm going to buy a pair of earmuffs so that I can continue writing outside the library's opening hours (white noise does NOT work for me). Chapter four is starting to come along nicely, but more intensity is needed. I've not been putting enough effort into the one thing that could change my circumstances forever – the one vocation I have!

Keep me posted on the move up to beautiful Barkisland (not ACTUALLY Huddersfield, of course!).

————

WhatsApp messages from Lomax to Fifi
Sunday, 14 May 2017

Translation from the original Italian

Lomax

As I've said now several times, I apologise for worrying you and thank you for your kindness.

16:24

However, once I'd explained that it was a false alarm, it was unreasonable to keep writing to me and trying to call me last night while I was at dinner.

16:24

> It was clear that I'd explain everything as soon as I could.
>
> 16:24

> We both must learn to calm down a little.
>
> 16:25

———

From: Lomax Clipper
Sent: Sunday, 14 May 2017 18:26
To: Katie Wetherden
Subject: Re: A remarkable evening

PS just remembered, I was going to call you about this, but I've taken the coward's way out and drunk two beers for a bit of Dutch courage and am writing it instead.

As you know, I rebuffed your remarkably kind and unsolicited £5k gesture of help. I have never asked anyone for money for myself. But I'm going to ask you the most awkward question I've ever asked, which is whether you would consider lending the same sum to Wen (perhaps best via me, given that you've never met or spoken to her!)?

———

From: Lomax Clipper
Sent: Sunday, 14 May 2017 18:55
To: Katie Wetherden
Subject: Re: A remarkable evening

That is completely understood. No need to apologise.

And no, I am fine – well within overdraft limit. In fact, I can probably give her a helping hand myself.

———

Wen

Lomax, what do you mean 'just take it'?

20:03

You don't have £3k to give me, you loon!

20:03

You better not have asked Katie!

20:03

I'm so upset that you thought I was asking for money

20:03

I'd never dream of it, was just sharing my frustration at my mum's little surprise from the taxman!

20:04

Hmm, not sure I believe that... you never mentioned these mysterious savings before?

20:15

Oh God, if you're really sure then I'll accept it for now, and I'm so sorry. Should never have mentioned this. But you're getting it all back with interest asap, even if I have to steal

20:25

And thank you. You've given us a lifeline and I don't deserve you as a friend

20:25

And Lomax, I wanted to add something

20:26

I know this is embarrassing for you to hear, but Aurora is abusing you

20:26

There's nothing wrong with you. All of us have Achilles heels and all of us are capable of finding someone who does this to us

20:26

Please remember you're worth so much more than this. Remember that you are not to take her back this time

20:26

I wish you'd fly home right now, and forget her. If you insist on staying for the moment, then just finish that novel and, as soon as you have, get back here, where people love you

20:27

From: Julian Pickering
Sent: Monday, 15 May 2017 09:05
To: Lomax Clipper
Cc: Julian Pickering
Subject: Re: To be rotten at one's core

Dear Lomax,

Hello from Gresham Street. Don't you miss Monday mornings here in the City? The sweltering train stopping suddenly, seconds before it is due to reach the station, and not moving for the next five minutes, while angry, jumped-up, overpaid graduates and angrier, exhausted, middle-aged stressballs all packed in like sardines cough in each other's faces? Do you miss rushing down Moorgate reading a litany of arsey emails from clients on your phone, just to get the week going? What about arriving late for that first meeting? Aargh, the joy.

See, I'm human too. I'm aware I never got back to you on your charming email. That doesn't mean the email made no impression on me. It hurt me tremendously, gave rise to some bitter anger at being misjudged, and some consequent self-pity. I even thought about sacking you, but decided against it.

You have me quite, quite wrong but I'm not going to get petty and explain things to you. I thought I would let you know, however, that I have resigned. Following discussions with Mr Curtain this morning here in the office, the resignation is now with immediate effect. I'll be leaving the office shortly for the last time.

Your job, I'm assured, remains safe and ready for you when you return – although if I were you I'd get the bastards to confirm in writing. I'm told by Charles that I sound manic today, and perhaps unwell, and he's suggested I go to see a doctor. Yet the truth is I could not feel more enthusiastic – I have only ecstatic thoughts buzzing in my head!

I intend to travel now for a few months, dance, take in a bit of Spain, maybe even Italy. Any tips? Perhaps we can even meet up for a glass of wine if I happen to pass by Palermo? Come on, don't be boring.

In future, please get me on my Hotmail address in copy!!!

Julian

From: Julian Pickering
Sent: Monday, 15 May 2017 09:25
To: Toby Enslin
Subject: Re: Further points

Yeah, yeah, yeah! It's all hate, my dear. Why don't you fucking dance instead, Toby? Dance baby, dance! It'll do you good, you prick!

From: Julian Pickering
Sent: Monday, 15 May 2017 09:51
To: Martin Pickering
Subject: Embrace the truth

Dear Dad,

All I have ever done is love and love you and seek your love. I am not proud of myself for anything I've done in my life, but I know in my heart that I've been a good son to you. Victoria does nothing, never checks on you, what you're eating, whether you're well, and keeping warm. I do everything and I confess I'm proud to do it because spending time with you gives me such pleasure too. You're a bloody great guy! We could have been such wonderful friends!

You love me too, in your own way. But I don't think you want to be my friend, no matter how hard I try. Christ, it's not my fault that I'm gay, dad. Why not embrace it instead of tolerating it with a passive-aggressive fury? Can't you see how your coldness makes me feel? Do you know that I spent most of Christmas Day in tears?

I'm GAY, GAY, GAY. Get it into your thick skull. It's been thirty years you've known!!!

Wen

Oh my god, call me back! Julian has just jumped out of the fucking window!!!! WTF?!!

10:04

Julian Pickering survives his leap from the third floor of the offices of Curtain & Curtain, due to the fortuitous location of eight bin bags full of discarded foodstuffs. Nevertheless, Julian breaks one leg, one arm, his nose and eight teeth. For twenty-four hours he is front page news in the Evening Standard *and* City A.M. *and he trends briefly on Twitter under the disgusting and evil hashtag #SuicidalScrivener. More significantly, he is sectioned under the Mental Health Act.*

Ironically, as soon as his casts are set, he is transferred to The Priory – the same private institution that had treated his former partner, Toby Enslin, only recently.

Once settled in, Julian begins to tell the psychiatrists that a man named Lomax has the key. He urges them to understand that the book Lomax is working on is the only thing that matters, as it will contain Truth. He is prevented from writing to Lomax, who does write a long, empathetic and self-critical letter to him, apologising profusely for his previous email and general behaviour, and sending his sincere best wishes.

Letter sent, Lomax tries to focus only on his novel. He explains to Fifi de Angelis, as kindly as he can, that their meet-ups must undergo a brief suspension. He also suspends email communication to Katie Wetherden. In both cases, the suspension lasts over three weeks.

During this period, Fifi de Angelis is seen several times on Via Lungarini by Roberto di Mauro. Towards the end of the same period, in early June, Fifi de Angelis visits his father in hospital, in Agrigento.

Meanwhile, Wen Li, problematically racked with guilt at her own baiting of Julian Pickering, visits him to apologise. Indeed, she soon becomes Julian's sole regular visitor, other than his father.

Following the official end of her employment at Curtain & Curtain, Wen carries out some freelance translation work for TransWorld, the company owned by her university acquaintance, Bryan Taylor. She also secures an interview with a very small notarial firm based in Holborn, which will not take place until late June. Her private health insurance having expired, she begins her new NHS treatment with the psychologist Samantha Griffin at St Ann's. She also joins an OCD support group, where she makes a new friend.

WhatsApp messages from Wen to Nyala
Friday, 2 June 2017

Wen

Lovely to meet you too, Nyala

12:03

And agree, it was pretty full on last night, right?

12:03

I'd never been sure about these groups, especially without a professional being there. It had always seemed to me that the least likely thing a person with OCD would want to do was to talk in detail about their thoughts to strangers!

12:03

But it worked and made me feel weirdly free. Definitely up for a tea, whenever you want. You spoke very beautifully last night

12:04

Hey! Sorry about your ex. Seems like he didn't come with enough emotional intelligence to deal with someone like you. My ex seemed to be pretty understanding towards the end, but then I found out that I couldn't trust a word he said, so who knows?

14:05

> I do have one special friend, a former colleague, who I talk to about these things from time to time. He's the most wonderful man
>
> 14:05

> I only met him relatively recently though, and I totally get the loneliness thing. That's where I'm happy to come in, if you ever need!
>
> 14:06

Oh, loneliness. Fifi de Angelis is the loneliest man in the world.

Translation from the original Italian

From: Fifi de Angelis
Sent: Tuesday, 6 June 2017 19:51
To: Ignazio de Angelis; Rosaria de Angelis; Elisabetta de Angelis; Saveria de Angelis
Subject: Goodbye

Despite everything, I'm happy that papà's operation was a success. That can be the only thing I am happy about. You've all given me some bad days in the past – but today might just have been the worst.

I'm sorry that I caused such terrible suffering and stress to you all by daring to show my face at the hospital. Nonna still says I am right to have done so, and is very disappointed in you all. Especially in papà, for waving me away from his hospital bed.

And as for you, Betta, before I left the hospital, in the middle of that terrible row, you said something so evil to me. It was so evil that I want to write it down so we can all remember it forever. You called me a little beast fit only for the circus. A LITTLE BEAST FIT ONLY FOR THE CIRCUS. How could you have said that, Betta, as a human being? Saveria, how could you have laughed, with such hatred in your eyes?

At least I can honestly say that I tried – for Nonna's sake. She is my family. None of you are.

To hell with you all.

————

WhatsApp message from Fifi to Lomax
Tuesday, 6 June 2017

Translation from the original Italian

> **Fifi**
>
> Hi Lomax, I've had a very bad time with my family. I do hope you'll still be able to see me for focaccia this Friday. It will be very sad if you can't, I have so much to tell you
>
> 19:58

————

Oh, Fifi. But he is not alone in his loneliness.

WhatsApp message from Wen to Nyala
Wednesday, 7 June 2017

> **Wen**
>
> Hi Nyala, I enjoyed tea too. Yeah, what a pair we are, right? Very happy to start swapping horror fears if you think it will help! :) Night
>
> 22:50

————

Some find it hard to admit that they are lonely.

From: Lomax Clipper
Sent: Friday, 9 June 2017 20:21
To: Katie Wetherden
Subject: Yo!

Sorry about the silence, but I have been stranded on Easter Island, only occasionally escaping into a whirlpool of self-loathing about the way I treated poor Julian. It turns out he's gay, by the way – I never realised. Anyway, worryingly, Wen tells me that his latest thing is that as soon as they let him out he's coming straight to Palermo to help me finish the book! Poor git, he has completely lost his mind.

Nothing from Aurora. She has blocked me again on WhatsApp and Facebook, but unblocks me from time to time, revealing a new profile pic of herself, which shows her having a GREAT time. As you can glean from this, I am as bad as she is, checking intermittently on my blocked/unblocked status! But I genuinely think that my emotions have abated, and that this has fizzled out for me finally – the occasional checking is just idle curiosity!

I enjoyed the photos of the rented mansion in Barkisland. How is David finding his new home? Bet he's loving all the new crawling space! It feels so surreal that you and Ross are – more or less – back living in my old corner of the world.

Surrealism is the name of the game here in Palermo too. Indeed, at times it seems to me that the only credible people and events in the world are on Easter Island. Outside the book, everything seems a little suspect.

Three new chapters have JUST been sent to Professor Melanie

Nithercott – so six chapters now done. I don't know how I wrote these three chapters in such a short space of time. I've been on fire, truly in the zone. I await Melanie's reaction with a quiet confidence and in the meantime am going to plough on. I'm not sure anybody has written something as funny as this in years.

I have now incorporated you into the novel, in the character of The Dubious Fisherwoman. I trust that is OK. When this does get published, someone might have fun tracing the characters back to people in my life. The Dubious Fisherwoman is you, Detective Carla is Melanie, The Good Samaritan is Wen... The Rodent is now Mr Curtain, not Julian (and the character's name is now The Shitty Rodent). It's shocking, by the way, what I've learned about the way he treated Julian.

The Narrator, I have realised, is me. His hatred of The Shitty Rodent is my hatred of Mr Curtain. His hatred of the novel is my deep and desperate desire to finish it; my hatred of the limbo in which I will remain until it is done.

On the subject of that limbo, back in the less concrete world of Palermo, it's been all about dizzying heat and smoke, the refuge of the old library, the earmuffs at home and that dickhead Roberto taking increasing pleasure in the idea that I am being stalked by Fifi. Apparently he's seen him hanging around here quite a few times during the moratorium that I imposed – a moratorium that ends this evening. I'm not so worried, even if it's true – it's just sad. He's so damn lonely. It must be horrible to feel like that. I do think I need to get to the bottom of what's happened with his family.

There have been some other minor, equally weird events punctuating the trippy monotony, but nothing much of substance. My parents are still planning to come out next month.

Anyway, must go – right on cue, my phone is ringing. It's Fifi and focaccia time. It's fair to say the poor sod has missed me – he's wildly excited! I'm going to go for *sfincione*, which is a mix between pizza and focaccia and comes with *caciocavallo* cheese.

————

Oh, loneliness. Letter from Julian Pickering to his father, Martin Pickering, sent from the Priory. Letter is dated Friday, 9 June 2017

Dear Dad,

It was so lovely to see your face and hear your voice. I am sorry that I let you down. Just a blip, and I will be out of here soon. But my head hurts today and I'm told I'm not quite myself. In the meantime I've gone against your orders and had people here help me organise a Waitrose delivery for you. When it arrives, please check everything is safe.

And please don't apologise again. It BROKE MY DAMN HEART to hear it.

Anyway, forget all that. I have a new project, related to a book that someone is writing. All attention focused on that at present – a game-changer!

Love,

Julian

PS My doctor has such a solemn face that, to myself, I call him the walrus. But he must not take offence as he is very handsome and I am not just saying that because I know he reads my letters.

———

Wen

Nyala, I know that you know this, but it's only because God is so important to you

21:23

Hence the bully in your mind making you question whether you want to say something terrible while you pray, whether you're about to. I can sooo relate, even if it's not my specialty :)

21:23

I had a relatively calm day

21:23

Saw Julian and, while doing my best to say the right things, inside I was obsessing about whether I wanted to laugh at him because I was evil

21:24

Then this evening my mum asked me to watch the soup and turned her back and so I considered in depth whether or not I secretly wanted to throw the contents of the pan over her and scald her

21:24

———

From: Lomax Clipper
Sent: Friday, 16 June 2017 19:33
To: Katie Wetherden
Subject: Heat is SPECTACULAR!

I am writing this to groans drifting in from the *salotto*. Lina tells me, between puffs on her cigarette, that this heat is terrible for her throat.

Everything is the novel here. Outside it, very little has happened again this week. I've realised that I've truly stopped thinking so much about Aurora. It's sad, of course, that I nearly got welcomed into her family; that I nearly got to know properly her lovely parents, whom I am not at all sure she deserves. Sadder still to think that somewhere inside her there's the person who once smiled at me, across a crowd of protestors, on a balmy summer evening in Milan.

Meanwhile, Wen tells me that Julian seems to be suddenly improving, and might be out soon. This gives rise, selfishly, to some mild alarm.

I ended up having a very moving chat with Fifi last week. He'd been treated terribly by his family at the hospital. After some delicate probing by me, he finally told me the background to the family situation and why they've disowned him. Basically, all the poor guy did was become great friends with the son of the local prosecutor in Agrigento! Somehow an unforgivable sin, given that the prosecutor is hated in the community for having successfully closed down a construction company,

243

which led to multiple job losses including in Fifi's wider family. Fifi won't renounce his friendship, and therefore won't be forgiven. Mad, right? Isn't this place absolutely nuts?

Which reminds me – focaccia time. I'm limiting our meet-ups to once, or maximum twice, a week. Otherwise it all goes a bit strange.

Lomax

————

From: Lomax Clipper
Sent: Friday, 16 June 2017 19:45
To: Katie Wetherden
Subject: Re: Heat is SPECTACULAR!

Why do you think Fifi's story is 'suspect?' Christ, you're more paranoid than I am, Katie! That made me laugh!

————

Letter from Julian Pickering to his sister, Victoria Pickering, sent from the Priory. Letter is dated Friday, 16 June 2017

Dear Vicky,

Kind of you to write and ask – it's only been a month, after all. I'm happy to report that I am doing a little better each day – with the occasional little wobble, it must be said!

Your job is to look after Dad while I am in here. Please be sure to do so.

Very little free time, for I am busy thinking about a book that could change everything.

My love to you, Chris and the children.

Julian

––––––––

Funnily enough, I don't actually know Fifi's surname. He's not on social media. Remember, you're not Detective Carla, you're The Dubious Fisherwoman!

Given you're so chatty this weekend, I'll give you a Sunday special edition. Never quite finished my update on Friday.

In the novel, a lot is happening. I am charging ahead while awaiting Melanie's feedback, and I can see the quality improving by the paragraph: I am surprising even myself. And this all despite the fact that a large group of students have appeared out of nowhere to shatter the library's peace. They sit on the desks, and sometimes throw things at each other. Their sudden appearance is mystifying. I spent hours last night on Google, trying in vain to understand Palermo University's term times.

I guess I should also fill you in on some trivia from that near-month of email silence. I can only recall two pieces worthy of mention.

First, Evil Enzo, the Italian notary in his twenties but with a 1940s hairstyle, came down from Milan to see his parents. I am not at all sure why I agreed to meet up with him – some sort of masochistic yearning, perhaps. He took me to a 'very

245

London' place, which did 'the sashimi and the biological wine'. Inside, a young woman at the bar ignored his flimsy chat-up line. His unblinking eyes became haunting as he told me that they do not make women like our mammas any more. I replied that Aurora was a communist. I added that I really did live on Via Lungarini in La Kalsa, and that my only friend here was 130 cm tall.

He kept laughing, then frowning, laughing then frowning. I am not sure he is right in the head. A bunch of Americans, who had clearly heard us speaking in English, came up to us a short time later. One of them was Pakistani American and Enzo concluded that he must be trying to sell us flowers. He waved him away, with a disgusted shake of his head. Naturally, the whole group looked deeply shocked and the poor Pakistani American, very hurt and upset, rebuffed my attempt to apologise on the bastard's behalf. As they walked away, I necked my cocktail and, in a moment of wonderful creative weirdness of which I am proud, asked Enzo whether his mother had found it easy to adapt to Italy as a Romanian woman (the racists despise Romanians here, for reasons unknown to me).

It worked – won't be hearing from him again. Indeed, he sent me a rather sinister text message afterwards, calling me insane, and demanding once again to know who in the Milan firm had told me that his mother was Romanian (nobody had). He added that if I ever spread this false rumour, there would be trouble for me. All in all, a cracking night.

Second, a couple of weeks ago I took a few hours off to visit Mondello, Palermo's main beach resort. It's a short taxi ride from the city and a dazzling stretch of sand. A bunch of university students were playing football on the beach. As I watched the game from afar, alone at a table with a bottle of wine, suddenly the melancholy aspect of this island hit me. The successful ones, I thought, would all soon be off, to Rome or Milan. Only oddballs choose to live here.

———

WhatsApp messages from Wen to Nyala
Sunday, 18 June 2017

Wen

I agree, Stephen was looking hot at Thursday's session!

17:23

As for me, scalding soup is now definitely a thing

17:23

And yeah, interview for new job is week on Monday

17:23

Mum meanwhile getting more and more depressed

17:23

Still won't see GP

17:23

Sometimes I try to make myself see the absurd side of life. Me, Julian, her… what a world!

17:24

Although Julian is sounding at least a bit better

17:24

247

> Hey Nyala, can you delete that thing I just wrote about my mum?
>
> 17:46

———————

From: Lomax Clipper
Sent: Friday, 23 June 2017 23:41
To: Katie Wetherden
Subject: Ciao bella

The novel is still of absorbing interest, but life in all its violent shades intervened this week. Aurora turned up at the *palazzo* and said we needed to talk!

Now, first I want to apologise, for it is undoubtedly true that I've portrayed Aurora unfairly to you. You've always heard only my side of things, and usually when I'm angry or upset with her. In particular, back in November I should not have sent you that translation of her messages. They were messages she'd written while she was clearly worked up, and were misleading when you consider her behaviour as a whole. I remain ashamed of myself for having sent you the translation. She's capable of incredible tenderness. As I've said, she is indeed highly temperamental, but then she's Southern Italian.

I know it must be annoying to read this, and you might feel that I've wasted a lot of your time. But I myself have also been too 'temperamental', both when things have gone well and when they have not. The real story is no more complicated than this: she perhaps has a few issues, but inside she's a good person.

And it is true that I behaved badly at her place – how would

248

you like it if there was a psychodrama going on between you and your parents and Ross took their side? Aurora said that if I was prepared to apologise, she would consider giving things one last go. She had tears in her eyes when she emphasised how much I had upset her. Whether or not those tears were merited on an objective level is irrelevant – the fact is that the tears were real and when they started to fall I felt an unbearable desire to protect her.

She has a lake of torment inside her, and I want to take our relationship, or whatever it is, to the next level – I want to elevate it from a crappy story about an Englishman who is wildly in love with a beautiful Sicilian. I want to understand this torment. When I apologised, she smiled suddenly and it was as if her personality and the whole world had changed in an instant: as if the sun had emerged from a total eclipse. If it is true that the underlying sincerity of her emotions has a direct and unhealthy impact on my own, it is also true that I should be able to look beyond my emotional reaction, and help her.

And so we're back on, I think, although part of me knows that it could end again at any point: I am walking on eggshells. She is not yet comfortable with me broaching the subject of her temperament, which is understandable. But we've had some lovely moments this week, including my second trip (this time by bus) to Mondello and an evening spent on the beach, under the stars. There's been no resurfacing of hostility, save for a disgusting comment she made about Fifi: she said it was odd I hung around with a dwarf, and not fair on him if I was doing it just because I had no other friends here. So disappointing, although I'm worried now that she may have a point about the selfishness.

Also, the work involved in finishing the novel now seems to frustrate her, but that's again understandable: it frustrates me too! And who the hell would want to date someone who spends ten hours a day writing? She thinks it's amazing I still haven't finished it, and I tend to agree.

Anyway, I apologise again for mixed messages to you about her – recalling my past reactions, and your kindness about them, has made me a little pensive. Yesterday, on the way home from the library, I was drawn again to the lovely faded world of Palazzo Mirto, which is just a minute from the flat. I went in, again the sole visitor walking through its silent rooms of tapestries and maiolica. I stopped before its quirky Chinese salon, and gazed at the silk, the pagoda furniture, the ceiling depicting genteel men and women ambling through gardens and looking down upon the room...

And I thought of you and Wen. I thought how you'd have said, 'How fascinating!' And how she'd have replied, 'WTF? So random.'

Oh, how I miss you both!

————

From: Lomax Clipper
Sent: Friday, 23 June 2017 23:59
To: Katie Wetherden
Subject: Re: Ciao bella

Fair enough – in that case I will not bring her up again in my correspondence.

————

WhatsApp messages from Wen to Nyala
Friday, 23 June 2017

Wen

Definitely up for the church party! I'll get to Kilburn for midday

18:23

Mum's been a bit better this week. Possibly I overreacted when I said she must go see someone. Because of my own problems I sometimes project, I guess. And there's a fine line between negative, stubborn pride and positive mental resilience

18:23

Saturday, 24 June 2017

That was a lovely afternoon. So chill!

15:45

It hit me how you could be anyone, from any walk of life, and you'd be welcomed

15:45

The vicar seemed such a kind man. Can't believe he's been there thirty years!

15:45

Ha! Tomorrow am prepping for Monday's interview, but you're welcome to come over for a Suzhou special?

16:00

Yeah, my friend Lomax is just the best. Bit worried about him at the mo. That horrible Sicilian is back in his life. I should be cross with him for being so soft, but I get how this can happen

16:13

Did I really talk about him non stop? Oh shit! Truth is, my feelings for Lomax are totally different from what I felt when I was with Rob. It was exciting with Rob, for sure. But what I feel for Lomax must be what real love is, I think... oh dear, feeling a bit emosh! :)

18:42

He has got to such a deeper part of me. I want to put my arms around him and hug him for hours. I love his big crazy dreams and his originality and this, like, romantic determination he has. I even love his silly pride and his chippiness and the sadness that just sometimes I hear in his voice

18:45

He's not aware at all of his actual qualities. His emotional intelligence and kindness. How much he makes me laugh. This charming thing he has of living in his own colourful world

18:46

But this Sicilian girl, fuck! Nothing to be done about it

18:46

Wen

Hello, my precious and brilliant writer. I got the job!!

11:23

On the way to bank on Seven Sisters Road. Remember that still?

11:23

They'll now grant overdraft, so I'm going to be paying you back, with interest, within a month. Thanks again, you saved us!

11:23

From: Wen Li
Sent: Monday, 26 June 2017 14:30
To: Dominic Corcoran
Subject: Quick update

Dear Dominic,

Hope you're well. Quite a bit of time has passed since our final session. I'm worried that in the session I thanked you in a way that wasn't really good enough, especially considering all your help in arranging the transition. It was also a brilliant idea of yours about the support groups. They're really helpful.

I wanted to let you know that I've got a new job. I start next month. I don't know if their health insurance will be as good as Curtain & Curtain's, but I will be earning again so I guess

253

that, if I came back as your patient, I should be able to pay you myself for, like, a monthly session. Might not be able to afford more than that though.

Anyway, your decision. To be super clear, Samantha is amazing and I'm totally happy with her. Please let me know what you think's best.

Anyway, as I say, I never got my words out right during our last session. You took me on such a journey, and my insight into what is going on in my mind improved so much. You always treated me with such kindness. Thank you for being an exceptionally brilliant and intelligent specialist but also a person with a very big heart. I'll never forget what you have done for me.

I'll wait for your advice,

Wen

———————

From: Julian Pickering
Sent: Thursday, 29 June 2017 18:14
To: Lomax Clipper
Subject: Hello, hello!

Dear Lomax,

I am out of the woods and allowed back on email. Thank you for your kind words – all apologies immediately accepted. What happened is the past. I am far more interested to learn about the progress of your novel. Wen continues to fob me off, telling me it's a light, comic piece. But some sixth sense convinces me that this is untrue. Call it instinct, but I think I know what you're up to, you bloody genius!

You're seeking to write the novel of our times, are you not? You are seeking to reveal the vileness, the lack of empathy, the bitter confusion of it all by putting down ACCURATELY and without emotion the status of things. The erosion of truth, the pitting of people against each other, the re-emergence of the charlatans and the hard right.

This email is in part an application. I am here to help. I have real understanding, and would be very happy to pop over to Palermo once I leave Alcatraz, in order to work on this with you. The book needs to be out there as soon as possible: I suggest self-publishing the thing.

Must go for now. But please let me know.

Julian

––––––––

WhatsApp messages from Wen to Lomax
Thursday, 29 June 2017

Wen

Lomax, I'm very upset about that phone call

18:30

You've never spoken to me like that before

18:30

I've not told Julian anything about your book except that it's comic fiction. And of course I wouldn't tell him where you live in Palermo!

18:30

––––––––

255

From: Fifi de Angelis
Sent: Thursday, 29 June 2017 19:51
To: Ignazio de Angelis; Rosaria de Angelis; Elisabetta de Angelis; Saveria de Angelis
Subject: Nonna

I will speak to Nonna whenever I want! Any of you try to break that bond, and put sick ideas in her head, and you will pay!

————————

From: Wen Li
Sent: Friday, 30 June 2017 15:12
To: Dominic Corcoran
Subject: Re: Quick update

Dear Dominic,

Thanks again for our call. I've thought about it and very happy to go with the plan i.e. have you in the background and see you every two months for a catch-up, and continue to see Samantha more regularly.

Have a nice weekend.

Wen

A brief editorial intervention: there are only two months now until the murder.

We would note here that, during the editorial process, some argued strenuously against these constant reminders. It was submitted that they underestimated the reader's ability to concentrate; and that the intelligent reader might take offence.

We apologise for any offence caused. However, for a publisher, commercial considerations are not unreasonable considerations. We wanted this Selected Correspondence to sell.

From: Lomax Clipper
Sent: Friday, 30 June 2017 23:16
To: Katie Wetherden
Subject: The Novel or Bust

Hi Katie,

Have you calmed down on me yet?! It's now obscenely hot here. I'm afraid this week's dispatch won't be one of my rosiest. Things have combined to lead me to the conclusion set out in this email's subject line.

I want the novel to succeed more than I can describe. I don't want to discover that I'm a man with ambition and narcissism sufficient to make it but talent that falls short. If I became an even moderately successful author, I could stay here with Aurora, be myself, elude the damn system that seeks to claw you back in. Even moving to another land, another culture fails – for always looming is the need to soon make some money. It's always about money, money, fucking money. The system fucking traps you and panics you into the wrong decision unless you FIGHT. I want to prove to myself that I was right – that you can beat the bastards if you really try. Anyone who has ever become truly successful must have had the same feeling. You can't do it by following the rules!

I received Melanie's feedback on Tuesday. I began to read her email in a distant, almost dreamlike state, shaken by the thought that, if she had savaged it...

And yet she loved it! I went wild and did a jig around my room. She concluded by saying that I should just keep going, as I am not far off.

But later I returned to the thought. What would I have done if she had savaged it? And what would I do now instead if I did not keep going with it? What would life look like without the novel and all my dreams that are bound up with it?

Without wishing to be melodramatic, I think the answer is that I would snap, crackle and pop. I clearly have a form of megalomania – I simply can't bear the image of myself as a nobody.

You won't want to hear this, but it's going OK still with the lady whose name I won't mention. Indeed, the only negative is that I'm feeling increasingly guilty about the way I've depicted her to you, which is the sole cause of your current hostility. Christ, if I end up marrying her you'll have to delete all those emails!

The one frustrating thing is that she isn't sure that she will be around next week when my parents come to visit. I know what it's about – I think at her core she suffers from an almost pathological shyness, which she conceals by feigning indifference. I said it would mean a lot to me if she met them, and to be fair she did say she would think about it. I so hope she finds the courage. I can't bear to think of how it might go – but if this is to work, they all need to meet.

Last night I got the surprise of my life: an email from Julian! He's soon going to be out, which he should not be: he's clearly still unstable. I'm considering writing to the Priory but it would be a harsh move if it resulted in a longer internment.

His email also reminded me that there are only two months left of the sabbatical.

As for the rest, all grim. Roberto continues to refer to Fifi as my dwarf and continues to claim that, on the evenings I don't see him, he walks up and down Via Lungarini.

Then, this evening, Nino poked his head out of his cabin as I passed and asked me if I was off to see my dwarf. Then, when I got back from the focaccia place, the lover asked me how it had gone with my dwarf.

Then Lina coughed so much that she was sick on the chaise longue.

Then I had a long call with Fifi, as a sort of follow-on from dinner. I explained again that he was a dear friend to me, and if I get the chance to introduce him to my parents next weekend I'll be delighted to, but he can't hang out with us ALL weekend or give us the full, day-long guided tour he wants to give us. I emphasised that it would be too much for my parents to meet Aurora and Fifi together for dinner, and he must understand that. Anyway, I promised I'd try to make something work.

Lomax

———

WhatsApp messages from Wen to Nyala
Tuesday, 4 July 2017

Wen

Yeah, start at new place next Monday. They seem very… normal!

23:31

260

New guy sounds nice! Nothing more romantic than a stroll along the South Bank. Brings back memories!! Have you told him about the OCD?!

23:31

Wednesday, 5 July 2017

Yeah, makes sense. All in good time! Sorry for silence today. Have been stressing. Julian has insisted on discharging himself and has somehow got his way

21:31

He's leaving Priory tomorrow. He went on and on about Lomax's 'very distant' reply to him and how he can, like, help him!?

21:31

Am beginning to think he really does want to go out there. I'm overthinking this, right? Don't know whether to tell Lomax

21:32

From: Lomax Clipper
Sent: Thursday, 6 July 2017 23:46
To: Katie Wetherden
Subject: The parents are in Palermo

Your weekly dispatch is coming a day early this week. My parents arrived this evening – they're here for four nights. I'm just back from their hotel.

Shortly before taking off they informed me that there was no need to come to the airport, as they had booked a hire car. I urged them to cancel it and said we should stick to the plan. My dad refused to listen.

They touched down in Palermo just before five. Three hours later, I received my hundredth phone call. My mother's dazed voice, with its lovely French accent, murmured that they had arrived on Via Alloro and were just parking.

I rushed to their hotel to find a Fiat Panda attempting a U-turn outside it, blocking the traffic. Sicilian men were hurling abuse from their cars. My mother was in the passenger seat, her head lowered. The car windows were open, and I heard my dad shouting:

'PISS off, all of you!'

The car then stalled. I went to get a member of staff from the hotel, who offered to park it for them. Your former headmaster finally broke under the tremendous pressure from all sides and stepped out of the car in his white shorts, white socks and a blue polo shirt, drenched in sweat... an unaccountable expression of victory on his face. My mother followed – she was wearing the lovely summer dress she bought in Lille many years ago. As I took in the picture of them both, I felt a lump in my throat.

My dad declared that it had been one hell of a journey. And that, wow, this street was like stepping onto the set of *The Godfather*. To evil stares from my mother, after I'd given them both a big hug, he said his dad had adored Sicily (creative licence there, I fear, as am confident Klopfer never visited it) and then, his Huddersfield accent having assumed for a moment that slight German twang, he rather excitably suggested having a beer.

He was unrecognisable from the Norman Clipper Who Used to Stare – exuberant! Even his repeated exclamations of 'this HEAT!' were said sort of positively, as if he were embracing the exoticism.

Later, in the bar, he tried his first arancini. My mother told me that they were so delighted about the eye, and that she SUPPOSED she was looking forward to meeting '*la communiste*' (I have told them a rather embellished story of how wonderfully it's gone with her out here). I felt tremendous emotion when I saw the love and hint of concern in their eyes, and had to pop to the bathroom to pull myself together – God, I'm a state at the moment. She better turn up for me tomorrow (she's still not confirmed).

When I got back, my dad jerked his head to the left. 'That guy over there,' he said, 'is the spitting image of Fredo.'

I said to my mum that this *Godfather* thing risked giving completely the wrong impression of the man I had always considered to be the most European man in Huddersfield. She told me something I had never known: that my dad and Klopfer had been addicts, and had watched the whole trilogy together many, many times.

To my dismay, my dad, who was not listening to anything we were saying, then announced that they intended to visit the town of Corleone during their stay. He said it would be a little adventure, and that Aurora was welcome to join. I cannot think of anything that would offend her more.

––––––––––

From: Julian Pickering
Sent: Friday, 7 July 2017 17:00
To: Martin Pickering
Subject: Plans

Hi Dad,

Was wonderful to see you looking so well – and your flat looking so clean!

I have just realised that my plan to head to Italy for a while on this project of mine might mean I have to miss the opening match of the new season. Can you talk to Victoria to see if Chris can come with you? If not, maybe ask Jerry. He still drives, doesn't he?

My best,

Julian

————

From: Lomax Clipper
Sent: Friday, 7 July 2017 18:16
To: Katie Wetherden
Subject: Further dispatch as requested

I should tell you that my dad agrees that Barkisland 'is not exactly Huddersfield, no'.

It has been a delightful first day here – I've never enjoyed Palermo so much! Parents are resting in their hotel at the moment, before tonight's dinner with me and Aurora. I am having pangs of nausea about the dinner, although I am indescribably relieved that she has finally agreed to come.

I received a very early call this morning. Norman Clipper was up. I arrived on Via Alloro to find him waiting outside the hotel. He was wearing wraparound sunglasses and a cap and getting into a very confused discussion with a street vendor who was selling fake or stolen Prada bags. My mother came out a short time later, and helped me to extricate him, before applying his sun cream.

'The way the men kiss each other on the cheek here scares the hell out of me,' he said, as she rubbed in the cream. 'Especially the old men. Not in a homophobic way, you understand. It's their faces, they're so stern when they kiss. Have you seen that, Lomax, hey? With their bloody chins sticking out... like this...'

The breakfast at their hotel had been 'sub-standard', so I took them to a bar I know near Via Lungarini. There, my dad expressed fascination at the sight of a croissant filled with ice cream. My mother – who, being French, is snooty/competitive about all Italian cuisine – forbid him from trying it.

Over croissants without ice cream, my dad asked about Fifi. I confirmed we'd be seeing him for lunch tomorrow, and maybe for a quick coffee again on Monday. My dad said he'd once had a pupil with restricted growth, and that he'd been bullied terribly. To my surprise he said: 'Hope you're treating him right.'

They were blown away by the Palatine Chapel. We then had lunch at one of Palermo's oldest restaurants, where to my disappointment my mum insisted on ordering a pizza (but my dad fell in love with chickpea fritters).

Anyway, it's all great. I just love, love, love them so much. With all my heart. Silently begging Aurora to be nice tonight.

Christ, got to go – they've arrived.

From: Lomax Clipper
Sent: Friday, 7 July 2017 23:55
To: Katie Wetherden
Subject: Norman Clipper plays a blinder

My dad is a star!

Christ, he was on form this evening! He wore his favourite short-sleeved shirt to dinner, its collar buttoned to the neck, just like Klopfer used to wear his. Rivers of sweat pouring down the poor git. On the way to the focaccia place, he made a line of middle-aged Sicilian men walking arm-in-arm in front of us collectively jump when he shouted to me: 'Tonight we meet Oroora!'

Just after we had sat down at a carefully chosen table directly under the big ceiling fan, Aurora texted me to say she was running late. My mother said: 'Hmm – she will be an hour!' But, only five minutes later, she arrived.

'Guud eeveneeng' she said, with a very sweet accent. 'Aurora.'

'Well, hello there!' my dad said, rising to his feet. 'Norman Clipper.'

Aurora had come as the real person she is – charming, exhilarating. There was an instant warmth between her and my dad. I began to act as interpreter as he told her the story behind his car journey through Palermo. Aurora, who I'm so damn proud of for tonight, adopted a very concerned and sympathetic expression, saying repeatedly: '*poverino*'.

'Tell her I'm fine,' my dad said, ignoring my mother's frown. 'I fought and I won.'

Aurora was pleasant to my mother too, and my mother was

pleasant, if a little distant, back. When Aurora popped to the bathroom, my mother did observe that she could have made more of an effort to dress nicely for dinner (if only she knew that this was the best dressed I've ever seen her, clean white top and jeans, even if the latter were somewhat ripped). But my dad told her that the girl was a free spirit, and to leave it be.

The positive vibe continued throughout dinner, until I couldn't believe what I was interpreting. Had my dad really just said that he'd like to meet her family one day? Had she really replied that maybe everyone could meet tomorrow? Had she really agreed to come with us on Sunday to Corleone?

Unbelievable! She mustn't have realised that my dad only wants to go to Corleone because he loves *The Godfather*.

So funny, right? I honestly believe I am HAPPY tonight!

———

WhatsApp messages from Wen to Nyala
Friday, 7 July 2017

Wen

Hey Nyala. Perhaps it was TMI for him, for now? Also, I think the problem is we end up believing that OCD is all there is to us. It's only a small part of you

23:56

I got from your message that you think our friendship is not going to help matters with him. I think you're going about this the wrong way. You can use me for this space, and leave OCD out of conversations with him?

23:56

———

From: Lomax Clipper
Sent: Saturday, 8 July 2017 09:13
To: Katie Wetherden
Subject: Re: Norman Clipper plays a blinder

Good morning. I'm about to head out for another day of sightseeing, before a drink with the two sets of parents this evening. For God's sake, Katie, don't put such a downer on things – it's going to be a lot of fun!

My mother wants to go to the marionette theatre before the drink. Which is to say that she wants to see a traditional puppet show. Not as odd as it might sound, as the Opera dei Pupi is a big thing here. Her guidebook notes correctly that catching a show is a thing to do.

God, I'm excited about the grand meet-up! Will write again this evening with a summary!

———————

From: Lomax Clipper
Sent: Saturday, 8 July 2017 22:50
To: Katie Wetherden
Subject: Not good

In all the hurt and humiliation this evening, I've been reminded of an inviolable truth: that an endless sea of love exists between my parents and me.

I should have seen this coming, to be honest. After a hilarious lunch with my parents and Fifi at a Sicilian street food place – my dad said he would go for the house special, the *pani ca meusa*, without even asking what they were, and then refused to row back when I explained that they were rolls filled with lung and spleen – I insisted my parents went back

268

for a rest before the puppet show. It would be a busy evening, because we would be going straight from there to see Luisa and Gigi. While they napped, I decided to thank Fifi for being so pleasant by buying him a beer. He was buzzing – never seen him as happy as he was this afternoon in that cobbled *piazza*, sipping his beer in the drowsy heat under the shade of a leafy trellis. My parents had been delightful at lunch – and I'd done another very efficient job as interpreter.

Anyway, over our beer I showed him some photos of last night on my phone. Then I remembered that Aurora had said she would post some photos on Facebook. She hadn't tagged me but I quickly saw on my notifications that she had added a new one.

It turned out that she had posted a very awkward picture of herself with my dad from last night. He looked very befuddled. I was certain it wasn't the best photo she would have of the night, so was disappointed she had chosen that one. Some of her friends' comments were cruel. I said to Fifi that the comments were a shame, as she was only being nice – Fifi looked up at me and made no comment.

Think I need a drink before part two!

———————

WhatsApp messages from Wen to Nyala
Saturday, 8 July 2017

Wen

Whoa, you're making me feel rather unwanted! Perhaps it's best if we leave this friendship then. I have no time for flaky people. Best of luck with your love life

22:53

And FYI I'm not needy at all. That was hurtful

22:53

From: Lomax Clipper
Sent: Sunday, 9 July 2017 00:45
To: Ross Wetherden
Subject: Re: Not good

I'm back, with some Dutch courage!

My dad got freaked out at the puppet show – he found it sinister. When a puppet was chopped in half, he wiped his brow and said he was just about done.

My mum feared he was going to have one of his old moments, but he perked up when we came out and had a quick bite to eat. He spoke of his coup in having the families meet. My mother was clearly less enthusiastic, but was putting on a brave face.

When we arrived at the bar on Via Maqueda, I saw Luisa and Gigi sitting at an outside table. They seemed nervous, but they greeted my parents very warmly when we approached. I could see my dad thinking, 'Brando' about Gigi, but my parents were very affable too. The goodwill around the table transcended the language barrier and was moving.

Then I saw that Gigi had tensed up. I turned to see that Aurora had arrived. Standing behind her were Diego and a female friend I had met at the Mazurka. I did not know why she had brought them. I had long thought Diego had been scared away.

'Mista Cleepa!' Diego said. 'My 'ero!'

They were all very stoned – Aurora far more so than I'd ever seen her. Luisa seemed close to tears. I said to Aurora that we needed a word, but she ignored me. She and her friends sat apart from us at the table. The two sets of parents – or rather, my dad and her parents – did their best to force the most stilted conversation imaginable, with me once again acting as interpreter, my heart beating fast. That was until Aurora pulled Diego towards her and kissed him on the mouth. Then we all stood, immediately.

I got my parents a taxi back. My mother put her hand to my cheek before she jumped in. My dad suggested a coffee back at the hotel and said, 'what a prat'. His voice tore at my heart. I managed to mumble that I would be with them shortly.

Aurora's parents were gone by the time I arrived back at the bar. Diego and the other friend were gone too. Mommo had been called out to pick up his lost and damaged sister. He was not friendly towards me, but he did leave the table briefly to give us some time alone. She was out of her head now and did not acknowledge me when I sat down. I asked her whether tonight had been revenge for the evening with her family, or whether the prospect of love, and a true relationship, had frightened her off.

As I was speaking, she looked up suddenly. Beyond the glaze, her eyes were abandoned and mad and poisonously angry. I understood finally that she was too much for me.

She told me that she had never believed in me and the truth was that I was just an English buffoon. I stood and left, promising myself that this was the end now; and, indeed, that she would pay.

Wen

Hey, just saw your message. Shit! Do you want me to come out to see you next weekend? I'd be happy to

09:10

———

Translation from the original Italian

Fifi

Hi Lomax, I'm so sorry. Of course, I would be honoured to accompany you all today. I've never been to Corleone. Tell me the time and place, and I'll be there

10:12

———

From: Lomax Clipper
Sent: Monday, 10 July 2017 21:07
To: Katie Wetherden
Subject: Sorry for the day's delay

Hi, I'm back in the flat but somehow it is Monday evening, not Sunday evening. The intended day trip to Corleone was extended a little due to unforeseen drama. Said goodbye to the parents at the airport a few hours ago. It has been an eventful day, which began at eight this morning with Fifi, my dad and a farmer trying to jumpstart our Fiat Panda with a tractor in the heart of Corleone – long story which I do not have the energy or the inspiration to tell. Suffice it to say that the farmer had towed the car to his rather euphemistically described *agriturismo* yesterday evening. By midday my mother was becoming frantic, so we paid a fortune for a taxi back to Palermo. The car remains on the farm.

At the airport my mum said that Fifi was a sweet guy, that it had been a hilarious time in Corleone and that she was very happy to think that I would soon be back in England, with the Aurora thing now 'brought to a close'. I can no longer look either her or my dad in the eye when they mention her name.

Things were unpleasant again when I got back to the apartment this evening. The lover had witnessed my parents, Fifi and me being dropped off in front of the *palazzo* earlier. When I came in, Roberto asked, re Fifi, whether I was planning to open a circus.

Incidentally, Fifi was indeed very nice during the adventure and we did have a lot of fun. But quite a weird thing happened late last night (he and I shared a room at the farm). It started off as sad, but then became jarring. Just as I was nodding off, Fifi sighed happily and said that we were like a family. But then he got out of his bed, came across to mine and gripped my hand – far too aggressively – and asked me to promise never to betray him. It wasn't really moving any more, at least to a man as jumpy as I am. Instead it came across as almost threatening. I said of course I wouldn't betray him, whatever that meant, but he didn't seem willing to let the matter go. He asked me to look at him and promise. When I did, he then asked me to say it again. He gripped my hand so damn hard that it's bruised today. Didn't like all that at all.

With respect to your suggestion, I couldn't come back to England immediately even if I wanted to. My tenants are not out until the end of August. (By the way, they're very angry with me at the moment because the roof has begun to leak just above the bed. That damn roofer!)

My actual plan is as follows. I am going to get some food supplies tomorrow morning and then hunker down in this flat until I finish the novel, regardless of the heat and smoke. It will not have ten chapters, but nine, and I am going to finish it this week. Literary agencies take six to eight weeks to respond to submissions to their slush piles. I am NOT yet clear how I will spend that time – but it won't be in London. Returning there at all, let alone early, smacks of an entirely premature acceptance of failure. There's a wealth of things to see on this island, away from Palermo.

Away from Palermo, and away from Fifi. I appreciate what my dad said about treating him right, and feel bad that I have perhaps helped cause this dependence on me, but I've had an overdose during the last day or so – and there have been five messages and counting since we returned to Palermo. Indeed, Nino shouted up gruffly from the courtyard earlier and, failing to understand him, I had a sudden electrifying fear that it was Fifi again. Instead, it was poor Luisa who had dropped off a letter of apology for her daughter's behaviour. A lovely letter. Poor woman is mortified.

Translation from the original Italian

From: Fifi de Angelis
Sent: Monday, 10 July 2017 23:39
To: Ignazio de Angelis; Rosaria de Angelis; Elisabetta de Angelis; Saveria de Angelis
Subject: Friendship

Just so you know: this weekend I met my English friend's

beautiful parents and they embraced me. They embraced my friendship with their son. And when they did, I thought: what LOSERS my family are!

You see, you were wrong.

Good night, losers!

———————

Translation from the original Chinese

From: Wen Li
Sent: Tuesday, 11 July 2017 13:39
To: Jin Li
Subject: Read this email carefully

Hi Mum,

I have read all your messages on WhatsApp. I can't believe you're doing this on only the second day of my new job. But let me leave your unique timing aside and make a few points to you.

First, I still can't believe that you actually opened a confidential medical letter addressed to me. Mum, I'm a grown woman!

The doctor, Dominic, whose secretary's letter you outrageously decided to open and read, has been my psychologist for over a year. I stopped seeing him when I lost my job because he's very expensive.

To shock you: I have seen many doctors over many years about this. Dominic is the best.

What I have is obsessive-compulsive disorder. I never wanted to tell you, because I thought you would judge me or worry about me.

It's disturbing and horrible but the medication and some of the therapies are an excellent help. When it's at its worst, this is when I pretend to have my migraines and rest in bed. They were always a lie.

At its worst, I'm scared to hold a knife. I think about pushing people in front of trains, asking myself again and again whether I'm absolutely sure I don't want to. I worry about whether I want to throw boiling water over people.

I become plagued by the weirdest fears. Sometimes, I sneak into the bedroom at night just to double-check you are alive. Then, when I'm back on the sofa bed and trying to sleep, I start asking myself whether I really checked properly; whether I can trust my memory. So, soon I sneak back into the bedroom, just to triple-check. And then, when I'm satisfied you're OK, I think, am I really in the bedroom because I want to kill you? And then I rush out.

So, I'm a mess. But at least now I'm aware of what is happening. Dominic taught me that we all have thousands of thoughts every hour of every day. The problem for people with OCD is that we notice any weird thought, and are upset by it, much more than a normal person is. A big red flag is raised in our heads. Ironically, of course, this makes us think about it more and more.

But, as Dominic said, it's what we do, not what we think, which makes all of us who we are. He also told me that people with OCD are usually very responsible and caring people, who impose very high standards of behaviour on themselves. This is the reason for red flags when we have any odd thought.

I'm going to send this to you now, without thinking. I'll not be able to come back to the flat tonight until you've replied.

Wen

———————

Translation from the original Chinese

Wen

Hi, just saw your email

15:05

I love you too. But the reason I never told you was because I just knew you wouldn't understand

15:05

See what I mean? You just don't get it

15:35

Obviously you don't need a lock on your bedroom door. Jesus!

15:35

I promise I won't come in again, if that helps

15:35

You have a special way of making me want to laugh and cry at the same time

15:35

What??! You'll love me even if I try to kill you? I mean, who says that?

17:29

I'm still laughing. You're insane! See you tonight

17:29

Wednesday, 12 July 2017

Translation from the original Chinese

Mum, we talked a lot last night and I thought you'd understood me by the end

09:11

Silly me

09:11

No longer finding this funny

09:11

This morning you jumped away from me

09:11

Last night I heard you barricading yourself into bedroom

09:11

Do you get that these reactions are maybe not helpful?

09:12

———

WhatsApp messages from Wen to Lomax
Wednesday, 12 July 2017

Wen

Hey, how's it going?

12:52

Realise you're busy writing but was wondering if we could speak about something?

12:53

Mum found out about my OCD

12:53

She's totally incapable of getting it. Is now constantly on her guard around me :)

12:53

Sort of funny but not great

12:53

Would be lovely if we could chat, even for 2 mins?

12:53

———

WhatsApp messages from Wen to Mum
Thursday, 13 July 2017

Translation from the original Chinese

Wen

Morning! I'm so happy to hear that!

09:59

Were you really reading until 2 this morning?!

09:59

It was Lomax who suggested finding some proper info for you in Chinese!

09:59

WhatsApp messages from Wen to Lomax
Thursday, 13 July 2017

Wen

You're a genius! She's much calmer today :)

11:54

Best of luck finishing the novel. Do let me know about coming out to see you, and whether it might do you good

11:54

A brief editorial intervention. Things speed up from hereon in. There will be no further explicit editorial reminders that a murder is going to occur (although we might refer to the murder in passing). Our view is that, if the reader isn't clear on it by now, the reader never will be.

From: Julian Pickering
Sent: Thursday, 13 July 2017 17:07
To: Lomax Clipper
Subject: A trip to Italy

Dear Lomax,

I have decided that my trip will encompass beautiful Sicily. I touch down in Palermo next Monday. I plan to see plenty of coast. My idea is to travel east, maybe get all the way to Taormina. Will you be around to say hello to your old boss when I'm in Palermo?

You didn't sound enthused by my suggestion of working on finishing the novel together, but the offer remains open. In any case, please do email me across a draft!

Julian

WhatsApp messages from Fifi to Lomax
Thursday, 13 July 2017

Translation from the original Italian

Fifi

Hello Lomax, I'm worried that you're working too hard. Remember to sleep. I know you need your peace, but consider also a pause for a sfincione, with extra cheese! :) Let me know

18:48

I've been looking at the photos of us in Corleone. One of the best and funniest times of my life

18:48

WhatsApp message from Wen to Lomax
Thursday, 13 July 2017

Wen

I wish you'd stop blaming me about Julian. And you're still not saying whether you'd like me to come out to see you!

20:22

Further WhatsApp messages from Fifi to Lomax
Thursday, 13 July 2017

Translation from the original Italian

Fifi

OK, Lomax. No problem

21:44

I can't wait for you to finish the novel on Friday! Shall we celebrate on Saturday? What's your plan after you've sent it to the agents?

21:44

From: Lomax Clipper
Sent: Thursday, 13 July 2017 23:07
To: Katie Wetherden
Subject: Re: All OK?

Hi Katie,

Yes, I'm just about OK. Superhuman efforts going on here on the novel. I have slept around seven hours since Monday.

And yes, my arrangement with Lina officially expires at the end of August. While waiting for verdicts on the novel I intend to visit some other parts of Sicily – alone! Palermo has got a little HOT, in every sense. What I do after that – which is to say, my more general life plan – depends entirely on how the novel is received by the agents.

All around me confusion and angst reign supreme, with messages streaming in from all quarters, but I am about to embark on the final push to finish my opus. My self-imposed deadline is 3 p.m. tomorrow. The novel will then be emailed out immediately to a raft of top literary agencies in the UK.

Professor Melanie Nithercott has written to me that it's madness to rush things like this, and has demanded a chance to review the final three chapters before the novel is sent. She does not understand that this needs to be over, ASAP, as I have had just about enough of everything. In any case I know I am on a roll and am writing as I have never written before.

There will be no sleep tonight.

From: Lomax Clipper
Sent: Friday, 14 July 2017 04:40
To: Katie Wetherden
Subject: Re: ALL OK?

Am in a state of extreme agitation here.

Why have I continually introduced new characters throughout the novel, when Agatha Christie's classic has all the characters arriving at the beginning?

How has Melanie missed this?

———————

From: Lomax Clipper
Sent: Friday, 14 July 2017 14:48
To: Katie Wetherden
Subject: NOVEL IS DONE!

———————

From: Lomax Clipper
Sent: Friday, 14 July 2017 20:18
To: Wen Li
Subject: Thanks again!

Thanks for your call earlier, Katie. I'm sort of beyond tired. After all the drama, I then find that literary agencies only request the first three chapters! If they like the first three chapters, THEN they ask for the whole novel.

How did Melanie not know this?

She wrote to me that the news was a relief because she shuddered to think what chapter nine must look like. However, I emphasised to Melanie that chapter nine is the best of the lot and borderline genius. I added that, while I intended to dedicate the novel to her, it was now closed and must remain closed for the sake of – yes – my sanity.

I fired off almost identical submissions to ten of the top agencies in the UK. It is strange to think of the novel being sent from a dusty room on Via Lungarini, La Kalsa, to some glamorous office in Bloomsbury. So far, the only agency that will definitely reject the submission is The White & Presswood Agency, because I forgot to tweak the covering email that I'd sent to the previous agency!

I am off to bed, to sleep for at least twelve hours. Immediate priority is to get out of this city and do a tour of the WEST coast of the island (see below as to why), while I await verdicts. San Vito Lo Capo, Trapani, Marsala…

Fifi is pestering me with a ferocity that is beginning to scare me. I'm meeting him for focaccia tomorrow, with a slight resentment that I've been bullied into doing so. I'm going to explain to him most gently that he's likely not to see me now for a few weeks. I'm going to try to avoid any discussion of my longer-term plans with him as I fear that the idea of me leaving Palermo for good, even to go to another part of Sicily – and not to mention the possibility of me returning to London – would break his heart, and I'm currently ill-equipped emotionally for the scene.

Meanwhile, to complement Fifi's persistence, a certified lunatic of a former boss has asked to meet in Palermo when he arrives on Monday – I'm going to limit this to a coffee near to whichever hotel he's staying at. Following which, I'll board a train for the west coast, as I say (because he says his tour will involve him going east).

In addition, both Roberto and Nino are sort of growling at me again, for reasons unknown. Could be just my paranoia, I suppose. But, to top it all, on the subject of not-so-stable people, there's needy Wen who is now also pestering me, wanting to come out and visit. Dressing up her loneliness in a rather earnest implication that I could do with some support!

The one thing I must do is respond to poor Luisa's letter of apology. The more I think of what her daughter did to her and Gigi, and to me and my parents, the more I become filled with rage.

———

WhatsApp messages from Wen to Lomax
Friday, 14 July 2017

> **Wen**
>
> Nice email meant for Katie and sent to me
>
> 20:50

> The one person in the world I thought I could count on
>
> 20:50

> I hate you!
>
> 20:50

———

From: Lomax Clipper
Sent: Saturday, 15 July 2017 10:18
To: Wen Li
Subject:

Wen, I appreciate why you're refusing to answer the phone or respond on WhatsApp. I can only say I'm profoundly sorry, and moreover that I don't know what the hell I was thinking. The reference to your not being stable was related to the cruel (and somewhat hypocritical) accusation of neediness – Katie does not know about your actual and serious problems.

It was a perverse comment that I can only blame on overtiredness and on my own emotional state here, which is not great. I care for you deeply and I apologise.

———————

From: Lomax Clipper
Sent: Saturday, 15 July 2017 16:20
To: Katie Wetherden
Subject: Re: Thanks again!

Thanks. Can you believe I sent the below email to Wen first by mistake?

I didn't say that I was going to go and live in a different part of Sicily, Katie. I've told you, I haven't decided on my long-term plan. I confess though that if my fantasy becomes true and the agents all ask for the full manuscript, I may follow my heart.

And as for Fifi, fine, yes, I will find out the git's surname tonight. Did I not make clear in my earlier email that my paranoia is already flourishing here and in no need of any encouragement?

———————

From: Lomax Clipper
Sent: Saturday, 15 July 2017 22:01
To: Katie Wetherden
Subject: Re: Thanks again!

Just back from focaccia with Fifi. Weird night. Told him I

would be leaving on Monday and would be away for a few weeks. He asked me to be specific i.e. to tell him when I'd be back in Palermo, about a thousand times. I said I didn't know yet. No laughs tonight, just tension, tension, tension.

I didn't know how to broach surname but spotted it on his bank card. De Angelis. Will do some Googling now, just out of curiosity. Bet you a hundred quid nothing comes up.

———

From: Lomax Clipper
Sent: Saturday, 15 July 2017 22:39
To: Katie Wetherden
Subject: Re: Thanks again!

Oh, Jesus Christ. *La Cronaca di Agrigento*. Long article. Oh, Jesus Christ.

———

From: Julian Pickering
Sent: Monday, 17 July 2017 15:18
To: Lomax Clipper
Subject:

Good to meet, but you were a little cold earlier, Lomax. It's silly being so secretive about the novel when I'm here to help. Your reluctance to name your area of Palermo, and even your current travel destination, struck me as unfriendly and weird too. I'm not stalking you, for God's sake!

I do firmly believe that the novel will not work without my input. I need to read it please.

Anyway, enjoy your trip.

There follow over three weeks of silence from Lomax Clipper. Despite his initial plans, and his representations to Fifi de Angelis and Julian Pickering, Lomax Clipper in fact remained in Palermo throughout this time.

The real reason for Lomax's decision to remain in Palermo is not entirely clear but is likely ascribable to his general mental state during this period. What is clear is that on Monday, 17 July, which is to say his planned day of travel, Lomax received a flurry of immediate rejections from literary agents. There is evidence that, during the subsequent weeks, Lomax submitted his novel to a further forty-three literary agencies around the world.

From: Lomax Clipper
Sent: Friday, 11 August 2017 20:59
To: Katie Wetherden
Subject: Re: Is anybody there?

Sorry. I began to reply to your email but became distracted by the sound of the church bells. I have taken to dancing the Mazurka alone in my room when they ring out.

I never bothered with my little trip. Instead I became seized by a vast and dreamy apathy, punctuated by little bursts of extreme anger – a state that continues to this day. All I know how to do is submit my novel to literary agencies.

Bizarre, I know, that I remained: I could have fired out submissions from my laptop in Trapani. Especially bizarre given that I only dare leave the flat out of absolute necessity, and even then with a cap and some super-sized sunglasses on. Julian could still be out there, so far as I know. The man-biting devil of Agrigento undoubtedly is. I wrote to him, by the way – while claiming to be in Trapani. I said that I would be heading back to London soon, forever. He replied asking me why I was so distant and what was wrong and saying that we must meet before I go. Like hell! Then, last week, Roberto told me that he'd bumped into him near the focaccia place and had told him to keep away from the *palazzo*, as nobody wanted to get bitten. I shouldn't have told Lina what I'd discovered on Google, as it was obvious she would tell her dick of a son, but I was in a state that night. Anyway, since then I've not heard from Fifi.

Wen's still refusing to reply to any message or email or to answer my calls (I've now stopped trying). I miss speaking to her so much and I'm very upset about it all. I can't even bear to reflect on it for too long, if I'm honest, the idea that I hurt her with that email. Any other suggestions as to what I could do?

I've become a smoker, by the way. This afternoon I sat on the antique chair opposite the chaise longue, and Lina and I smoked for three hours. When the heat reached its zenith, I began to imitate her groans.

Soon afterwards, the lover came in, glaring at me. He asked whether it had been me who had been barking yesterday evening. I said that it had been. Lina agreed with him that the nocturnal screaming was getting louder too – and that I should see someone about that.

And yes: this coming Monday is indeed my birthday. A present arrived today from Melanie, how sweet is that?! It was Goethe's *Italian Journey*. Already got it. Told her many times I have it too. Still, a lovely thought.

My mother then phoned and said to get back home ASAP and that she genuinely feared that if I stayed out here much longer I would lose my mind. I replied: 'Perhaps I was mad BEFORE'. I don't think she got the Goethe reference.

The main news is that rejections of the novel are coming thick and fast. So much for having to wait six to eight weeks. Three weeks in, my Gmail has never seen such traffic. I've worked up a standard response to the rejection emails. It goes like this: 'Next step is transfer money for book to Cayman branch, then have poo. Account 00000000'. The poo bit I added only recently. I'll admit it's quite odd.

Oh God, Katie, am I just another of life's dreamers after all? Is this whole novel nothing more than a deep embarrassment? Surely, Melanie knows what she's talking about and wouldn't have encouraged me if she didn't feel confident?

Finally, I've taken your advice about not responding to Luisa's letter of apology. I'll save the response until I leave Palermo. It is strange how I can hold two different versions of her daughter in my head. The Aurora who humiliated me, lost in her own bitter song – a young woman on whom I still intend to get my revenge. And then the young woman of last summer, on an island outside of time.

———

From: Lomax Clipper
Sent: Monday, 14 August 2017 20:59
To: Lomax Clipper
Subject: Happy birthday, Lomax

Dear Lomax, I just wanted to say that you are an extraordinary writer, an all-round fucking great guy, and I wanted to wish you a VERY, MERRY happy birthday.

All the best,

Lomax

———

From: Julian Pickering
Sent: Wednesday, 16 August 2017 12:47
To: Toby Enslin
Subject: An instruction from Sicily

You better be out of the flat by the time I get back to London,

Toby. Don't push too hard. You may end up wishing you hadn't. You are playing with a rejuvenated tiger.

———————

From: Lomax Clipper
Sent: Friday, 18 August 2017 18:24
To: Katie Wetherden
Subject:

Nothing still from Wen, am so beaten up about it.

I received twelve rejections today. TWELVE. And nobody explains why it has been rejected.

I just need one agent at a big gun to like it. Is that too much to fucking ask?

Christ, Katie, I think I really am a failure. I am not good with that feeling. I've always believed I have something special. I fear this must be the same feeling that deranged psychopaths have. Perhaps I do have narcissistic personality disorder – or perhaps I'm overthinking. Regardless, this growing rage is not normal.

———————

From: Julian Pickering
Sent: Thursday, 24 August 2017 12:18
To: Lomax Clipper
Subject: Ciao

Dear Lomax,

I've had a most wonderful trip. My God, the history here! And the colour and warmth of the sea! I'll be back in Palermo next week before I fly to London on the Saturday. Are you back too? Fancy meeting up for something a little stronger than a coffee?

Have you had any luck so far with literary agencies? If only you'd let me review!

By the way, have you ever learned to dance? I intend to take dancing lessons when back in London. There is a truth in dancing that goes beyond even literature.

Julian

———————

From: Lomax Clipper
Sent: Friday, 25 August 2017 11:03
To: Katie Wetherden
Subject: A dark night

The World of Smoke and Heat is not the ideal place in which to wake up hungover. Cabin fever finally broke me and last night I decided to venture out. It is fair to say that the experience that followed was a little bit special.

Thanks again for your call yesterday. To confirm, <u>unless a miracle intervenes with the novel, I am now resigned to the horrific prospect of coming home and returning to work at Curtain & Curtain.</u> This will involve me flying back next Saturday, which is most unfortunately the same day that Julian will be at the airport.

There is now only one literary agency left in play – Erskine & Price. I have one minor quibble with your argument in relation to my rapidly failing literary career. I appreciate that, even if a literary agency took the novel, it might be months or longer before I made any money. But you're missing the point about the psychological effect it would have on me. It would galvanise me, and justify a decision to make a life for myself away from the notarial profession and away from London. Not Palermo, I agree – but Italy is a big place!

You're right about Wen. Just as I forgave you for your little email error once, she really should try and forgive me too. Hopefully she will soon. Her silence is beginning to get a bit perturbing.

Now, yesterday evening – an experience that underscores your point about leaving Palermo and partially explains why I've decided to take the risk of venturing out again this coming Monday, this time to see a psychologist. (The main reasons for this decision are a need to confront the intense anger I'm feeling about Aurora and the novel, and, I confess, a sort of curiosity about The Nightmare.)

So here we go. The sky was low when I rushed out of the *palazzo* and bundled myself into a taxi last night, with an eerie wind blowing in from the sea. The prospect of Albergheria, and an evening with a middle-aged, possibly alcoholic, language teacher, felt right. Sam had viewed my old, half-baked profile on a Freelance Tutor website and had got in touch, suggesting that he would have some tips. When we spoke on the phone yesterday – I rang him on a whim, out of intense boredom – I explained that I might be leaving Palermo in a week, but he invited me for a drink in any case, insisting, in a strong Australian accent, that I should come to his part of town. He sounded hammered, and it was a weird decision to agree to go. I fear that, in addition to cabin fever, it might have been out of a perverse hope of bumping into Aurora with the Mazurka crowd. Sam lives on a street that is perhaps Albergheria's worst.

I arrived already distressed. My taxi driver had claimed my cash was fake and had paced the dimly lit pavement while I had withdrawn more cash from a machine. I decided it was important to drink.

I sat down outside Via Orrore's only bar. Presently, Sam emerged from behind a plastic sheet serving as the main entrance to the building opposite. He was tall, and well-built for a man in his mid-sixties. He told me that he was a former banker.

He had the saddest smile I have ever seen. He spoke at length about Trapani and said he didn't understand why I hadn't gone there. But then he switched, seeming suddenly very drunk, and began to imitate the Palermitan dialect. It was funny at first – the Sicilians at the table next to ours found it so too. But then it was not funny any more.

After an hour of rapid drinking, Sam stood up and declared that he must go. He had a long walk ahead to the Foro Italico. He must have seen my face, for his went pink with shame. In a confused attempt to lighten the atmosphere, he told me a sickening joke about the curse put on the African prostitutes to bind them to their traffickers. Walking away he broke into a fit of laughter that reeked of anxiety.

Then I heard the violins. The music came drifting down the forsaken street. Thankfully, I did not try to find the Mazurka. Instead, I stood and then spun alone, like a ghost in a dream.

———

WhatsApp messages from Wen to Mum
Monday, 28 August 2017

Translation from the original Chinese

Wen

Hi, rubbish morning here in office

11:59

Anxiety levels not so good today. Not terrible, but not great

11:59

Can't wait to get home and drink some tea on sofa! :)

11:59

Love you too

12:12

———

From: Lomax Clipper
Sent: Monday, 28 August 2017 13:58
To: Katie Wetherden
Subject: The psychologist

Hello there, Mrs Wetherden,

Before I get on to the psychologist – do you remember that repulsive guy Enzo, the nasty little racist of a notary? The one I wound up by pretending I'd always thought his mother was Romanian? Well, it turns out that I foolishly inflamed things further when I got back drunk from my dark evening with Sam. I was so drunk that I have no recollection of writing the damn thing. But I noted this morning that he'd put some horribly sinister things up on Facebook about false rumours. In one of the photos he's sliding his index finger across his throat!? This then led me to the grim discovery of a weirdly angry Facebook message I'd sent him. 'Rumena, Rumena, mamma is Rumena!' What was I thinking? It's pretty damn bad taste too, as Romanians suffer terrible discrimination out here. In part, I suspect, because Romanian women tend to be even more beautiful than Italian women!

Anyway, the psychologist. Fair to say that today's session with Dottor Pietro Cusimano was, erm, interesting. Cusimano is old and terribly grand. Thin, with a sharp nose and silver hair. He wore an elegant grey suit and large glasses, through which he peered at me gravely from his desk. I sat on a low chair in front of him.

He asked me why I had arrived concealing my face with a cap and enormous sunglasses. I noted indignantly that it was standard Sicilian attire and that I had removed them as soon as I had come in. Incidentally, I do believe that if I had said that it was because I feared that I was being stalked by an Englishman and a man-biting Sicilian, he might have had me committed!

Anyway, Cusimano nodded pensively, then told me that I was the first Englishman he had seen. I assumed he meant in the professional sense. He insisted on speaking in English, which was a shame because his was so strange. It became clear that he liked his Latinate words, which he pronounced slowly and pretentiously, misusing many and inventing some. His colloquial English was appalling. His grammar was not so hot either.

Once we had exchanged pleasantries, he said: 'Is optimal to conversate. But please now you explicate. Why you decide see a shrimp?'

I told him as calmly as I could that the word was 'shrink'. This clearly infuriated him. He projected immediately, telling me: 'I see it. You manifest the periculous rage.'

He then continued to suggest that I had tremendous anger inside and, as I began to tense up, I continued to agree. He asked me to tell him more about myself. After I had given him an outline, we agreed that he should seek to 'provocate the monster'.

'Let be considered the book,' he said.

I did not bite.

'Let be considered Aurora. Seguish Aurora to Palermo, and she not dedicate. She not fidanzate. She Diego a kiss.'

I felt my fists clenching.

'Think 'ow is to be Katie,' he said. 'Think Katie, the money.'

Here I interrupted, insisting that he stop, as I was not bothered about money. At this, Cusimano stood and walked over to my low chair. He then began to circle me. Suddenly, while behind me, he bent down and screamed into my ear: 'You no 'ave the money!'

I shot to my feet and yelled at him to get the fuck away from me.

'*Ecco*,' he said, his face failing to mask his glee. 'We 'ave provocate.'

He then charged me ninety-five Euros and said he would see me next week to discuss The Nightmare. I can assure you he won't!

Another sorry little story – apologies if it bored you. It's the quietest and most boring time of day here on Via Lungarini. There's nothing to do except hit a pillow, or daydream about an email from Erskine & Price, in which they tell me that the book is magnificent. An email that would change everything.

———

Translation from the original Italian

From: Fifi de Angelis
Sent: Monday, 28 August 2017 14:00
To: Lomax Clipper
Subject: The Truth

Hi Lomax,

So yes, I am Fifi de Angelis. The terrible man from Agrigento who assaulted Damiano.

Excuse me for searching for your email address. It is very easy to find on Google. You should put more privacy on your social media accounts.

I am forwarding you the attached emails from me to my family. Now you will know the truth. You will understand how my family behave, and also why I did what I did to Damiano. I want you to know everything because I know you are good.

I hope you are not back in London already. Even if you are, once you have read these emails, perhaps we can speak again.

Fifi

———

From: Lomax Clipper
Sent: Monday, 28 August 2017 16:23
To: Katie Wetherden
Subject: FW: Your novel

From: Cynthia.Mirren@erskineandprice.co.uk
Sent: Monday, 28 August 2017 14:59
To: Lomax Clipper
Subject: Your novel

Dear Lomax,

Thank you for sending me the opening chapters of *And Later on Easter Island*. Isabella mentioned the particular urgency so I have sought to prioritise the submission over the past days.

Isabella also mentioned that your email was one of the most passionate she had ever received from a writer seeking representation. I am sensitive to the novel's importance for you and your ambition makes this email difficult to write. However, I am afraid that the novel is not for me.

Please don't take this as a comment on your ability as a writer. Remember that ours is a highly subjective business: another agent may well respond differently.

Best wishes,

Cynthia

Cynthia Mirren

Wen

Are you OK? Answer the phone please!

21:50

You sounded totally wasted in that voicemail

21:50

I miss you too, you know that. All forgiven

21:50

But what do you mean, you made a terrible mistake when it came to me?

21:50

Do you mean what I think you mean?

21:51

I just can't wait for you to get yourself home. We can talk then, about everything

21:51

Don't be down. You're so much more precious than a fucking novel

21:51

And don't even think about 'resolving things' with Aurora before you leave. What does that even mean? Call me!

21:51

From: Lomax Clipper
Sent: Tuesday, 29 August 2017 12:42
To: Julian Pickering
Subject: Re: Anybody there?

Julian, I have no idea why you think I live in La Kalsa – your hunch is wrong. Anyway, I'm sorry but I'm not around. Hope you enjoyed your trip.

———

WhatsApp messages from Wen to Lomax
Tuesday, 29 August 2017

Wen

Why won't you answer when I call?

16:50

Anyway, please chill

16:50

There's no need to keep sending me your apologies for the voicemail

16:50

I know you were drunk and we all say shit we don't mean with alcohol. Voicemail deleted and forgotten. Won't mention again, I promise

16:50

But you promise me something back

16:51

Promise me you're still coming back to London on Saturday

16:51

WhatsApp messages from Lomax to Fifi
Tuesday, 29 August 2017

Translation from the original Italian

Lomax

Hi Fifi, I've tried to call a few times.

18:03

I've read all the emails from you to your family and I was heartbroken.

18:03

Anxiety is a terrible thing, and mine led me to behave disgracefully towards you. I'm so sorry.

18:03

In my defence, many people would be perturbed by a story about you hospitalising a man through biting.

18:03

Anyway, the novel failed.

18:04

I'm in Palermo and feeling very lost. Have made up my mind not to return to London.

18:04

I'm leaving Palermo on Saturday and going to go to the other side of the island, to Syracuse, for a couple of months for a fresh start.

18:04

If I like it there I'll stay. If not, I'll move on to some other town or city. After all, as you know, I love Sicily.

18:04

And of course we should keep in touch, if you'll accept my apologies. Would be lovely to see you before I go.

18:05

From: Lomax Clipper
Sent: Wednesday, 30 August 2017 14:25
To: Katie Wetherden
Subject: Re: Hey

Hi Katie. Thanks for your email. Apologies for missing your call.

I am still leaving Palermo on Saturday. But after serious reflection I've decided that I won't be returning to London. I've just told Mr Curtain. Instead, I'm going to enact my fantasy – what I would have done if the novel had been immediately accepted. Of course, things are different now: an about-to-be published writer wandering around Sicily would have been a charming image. But drifting is not all bad. I'll teach English here and there, and there's quite a bit of the overdraft left for now.

I informed Melanie this morning and sent her the full novel with the final chapters. Then I deleted the document from all systems, including email.

Last night I told my parents that my return to Curtain & Curtain had been pushed back a further fortnight for administrative reasons, so I was staying here a bit longer. This was to buy myself some time to think of an explanation that might ease their worrying once I reveal the truth. But, judging by their anxious tone, I'm not sure they believed me.

I also lied to Wen so that she'd get off my case at this delicate moment. It felt so wrong to lie to her, but it'll be easier to defend the decision once I've had a bit of time to digest it myself.

I'm taking the train from Palermo to Catania on Saturday morning, then on to Syracuse. Lina has insisted that on Friday evening we have a leaving party at the flat and has imposed a three-line whip to get Nino, the lover and Roberto to come. I'm meeting Fifi after that, for what will be an emotional late-night farewell over some focaccia. By the way, we got him so horribly wrong, Katie. He's not dangerous at all. I had a wonderful time with him yesterday evening – I've apologised to him and we've made up. Long story.

On the subject of danger, though: Julian is still around – not leaving Palermo till Saturday. Also, Enzo the psycho-notary suddenly replied to my apology about the drunken message – it turns out he's here too, and most hauntingly he said all was forgiven, and that he would very much like to say hello again. Obviously, I am going to avoid. You should see his Facebook posts: the last one just says 'LIARS!' In English!!

I have just paid Nino's cousin five euros to deliver my response to Aurora's mother. More reliable than the post. It feels right to let Luisa know that I'm leaving Palermo on Saturday with no hard feelings. It also feels right to tell her about the novel, so that she won't grow old believing that her daughter missed out on the chance of marrying a successful writer. As for Aurora herself... I'm rather tempted to close this off in my own way. Aren't we always told it's unhealthy to bottle up anger?

During the two days leading up to the murder, Katie Wetherden continues to send Lomax emails and text messages, demanding that they speak. Lomax refuses to speak. He accuses Katie of ruining the build-up to his leaving party.

On the evening of Friday, 1 September, Katie Wetherden declares to her husband Ross that she has finally given up. She pours herself a large glass of wine. As she takes her first sip, she receives an email.

From: Lomax Clipper
Sent: Friday, 1 September 2017 22:44
To: Katie Wetherden
Subject:

A sad and grim little leaving party, with a melancholy Lina smoking in silence, and the three Sicilian men staring down awkwardly into their drinks. Power had gone again, so it was thanks only to the moonlight that I could even SEE the guests – there's a most extraordinary sky tonight. I was about to make it clear that it was home time for everyone, and then go and see Fifi, when Nino's cousin, who was standing in for Nino, called up to say that someone was here for me. I went down to find it was Aurora.

We stood before each other in the courtyard without speaking. The most jolting thing was that I felt nothing. All the affection, all the magic had turned to dust. I did think it was nice that she had come to say farewell, and I realised that, as always, just one kind gesture had led to all my anger dissipating immediately – it was exactly the same with Lisa. I felt so relieved that I'd resisted the temptation to get everything off my chest in an email.

But suddenly Aurora took from her bag what looked to be my letter to her mother, waved it in my face and began to shout and scream. There was nothing inappropriate in that letter. Nothing that justified her yelling at me to leave her and her family alone, and that it was indeed time that I got the fuck out of Palermo.

Nothing that justified her slapping me in the face, before shouting that she had always known that the novel would fail.

I asked her to step outside the *palazzo*, as I was embarrassed in front of the wide-eyed stare of Nino's cousin. On Via Lungarini she carried on shouting, giving vent to all the hatred in her heart, and I found it weirdly difficult to turn away from her and go back inside. I just stood there in silence, taking it, as passersby stared and people peered out of their windows. In the end, in her instability, she asked me if I loved her. To her clear dismay, I looked into her eyes and said no, I did not. I remained standing in front of the *palazzo* for some time, a good fifteen or twenty minutes, once she had disappeared into the darkness.

I've had an unremarkable life, but what happened next... well, I suppose it will go down as one of my few remarkable moments. I had turned to go back inside the *palazzo* but had discovered that I didn't have my key or my phone. As I was pressing the buzzer with one hand, and banging on the main door with the other, a familiar, gentle voice said from behind me: 'Hey, Lomax.'

I spun around to see Wen. She had a little suitcase beside her. I don't mind admitting that I began to cry.

She told me that she loved me, and that she'd come to bring me home. She came up close, looked into my eyes and said that I was the nicest man she'd ever known. Her softly spoken words were like a thunderbolt in my head. I heard myself stammering that I didn't know what to say. That she was such a beautiful person, and that I simply wasn't good enough. That she was so gorgeous, so intelligent, she could have anyone she wanted.

She began to cry too, saying that I had it all wrong. She said that, if I felt the same way, she'd hit the jackpot with me. We hugged, more and more tightly. Suddenly we were kissing and I was confessing that I loved her and it felt as though I were floating in a dream.

From: Julian Pickering
Sent: Friday, 1 September 2017 22:45
To: Lomax Clipper
Subject:

Dear Lomax,

This was just to say no hard feelings. I will see you, I hope, back in England soon. I'm in a bar in La Kalsa, having a rest after dancing with some locals I've managed to befriend! Great choice of city you made for your sabbatical!

And what a sky. I've never seen a moon like it!

Julian

From: Julian Pickering
Sent: Friday, 1 September 2017 22:48
To: Martin Pickering
Subject: Re: Hello

Hi Dad,

Your email this morning had an indescribable effect on me. Your statement that you'd like to see me happy with another man... my eyes fill up every time that I read it.

I'm so proud of you. Feeling wildly joyous here in Palermo tonight!

Julian

Translation from the original Italian of a handwritten document found on Fifi de Angelis's person, and taken by Palermitan authorities. It appears to be a sort of script.

This is our chance now, Lomax. We have to take it. You're lost and I can help you, I can be such a good and loyal friend that you will wake from your lonely dreams. I insist on being your companion on your Sicilian wanderings. First Syracuse, then maybe Ragusa, wherever you want on my island we'll go. You have so much to see here, our friendship will grow and you will find yourself again.

Think of this unique opportunity. A true Sicilian adventure, experienced side-by-side. Think of the laughs, the experiences, the new cities. I don't care how long it lasts – whether it's weeks, months or even a year – you can count me in.

I will not take no for an answer. I need only a week or two to deal with things here. Then I will meet you in Syracuse.

———————

From: Lomax Clipper
Sent: Friday, 1 September 2017 22:59
To: Katie Wetherden
Subject:

Thanks, Katie. Very touched that the email brought a tear to your eye. Amusing scenes here in the flat. Nino, Roberto and the lover were befuddled by the appearance of Wen.

I'll call you when back in England. Must rush, as poor Fifi is still waiting for me at the focaccia place. I've told Wen to stay here because this is going to be delicate.

In fact, Christ, it seems he's lost patience and is now

downstairs! Or at least somebody is – Nino's cousin is calling again. What a night!

WhatsApp messages from Wen to Mum
Friday, 1 September 2017

Translation from the original Chinese

Wen

Mum, it went just as I'd dreamed!

23:05

Lomax and I love each other, and he's coming back to England!

23:05

He's just gone to say goodbye to a friend so I thought I would lie down and write you this happy news :)

23:05

The moonlight is pouring in through the apartment's windows and it's all so romantic... I'm wondering what I could have done to be so blessed

23:05

Postscript and Acknowledgements

Late in the evening of 1 September 2017, Lomax Clipper was horrifically beaten outside his flat on Via Lungarini. He suffered several serious injuries, including a punctured lung, and was rushed by ambulance to Palermo's general hospital, where he remained for over two weeks, until his condition improved sufficiently for him to be discharged.

Lomax's life had been saved by three men: Nino Messina, Franco Messina (Nino's cousin) and, in particular, Fifi de Angelis. Assumedly confused by Lomax's no-show at the *focacceria*, Fifi had made his way to Lomax's *palazzo*. Upon encountering the scene on Via Lungarini, Fifi threw himself at one of the attackers and bit him severely a number of times. Fifi was stabbed and passed away in Palermo's general hospital four hours after the attack.

Six months later, Mommo La Rosa and two accomplices were convicted of Lomax's assault, and Mommo La Rosa alone was convicted of Fifi's murder. It is accepted by all that Aurora La Rosa had made a serious allegation about Lomax to her brother. That allegation, vehemently denied by Lomax, has been neither proved nor disproved.

Fifi's family would like it to be reiterated that Fifi was estranged from them. The family's position is that they finally agreed to the publication of certain of Fifi's emails to them only out of respect for the last wishes of Fifi's grandmother, Nonna Liboria. Lomax Clipper would like it to be stated that, in his view, the request made to the family was only out of courtesy, given that Fifi had forwarded the emails to Lomax. This publisher makes no comment on such statements.

We thank the notarial firm Curtain & Curtain for its constructive approach towards the discussions held between the firm, this publisher and Julian Pickering over several months. We acknowledge that the firm does not condone the historical forwarding by Julian Pickering to his private email account of internal email correspondence. We further acknowledge that any depiction of the firm or of any of its partners in this correspondence is, of course, subjective.

Professor Melanie Nithercott is a retired lecturer in English at the University of Huddersfield.

Katie Wetherden is a partner of the law firm Reynolds & Hyde.

Julian Pickering is a former partner of Curtain & Curtain and is currently working on a novel.

Wen Li is a prominent writer and speaker about obsessive-compulsive disorder. She lives in Huddersfield with Lomax Clipper and her mother, Jin Li.

Lomax Clipper is a freelance translator of Italian to English, and in his spare time continues to work on his writing. Lomax returned to Sicily in order to meet Fifi de Angelis's grandmother in Agrigento, shortly before she died. Nonna Liboria told him that she had loved her grandson very dearly indeed, and that it was very soothing to her to think that this Selected Correspondence might allow him to become known as a hero.

About the Author

Tom Vaughan MacAulay is a solicitor. His first novel, *Being Simon Haines*, was published in 2017. *Countdown to a Killing* is his second novel.

BEING

SIMON

HAINES

TOM VAUGHAN MACAULAY

If you enjoyed Countdown to a Killing, you may also like
like Tom Vaughan MacAulay's debut novel, Being Simon
Haines.

Read on for an extract...

1

I flew to Havana in memory of earnestness. I was thirty-
two years old, professionally accomplished but lacking in
wisdom, financially secure but privately adrift, at the point
in life when a lawyer recalls Purpose, becomes indignant at
the stability afforded by general malaise. It was April 2012
and I had a moment: my eight-month 'Campaign' at the
law firm of Fiennes & Plunkett, that family-run, exclusive
financing and insolvency boutique of the City of London, was
over, and I had to wait for two weeks to see if I would be
voted in as a new junior partner; if this blue-eyed boy from
Lincoln would become a millionaire. During Campaign, the
firm, led by the long legs and mighty silver quiff of Rupert
Plunkett, had worked me to a level of nervous exhaustion
that required not only a period of recuperation, but also an
illusion of escape. Sophie Williams, my now *ex*-girlfriend, had
left me only recently. In London spring had been withheld and
even the April showers' vitality curbed, so that instead a fine
rain, incessant in its listlessness, drifted through cold, hurried
streets below a sky of gloom.

'Just disappear for a while, Simon – it'll do you good.
God, that sounds banal.'

Dan Serfontein and I had been friends since university –
all the way through law school, the training contract and the
associate years at Fiennes & Plunkett. Son of a fund manager
from Cape Town and his beautiful wife, Dan's towering alpha-

male physique held up a boyish, infuriatingly handsome face and a head of thick blond hair. Dan had poise, that special assurance of all of Belgravia's children, but unlike them he had an admirable, manic determination too – despite, or rather because of, the family money. All this Dan Serfontein had – but he did not quite have the mind, the obsessive attention to detail, the neurotic speed of thought, to go all the way at Fiennes & Plunkett. He had left just a couple of weeks before the horror of Campaign had begun, burnt out and unable to go on, and now swam the calmer waters of in-house law.

'No idea how you got through it, mate. You should be proud of yourself, whatever happens – you're far stronger than I am.'

After much pondering, one morning the apotheosis of strength that was Mr Simon Haines decided where to go. Selecting the age category of 28–35s, I booked myself on a group tour of Cuba, through an agency specialising in *bona fide trips for bona fide travellers*. Cuba was, I supposed, a place that I had always wanted to see; and those friends of mine who had made me wince when speaking of 're-connection with your spirit' did perhaps have a point, albeit atrociously expressed . For the idea of a faraway land, of new air, brought about a flicker of an old emotion that lay deeper than consciousness...

I had not been getting much new air. According to Tempo, the firm's electronic timesheet system, I had billed over three thousand hours in the previous twelve months. At one nebulous point, when matters had reached their peak of intensity, I had spent three consecutive days and nights at my desk. Thirty-two, the once attractive face now anaemic and haggard. The once big blue eyes now smaller, the curly brown hair turning grey, beginning to recede; and I was getting through a packet of cigarettes a day in the Fiennes & Plunkett smoking pit. I was still of reasonable, unremarkable height, just below six foot, but at times had the unnerving impression that I was slowly shrinking. Over half a stone in weight had gone since law school, but I had gained at the bottom of my stomach incipient rolls of fat, which seemed unsure of their identity. For years, my only exercise had involved sprinting back and forth to the lifts.

'No running,' Rupert Plunkett had whispered one morning, his distinguished, skeletal figure bending down towards me, minutes before Project Archer had been announced to the market. 'No running in these offices.'

Even before the final test that was Campaign, a sixteen-hour day had been standard for me at Fiennes & Plunkett. Twenty-four-hour days were not rare. Up on the ninth floor of that dome-shaped glass building – the first six floors were populated by an insurance company, and the top three floors belonged to the firm – I spent the end of my twenties and beginning of my thirties as an unappreciative witness of the cycles of nature; of the transience of the days and nights, the seasons, the months, the years. Often, as I made the final tweaks to a loan agreement, I would look up to see the night creeping away, once more defeated by a grey but penetrating light that promised a day of anguish. In the summer, distraught at the abstruse instructions of a man who only ever whispered, I would sometimes gaze out, hands to my temples, just in time to see the sun letting itself down gently into the Thames. During the early hours, in the refuge of the smoking pit, on occasion my head would rise up to the sky and I would see the moon, at which sight I would panic, and then feel terribly alone.

My relationship with the firm had become akin to a love affair with a narcissist – a beautiful sociopath whom I had courted with desperation, seduced by its lustre and the

321

indifference of its cold heart. Fiennes & Plunkett was far from being one of the big boys of the City – it sat way below the elite Magic Circle firms, below even the Silver Circle and the huge international alliances that came after that. Moreover – and unlike virtually every other serious law firm in the City of London – it had an offering of only two specialisations, with one support department. City law firms generally have corporate departments, finance departments, tax, competition, real estate, intellectual property departments. But at Fiennes & Plunkett...

'At Fiennes & Plunkett we do financing and insolvency,' Rupert Plunkett would whisper proudly, in his Annual Address to the firm – putting particular emphasis on the final two words. He'd whispered this in every Annual Address since the 2008 financial crisis, the time at which a simple fact had transformed into a slogan, a sort of battle cry. 'That is all we do. It's all we will ever do.'

At which point a partner would raise a hand gingerly and Rupert would grimace, then whisper:

'OK. We also have a small real estate department.'

And yet, despite these apparent limitations, Fiennes & Plunkett was the pinnacle of some law graduates' ambition. To the extent that the insolvency sector could be said to have its king in the City, Fiennes & Plunkett was it – and its general financing work was highly regarded too. Unaccountably still a family firm, it had been at the forefront of loans, restructurings and liquidations for four generations of a line of madmen, and was flourishing now under the latest of the line. It was a self- proclaimed 'inventor of market practice', renowned for its commercial approach , and then – let's get to it – there was the money. While its profits as a firm were dwarfed by the US firms and the players in the Magic and Silver Circles, Fiennes & Plunkett had an extremely tight equity structure –

there were only thirty partners – so that those who did make it earned considerable sums. Or rather, extraordinary sums – a newly made-up partner, people said, would take home over a million pounds a year. Over a million pounds! For this reason, the intensity of the competition among associates; on this promise, the incomparable demands made of them by the firm; on account of all this the fact that the firm, which had as its mantra the concepts of prudence and clarity, boasted more damaged individuals than any other institution in the City.

'At Fiennes & Plunkett we do financing and insolvency.'

Oh, the grave beauty of the whisper!

Infatuated, I had courted it. And the firm had given me its hand: I had been offered a training contract at the age of twenty-two, while still studying languages at Cambridge and knowing nothing about the law. A training contract that included sponsoring me through law school. Signing it, I felt the tingle of glory. I saw constant intellectual stimulation, the biggest restructuring deals, saving famous companies! I saw a million pounds a year, in my early thirties! For a moment I wanted to stop cars in the street… Back in Lincoln, amid the euphoria my parents invited some friends around – the couples who had babysat me as a child – and we had a party in the pleasant and understated sitting room of our small terraced house, which extended through a bright conservatory to a view of a back garden rich with flowers and deliberately imperfect, as if based on a fear of accusations of *petit bourgeois* tidiness .

'Fiennes and bloody Plunkett!' My father – a slight, dishevelled man who practised, in a not overly strenuous manner, as a local psychologist, and whose two distinguishing features would always be a bushy beard and an ability to fall asleep immediately upon sinking into his armchair – was wearing his old green cardigan and older creased corduroys, but his tired face was lit today by a lovely, proud smile. 'I've just read all about them – I can't believe it! Are you sure it's what you want?'

'What? Of course I'm sure!' Oh, the surly conviction…

After law school, there came the two years of training at the firm – years in which the illusions ebbed away but the infatuation intensified, the bond fixed by the glue of a bitter je ne regrette rien. They were the years in which we were revealed to one another, naked in the dawn that brings to an end an all-nighter. The firm was indeed an intellectual powerhouse. But it was also an asylum: a home of perfectionists, a sea of insecurity, an uncaring and selfish life partner who demanded dedication twenty-four hours a day. And I, who was I? I was a man who had become addicted, a man who had submitted. A man whose primary emotion was now *terror of getting it wrong*. And for this I was duly rewarded: at the end of the training contract, I was kept on as an 'associate'.

The road ahead, carved through desolate plains, promised soon to straighten out, but I had lost my parents' endorsement on the way: this time I saw only a worried couple, the same old neighbours and a cocky, adolescent cousin who was asking me why I couldn't talk for more than a minute without looking at *that* thing.

'It's the firm's BlackBerry,' I said haughtily. In those days, a junior associate carrying a firm-issued BlackBerry was entitled to be haughty.

'I know what it is, you prick!'

Less than six years of qualified life, I explained to the gathering. The last eight months of it would be Campaign and – if I made it through that – there'd be the possibility of partnership.

'Your dad's right, though,' said Sophie in a soft voice. 'We all just want to see you happy. Not so stressed all the time.'

I was betraying Fiennes & Plunkett. Sophie had been

my first girlfriend at school, the first girl I had made love to, and years later we had met again in London, where she now worked as a primary school teacher a couple of miles from the alternative reality of Rupert Plunkett's mother ship. Sophie was very pretty, radiating that transient promise of true beauty that all prettiness brings, and her gentle character concealed a fine intelligence and often sceptical nature that were nevertheless contained within that gentleness. But her most striking feature was her height, standing as she did at just over six feet tall. It was a height that, had she been wired differently, might have brought about a supreme confidence and hauteur, terrifying to men, but for Sophie it was instead a source of faint but perennial embarrassment. Her auburn hair flowed down in tender waves from that height, the fringe stopping above twin seas of dark brown that were the emotional pull of a lovely, captivating face, the charm of which came enhanced by her long, slender figure. Sophie had a teacher's honesty, an ingenuousness that did not allow her to let things go, and she was both alluring and infuriating in her conviction that the business world was an absurd, possibly unnecessary place. She guarded this view, defending it against the violence of reality, and in so doing she had become my hero ; and, perversely, a further base for those very ambitions to which she seemed so indifferent.

'You know, I'm not so sure you mean it,' I said. 'Would you *really* be content if I bummed around as – I don't know – an impoverished writer, waiting for you on the sofa when you got back home from work? Would you like that?'

'Simon!' She awoke from the catatonic state which the long lunch had induced in her, and stood up now from the sofa. 'Why wouldn't I like that? Anything would be better than—'

'OK, OK.' My mother's voice was both conciliatory and

protective. Like her husband, she was a sensitive soul – but unlike him she had beautiful blue eyes, which flashed under dark curls that belied her age, and an Irish DNA that didn't mind confrontation. 'Enough of that, you two. Come on now, Sophie, I want to show you my rhododendrons.'

And five years went by in seconds, like a confused and unhappy dream, and Sophie and I were arguing every day and of the forty Fiennes & Plunkett associates that had qualified there were only three of us left and then Campaign began. Eight months during which the contenders were required to work on no less than fourteen major transactions – and gain an unconditional endorsement from the client instructing on each. A vortex in which we were spun from deal to deal, from impending catastrophe to financial emergency, our talents and our defects exhibited to all. A major restructuring deal – with its list of documents to be drafted, negotiated, tweaked and renegotiated; its all-night conference calls and its completion agendas; its plaintive requests for approvals, its last-minute obstacles and its chaotic signings – leaves everyone involved broken. The trainees and junior associates are given extra days' holiday to recover. The partners sneak off to their country houses. The directors of the client fly to the Alps or to the beach, having put the noose back in the attic, safe for a rainy day. The lawyer on a Campaign, however, must go on. The lawyer on a Campaign tidies the desk, gets an early night and comes in early the next morning to join the next two major transactions.

Yes, there were only two others left. The first was Angus Peterson – a fair-haired, eerily pale young man with a cruel, wolfish mouth and grey, unblinking eyes that were particularly haunting on what was otherwise a baby face. Angus wore a fixed, very nerdy, very empty smile, the infelicitous façade of bonhomie serving only to underline the ruthlessness of his dream, his coldness. The second of the other two lawyers remaining was the Queen of Keen, Emma Morris – a plump, desperately ambitious girl from Walsall with mousy-brown hair, whose strength derived from both fear and an entire absence of imagination – a closed mind allows for no doubt – and who existed in a state of permanent hysteria, forever flushed, forever promising tears of fury. These two delights, my competitors – and all three of us were to be sent away to recuperate while the partners held the annual vote on whether any new partners should be admitted; and, if so, who they were to be. There was no guarantee that any of us would be admitted: at the tight-knit family firm of Fiennes & Plunkett, often years would pass without any new entries. The only thing for certain was that we had worked three or four times harder than the other lawyers in the building, and that for at least one of us this would have been in vain: there were only two senior partners retiring that year, and the partnership, of course, could never exceed thirty.

'We also have a small real estate department.'

We had not worked harder than *every* lawyer in the building. For there was one man who had worked like a lawyer on a Campaign every working day of his career. That man was Rupert Plunkett – the man who knew how to do nothing else. Each lawyer on a Campaign had a mentor and, to Angus and Emma's dismay, during the partnership meeting Rupert had pulled my name out of the hat. This had its obvious advantage – if he liked me, I reckoned that Rupert, as Executive Chairman, would hold sway when it came to the partners' vote. But he could just as easily blackball me. And he kept following me around as I worked for the different departments and partners, constantly interfering in the deals I was working on.

'I have read the email correspondence, and I believe your

deal will sign,' he whispered to me at some point during my final deal of Campaign. 'Where are you headed when this is over?'

'Cuba,' I said.

'Cuba?' The left hand to the quiff, the gaunt face peering down at me, concerned.

'Yes, Rupert. I thought — '

'Cuba?'

Three months earlier, Sophie had walked out of the rented flat in Fulham that we both so adored: it was located on the top floor of a pleasant house on Munster Road, with a skylight in the bedroom and a large roof terrace at the back with a low black railing from which there hung pots of flowers we would buy from a nearby nursery. I had arrived back at 5 a.m. one morning and, as I had entered the living room, I had seen a note on the table.

Can't do this any more. Have gone home to Mum's for the weekend.

The house back in Lincolnshire, up in Hubbard's Hills. Sophie's refuge of fresh green fields and a gurgling river that wound down into the ancient market town of Louth, the capital of the rolling slopes and gentle beauty of the Wolds. That white house high up there alone, that countryside that had bewitched me so long, only to then lose its appeal, quite suddenly, during one long winter's walk. However, by this stage in Campaign nothing evoked emotion, nostalgia, real thoughts. I considered the note for a while, drinking a large glass of whisky, and then passed out on the sofa. Three hours later, I was up.

'The distribution list,' a voice was whispering down the phone. 'Where the hell is it?'

Sophie had erupted a few days before the note. Having not heard from me for over thirty-six hours, and with my

328

secretary not passing on her messages, she had taken the extraordinary step of telephoning Rupert Plunkett, telling him that what he was doing to me was illegal.

'I'm so sorry, Rupert,' I had mumbled, upon my return from the lock-down meeting. 'This is very embarrassing.'

'Par for the course,' he'd whispered. 'It has happened countless – countless – times before.'

After her note, I had not seen Sophie again. One evening, while I had been negotiating the final terms of a warranty schedule, she had returned to that flat where we had lived together for over eight years and taken everything she owned – all her myriad classics and schoolbooks from the shelves in the living room, all her low-heeled shoes that spoke so intimately of her insecurity, all her pictures and her computer and the paintings the kids had given her for her birthday, all she owned, all of her – and she had moved in with those dreadful teacher friends of hers, Eleanor Cantle and husband. Eleanor, who was infinitely less intelligent, had trained with Sophie and, to my dismay, was now a geography teacher at a nearby secondary school – as was the husband. I could just imagine Eleanor, the bony frame perched still and tense on the armchair, her eyes gleaming below her short dark hair, her husband dozing on the sofa as she bitches about me with her special subtle venom...

'It's alright, lovely, you can stay as long as you want.'

Find out more about RedDoor
Press and sign up to our
newsletter to hear about our
latest releases, author events,
exciting **competitions**
and more at

reddoorpress.co.uk

YOU CAN ALSO FOLLOW US:

 @RedDoorBooks

 Facebook.com/RedDoorPress

 @RedDoorBooks